Paris Moments

A NOVEL

Apr. 27, 2022

To my dear Heyman family

Lynn Heyman

LYNN HEYMAN

Copyright 2021 Lynn Heyman

First Edition

Print ISBN 978-1-09838-754-9
eBook ISBN 978-1-09838-755-6

Printed in the United States of America

To my dear sister Wendy

"In the depth of winter, I finally learned that within me there lay an invincible summer."

Albert Camus

Chapter 1

When Brie checked in at the Air France counter at JFK airport, it was as if she was escaping from jail. The coffee she drank burned in her empty stomach.

The perfectly coiffed, auburn-haired woman at the desk viewed her with a pouting disinterest. "Passport, please, Madame." Brie's hand shook at she gave her the document. The woman's eyes scanned the passport. "Very well. And baggage?"

"No luggage," she replied. Brie brushed away the blonde hair from her eyes as she recalled leaving her residence in haste. She put on her oversized sunglasses to avoid the surprised and penetrating look from the attendant. She grabbed the boarding pass. It was her ticket to freedom.

The terminal lights dimmed, or perhaps it was her dark glasses. She felt numb. All she could hear was the click of her heels on the highly polished floor. Airports always had a dream-like quality for her. They were vehicles that bridged one place with another, and all seemed the same. One could be almost anywhere. She craved some humanity. Some culture. She closed her eyes and imagined a faraway place.

She breathed deeply several times as the plane took off, trying to calm her nerves. It wasn't flying she feared, but the uncharted waters she was about to enter.

Chapter 2

The damp Parisian morning air draped over Brie as she walked to the taxi stand and entered the first cab in the line. She spoke to the driver in French.

"St. Germain des Prés, s'il vous plaît."

Her stomach was in knots. Perhaps she could have slept more on the plane and finished her meal.

"Très bien, Madame," said the driver, who spoke with an Arabic accent.

Music played with a strong clarinet refrain. A blue glass evil eye hung from the mirror. The driver sang along with the tune.

The taxi ride was a blur until the city center appeared, in all of its splendor. Classic Parisian architecture stood in sharp contrast to the modern industrial outskirts of Paris. Despite morning traffic, Brie arrived in good time to the small boutique hotel on the left bank. The *quartier*, St. Germain des Prés, the sixth arrondissement, was renowned as the intellectual heart of Paris. It was home to the city's oldest church, Eglise

St. Germain des Prés, which housed the tomb of French philosopher Descartes. The church stood across the boulevard from the hotel.

She was greeted by an old friend, the hotel's General Manager Jean-Jacques, who kissed her hand. "What a pleasure to see you again, Madame Brie."

"The pleasure is mine, Jean-Jacques."

Her vision lacked clarity.

"Do you notice the changes to the lobby? No more antiques. We've modernized," he said.

She gazed around the lobby in a daze. "Lovely renovation. I liked your former Belle Epoque style and see the oil paintings are still gracing the walls," she smiled at him. "You've kept your antique vases with the fresh roses."

"Merci, madame," he said and offered her a white rose. Rose colors meant something important to the French. White represented new beginnings and she acknowledged this to Jean-Jacques, while she sniffed the enormous, fragrant flower. "I will have your room ready in about an hour, madame," Jean-Jacques added.

She imagined the bed where she could rest.

"Would you like to take your *petit déjeuner* in the cafe lounge?" He asked.

"*Oui, merci*, Jean-Jacques," she managed another vague smile. "I wish my usual room that faces the church." *Where Camus completed his final chapters of The Stranger*, she thought. She had written her thesis about Camus in that room during her university years at the Sorbonne. She rubbed her forehead, trying to soothe her headache and immense fatigue. She longed to lie down and close her eyes. Jean-Jacques brought her back to the present.

"*Oui, oui, la chambre de l'étranger*," he laughed. "It no longer has the peach walls, but I think you will like the new décor. Are you still teaching French literature at the university in New York?"

"I'm on sabbatical this year and writing a new book," she said and took a breath, making eye contact with him. *"Merci mille fois* for asking." But she stopped short of revealing details.

"At your service," he said, with a wink.

A young, petite woman, in a light blue starched dress, entered the lounge area. She set a silver tray in front of Brie, who sniffed the contents of the large, frothy cup of *café au lait*. Brie touched the warm, flaky croissants and covered one with crimson strawberry jam. Included on the tray, Brie noticed a square, white envelope with her name scrolled on it.

Chapter 3

When Brie awoke from her nap, the room had darkened. She glanced at the clock near her bed. Nine o'clock. Surprised it was already night, she vaguely remembered closing her eyes on the pillow that morning, after being informed that her room was ready.

She rose from the crisp white sheets of the double bed and opened the French doors, which let out onto a small balcony. She breathed in the air of the city she loved. The May evening was warmer than expected and the boulevard below was a maze of glittering lights of cafés that punctuated the four corners in front of the Romanesque church of Saint Germain des Prés. She could hear the distant clatter of silverware on plates. The Parisians were enjoying their evening meal. Dinner was a later event in Paris.

Brie moved back inside and noticed an envelope on the floor. The one that had been on the breakfast tray. She had neglected to read it earlier, assuming it was a card from the management, welcoming her back to the hotel. She was surprised that it contained a phone message from her dear Parisian friend Annick, who usually texted her. She decided to return her friend's call.

"*Bonsoir, ma chère*. So sorry. I have been sleeping all day," said Brie, attempting to sound upbeat.

"So, you did get my message?" Annick's voice quickened. "Welcome back to Paris, *ma chérie*. I was concerned. Your text indicated you would arrive in the morning, and we didn't hear from you."

"*Desolée*. I did arrive this morning, and then I fell asleep. I must've been more exhausted than I thought."

"How are you feeling now? When we heard your phone message, two days ago, it sounded urgent. I called you back and left a voicemail."

"I had to get out of New York, Annick. I didn't feel safe anymore," Brie said, as her heart pounded. "I've been depleted for months, from the surgery and then the drama with Jack." Brie sighed.

"Oh, my dear friend. Your husband has become menacing and unpredictable, but you're a survivor. You will get through this challenge," Annick reassured her.

"I've suffered a broken heart twice this year. One repaired by the heart surgeon and one caused by Jack," Brie's heart raced.

"I want to give you a big hug in person and so does Pierre," said Annick. "You know, we still have your valise from last time. We can bring it to you."

"*Merci*, but not tonight," Brie touched her chest. "It's getting late. Let's talk again in the morning."

"Of course. You must tell me the whole story. You know, Pierre and I want what's best for you," said Annick.

"Kisses to you both, and to your sister Chantal," said Brie.

She thought about the bond she and her French "sisters" had made so many years ago, as students of literature at the Sorbonne.

"And from us. I must call Chantal right away and tell her that you have landed safely. She's waiting to hear."

"It's comforting to be back in my second home. *A bientôt.*"

"See you soon. *Au revoir, ma belle.*"

"*Bonne nuit, ma chère.*"

Brie's stomach growled. She grabbed her carry-on bag of essentials. She had left New York in a hurry, taking only the carry-on bag she had ready for quick departures. She splashed some cool water on her face and brushed her teeth. She pulled a brush through her tousled blonde hair. She smoothed her grey silk blouse and skirt, added pearl earrings and a light pink sweater. She sprayed on her Dior scent, and applied Chanel Red lipstick. It was Paris, after all, and she needed to be presentable. She was famished and the renowned Café des Deux Magots was just across the street.

She entered the café and motioned to the waiter. She would take a table on the covered terrace, facing the boulevard.

The waiter placed a white tablecloth on the small, round table. She slid onto the banquette, as he offered her the menu.

The waiter was tall and lean, with black tailored pants that hugged his derrière. He wore a pressed white shirt, black vest and tie. A classic French waiter with perfect posture and a Gallic profile.

"*Vous désirez*, Madame? Un apéritif?"

"*Un Kir Royale, s'il vous plait,*" she said.

"Very well, Madame," he said and took his leave.

There was a fair amount of traffic on the boulevard. Brie felt more awake, as she viewed the parade of splendidly attired locals glide by on the sidewalk in front of her. Every so often, tourists in jeans and sport shoes, some speaking loudly, broke her mood and brought discord.

The waiter returned with her drink and added champagne to the Framboise raspberry liquor at the bottom of the glass. She took a sip. Her headache began to clear.

A while later, she ordered *la soupe à l'oignon* with crusted gruyère cheese. She licked the salt from her lips and savored the flavors. The next course was smoked salmon on blini with capers and sour cream. The taste of the salmon was smooth and subtle. Brie remembered the French pace. No meal was rushed in France. Eating was like lovemaking, details important. For the first time in weeks, she felt her body relax. Her shoulders were no longer up at her ears.

She requested the check. *"L'addition, s'il vous plaît."*

"Madame, your bill has been paid by the gentleman at the end of the *terrasse*," the waiter grinned at her.

Brie gasped. Her eyes widened as she glanced to her right. There, she saw the Prix Goncourt award-winning writer Michel Houellebecq, with his eyes gazing down at a small leather journal he was scribbling in. She recognized him from the numerous photos in the French press and from the back cover of his book *Poésies*. By coincidence, she had been reading the same one on the plane. Many authors frequented these Paris cafés. She knew the café was where the artist and writer could go to leave their creative solitude and find human contact. After all, she was at the famous Les Deux Magots. Camus, Sartre and de Beauvoir had been regular clients here.

She flashed on a memory from her university days of catching a glimpse of Jean-Paul Sartre at this same cafe, wearing a black cape and round wire rimmed glasses, looking existential. Brie had been in awe of this experience in the past.

As she rose to make her exit, she looked back at Monsieur Houellebecq, who, this time, met her glance and smiled at her. She took the book of his poetry out of her purse and waved it toward him. His smile broadened. She walked over to his table and said, *"Merci, monsieur,"* meeting his gaze. He offered her his hand. "I'm a fan of your work, as you can see," she said.

"I'm honored," he said. "Perhaps our paths will cross again?"

"With pleasure," she said. She continued out of the café, with a smile on her face and crossed the boulevard. She was back in Paris. Magic could happen at any time.

Chapter 4

Annick called mid-morning the next day.

"Ma chérie, I wanted to let you know that Pierre dropped off your valise at the hotel early this morning, on his way to Versailles for a meeting. We didn't want to wake you. I know how stressed and fatigued you have been."

"How nice of him. *Un grand merci*," she was still waking up.

"We thought you would like to have your things," said Annick.

"I left New York with only the clothes on my back. I didn't want to risk returning to my apartment and was frantic to escape."

"No person should have to live in fear. We will see each other soon and listen to your story," said Annick.

"I'm relieved to be back in Paris. It feels like a refuge," said Brie.

"It will always be a safe place for you. *Bisous!*"

"Kisses."

She thought about her troubled marriage and her angry husband.

She wanted to focus on the positive. On being three thousand miles from all the chaos.

She reflected on last night and on the author Monsieur Houellebecq at Les Deux Magots. She thought Frenchmen were so gallant and flirting was an art form in French culture. There were no expectations. She had lived for so long with a critical, angry man and had forgotten what it was like to be treated with respect and even admiration.

Just then, there was a knock at the hotel room door. She put on her raincoat, for lack of a robe to cover her undergarments. She looked through the peep hole, which was part of her New York training since birth. The bellman was standing outside with her suitcase and a breakfast tray. When she opened the door, the young man smiled at her.

"*Bonjour, madame.* Jean-Jacques wants you to have this valise," he said. His voice was heavily accented and halting, as if he had been practicing the words beforehand.

"*Merci, monsieur.* I speak French. Place it here, *s'il vous plait.*"

The bellman looked relieved as he put the suitcase on the wooden bench at the foot of the bed. He placed the silver tray on the table near the French doors. He then opened the curtains to reveal a sunny spring day. Along with the French breakfast was a petit silver vase with lilies of the valley, the flowers that honor the first of May in France. She took a deep breath. The fragrance was hypnotic.

"*Bonne journée, madame,*" the bellman said and left in haste, but with the grace of a butterfly.

She opened the doors to let in some fresh air. She breathed in Paris once again and breathed out the pain from the recent events in New York. The white clouds and partial blue sky were an omen of a good opportunity to take a long walk. First, she would wash off the negative energy she left behind.

She entered the blue and white tiled shower and let the warm water wash over her. She used the Balmain gel, which had a multi-layered scent of lemon and floral bouquets. She had learned about perfume making in Grasse one summer: the head, heart and base notes. It was a symphony.

On the back of the door to *la salle de bain*, she found a fluffy white terry cloth robe embroidered with a scrolled "M." It was the hotel insignia in gold thread. It reminded her of the initial "M" for Marie-Antoinette, engraved in stone on many of the chateaux of the Loire Valley.

She wiped down the large oval mirror with a hand towel, where she caught sight of her own reflection. Her rich brown eyes, with golden amber highlights, had a serious expression, as she gazed at the long incision on her chest. The scar was from the life-saving heart surgery a year ago. She shivered. Tears rolled down her cheeks, as she blotted them with the towel. Now, she could see a glimmer of *joie de vivre* in her face, and she was grateful to be starting another new day.

*　*　*

Brie turned right outside the large, automatic glass doors of the hotel. She walked down the Boulevard St. Germain toward the sumptuous gardens of the Jardin de Luxembourg. As she strolled, she noticed *les muguets*—lilies of the valley—being sold on every street corner. The *quartier* was festive, with many couples and families taking their holiday walks. She felt a pang as she noticed the happiness around her. The cafés were animated, with every table filled on the *terrasses*. She became part of the parade, in her beige trench coat and bright blue silk scarf. Her pace was slow, unlike the quick New York variety, which was fast and determined.

When she reached the Jardin, she passed through the huge metal gates and walked alongside the Palais de Luxembourg. The chestnut trees were lush green, as were the low chained off lawns. Pink and fuchsia flowers were in bloom all over the landscape. In the midst of this city, there were many large green spaces that brought relief from the urban feeling. It was a stark contrast to Manhattan, where Central Park was the only major respite in a vertical sea of skyscrapers and concrete sidewalks. You could barely see the sky, so many stories above. While in Paris, with their six to eight story buildings and wide green expanses, Brie could look out and view with ease the rich blue sky and white cumulous clouds.

She was drawn toward the boat basin, where young children, with the help of their parents, were sailing their little wooden boats. Many were jumping with excitement. The clouds reflected in the basin in a true mirror image. She noticed many breeds of dog gallivanting in the park. Brie was careful not to step in any droppings that may have been left by a poodle on the loose.

On the far lawn, past the chairs on the pebbled walkways, she could see a bride, with her wedding party and a photographer, who was taking photographs. The bride's bouquet ribbons were trailing on the ground. She froze, recalling her own wedding, ten years ago, at a time when she had been happy. Her body tensed. She swallowed her hopelessness. So much had shifted in her life. Aimless, drifting, she had come to Paris to make sense of it all.

There was a sudden change in the sky. Foreboding, dark gray clouds moved in, and a light spring drizzle entered the scene. The bride and groom picked up their colorful umbrellas from the lawn and continued to pose for pictures. The couple laughed in the rain. They embraced each other and seemed to enjoy the changing sky. Brie trembled as she pulled out her own umbrella, which she learned to always carry in Paris. No matter the season, you could have all four in one day. She shifted her view from the joyful wedding party. Anxiety tightened the muscles in her body, as she recalled her own joyous wedding of ten years ago. She searched for a respite.

Brie remembered Café Angelina, a tea salon, famous for their teas, dense hot chocolate and elegant pastries, had a small shop near the edge of the park. A hostess seated her at a table next to a vast window, as many people from the park crowded into the small salon. A female server approached, in a pink frilly apron. The woman was hurried and brusque.

"*Bonjour, madame,*" she mumbled. "We have a special patisserie this month, an apple mousse, with red crème in honor of Cézanne." She put out her hand to indicate that several clients were having that specialty.

Brie turned toward the immense glass counter filled with pastries. "I would like to have the raspberry tart and a cup of rose and jasmine tea. *Merci.*"

"Very well," said the server, scowling, visibly disappointed that Brie hadn't taken her suggestion.

Now, the rain was coming down in sheets. The patter on the windows fogged the view and Brie was relieved to be sheltered, sipping hot tea. The light green leaves on the trees glistened through the fog.

Brie barely touched her raspberry pastry, pushing the berries aside with her fork and tasting a few. Her fatigue returned as she thought about the long walk back to the hotel. She sat and watched the rain, as the salon emptied of most of the clientele. The clouds darkened further. The weather matched the frisson inside her heart.

She decided to take a cab back to the hotel instead of walking for miles in the pouring rain. Her feet were soaked. She stopped at the small Italian restaurant she knew, next to her hotel. She felt comfortable there and didn't want to be alone. The place was formerly owned by a well-known Italian family of restauranteurs from Rome. Several years ago, they had retired and sold it to two Portuguese brothers from Porto. One of the brothers was the chef, the other was the manager. The Italian grand-mother's recipes were included in the sale.

Antonio, the restaurant manager, met her at the door. "*Bonsoir, madame!* Welcome back. Let me take your wet coat." He recognized her. "So good to see you again." His French was heavily accented with Portuguese. His black hair gleamed in the soft light. He had a strong, squared chin.

She ordered her favorite, eggplant with homemade marinara sauce, melted cheese and artichoke hearts. She ate with appetite, as it was as delectable as she recalled.

The manager approached Brie at the end of her meal. He pulled a chair around to sit next to her and placed his hand on her arm. She knew Latins liked to touch. She bowed her head, so as not to meet his penetrating gaze.

"I recall when you and your friends would sit in the back room and discuss literature for hours. Do you remember?" He had been a waiter under the original French ownership.

She nodded with a smile. "Yes."

He continued. "How long will you be in Paris this time?"

"I'm uncertain," she said, glancing at him and then to the side. She asked for the check, and he indicated it was not necessary.

"I hope we see you again," he said, helping her on with her coat. "*Bonne soirée.*" He was so close, she could smell his cologne, which reminded her of her estranged husband Jack.

"*Merci, Antonio,*" *she blushed.*

"*C'est mon plaisir,*" he said and walked her to the door.

It was a short block to the warmth and safety of her hotel room. Once there, Brie removed her wet clothing and shoes and fell back onto her bed with its numerous white pillows. She closed her eyes.

Chapter 5

The morning brought several frantic texts from Brie's daughter Chloe in California.

"*Maman*, where are you? You haven't responded to my texts in days. Please contact me!"

She made a phone call to Los Angeles.

"*Ma chérie*! I'm in Paris!"

"*Maman*! I was concerned." She heard her daughter out of breath on the other end of the line. "Did you have a last-minute conference to attend?" asked Chloe.

"No, no! I just needed to clear my head. To take a break from New York and recharge," she tried to sound cheerful.

"Recharge?" asked her daughter. "From what? Are you okay?"

"I think I'll be fine. It's not a physical health issue. I'm just mentally tired," she sighed.

"Did you call your surgeon? Did he think it was advisable for you to travel so soon?"

"It's already been a year, sweetie. I'm no longer so fragile."

"Mom, you were close to death! The doctors wrote a book about your case," her daughter's voice had turned serious. "Do not take this lightly!"

"You know the best medicine for me is France," she said, trying to reassure her daughter. Then she changed to a positive subject. "How is your film, honey? Working with the great director?"

Her daughter had graduated a few years before from the UCLA School of Film with a major in direction. After paying her dues at low levels jobs, and making contacts in a competitive industry, she was tapped to be an assistant director for a major project with a prominent Hollywood filmmaker.

"He's intimidating, but I'm learning a lot—in a short time," said Chloe.

"Oh, you've got this, baby. You've been a director since you were two years old," Brie laughed.

"Dad's coming out tomorrow. He has some business in town, and he'll be visiting me on the set."

"Oh, that's great, honey," Brie said and tried to continue her upbeat tone.

She was divorced from her first husband, Carter Sandstrom, for several years. They had become friends again, over time, and had succeeded at co-parenting. He was a wonderful father to Chloe. He had sometimes made fun of Brie's romantic view of Paris, preferring the German-speaking countries for their organization and predictability. His major concern was the health of the stock market. Still, he was a good man, in his core. He had shown that when he was by Brie's side throughout her recent health crisis. Chloe could depend upon him to provide emotional support.

"So, mom, is Jack with you?" There was a pause on the other end of the line. Brie could feel her head pounding.

"No." Several seconds passed and Brie's pulse quickened. "I have to go, sweetie. I have to call Annick."

"Okay, Mom. Enjoy! And say hello to everyone from me."

"*Bien sûr*, of course, I will. Kisses," said Brie and took a deep breath.

"I love you, Mom."

"I love you, too, sweetie."

Brie didn't call Annick, as thoughts scrambled in her brain. Nor was she ready to talk about the recent events with Jack with her daughter Chloe, who harbored mixed feelings toward her stepfather.

* * *

A clear Paris sky nudged Brie to walk the couple of blocks to the Seine River—the heart of Paris. Her wanderings often helped her process her thoughts. She hoped she could rid herself of the agonizing pain caused by her challenging relationship with Jack. She couldn't comprehend his insensitivity toward her cardiac condition and subsequent massive surgery. Brie's thoughts flashed on being in the hospital bed a year ago, unable to move, attached to so many wires, tubes, and machines that she needed a nurse's assistance to perform her basic tasks of eating and washing. She had been there for two weeks, and Jack had only appeared once, never speaking to her directly. The surgeon mistook her ex, Carter, for her actual husband Jack. To her, that spoke volumes about the two men.

Brie strolled from the left Bank—*la rive gauche*—onto one of the many bridges that connected the two banks of the river. She could see Notre-Dame in the distance. The grand lady was recently refreshed by sandblasting and was as creamy white as the day she was built. The stone glowed, the gargoyles on guard for protection. Brie pulled her coat around her in response to the strong Parisian spring breeze. She closed her eyes in prayer to the spirits of Paris for healing and clarity.

Brie continued her walk until she found herself in front of the Louvre. She admired I.M. Pei's glass pyramid as the perfect addition to the historic palace turned museum. She remembered all the fuss about the new, modern entrance. At the time it was first completed, the Parisians were not complimentary. There was a time when the restless locals wanted to tear down the Eiffel Tower, which they viewed as an eyesore. The world cried out in revolt. The French, having great respect for revolution, backed down.

Once inside the Louvre, she felt the "Winged Victory of Samothrace" calling to her. She found it, as always, at the top of the marble staircase. The statue was bathed in natural light and gleamed like a headless angel. It was in the morning, midweek, so, the tourists, usually buzzing around the statue speaking a variety of languages, were absent. Brie had the beauty of classical Greece all to herself.

She decided to make the climb up the stairs, stopping intermittently to take frequent looks at the statue from various levels. She was at last at the top, close to the stone itself.

"*Très belle, n'est-ce pas?*" said a resonant male voice.

She was startled to see a handsome, distinguished looking Frenchman, in a navy suit, white starched shirt, and rich French blue tie. His gold cufflinks shone in the natural light from above. Brie and the Frenchman stood on either side of the winged statue.

"*Oui, très belle*, very beautiful," she said. She lowered her eyes from his intense gaze. "I adore this statue. She is a mother figure to me."

"You are French?" he inquired, studying her, with his unique turquoise eyes.

Brie hesitated a moment before speaking. She was under the spell of the statue and assumed she was alone, a rare moment in the Louvre. She was a middle-aged woman, used to being invisible in New York.

"*Américaine.* From New York. *La Victoire* is one of my favorite sculptures in Paris."

"Mine, as well." He smiled into her eyes. "You speak excellent French."

"*Merci*. I studied at *La Sorbonne*," she blushed, continuing to take in his commanding, yet youthful presence.

"*Ah, je comprends*." The man offered her his hand, after complimenting her. "Here is my card. If I can do anything for you while you are here, please do not hesitate to contact me." She didn't understand why he thought he could *do* something for her.

He spoke in perfect British English. The French studied British English in school. They considered American English to be a dialect and too informal.

She placed the card in her purse without looking at it. She couldn't take her eyes off his eyes. Her knees were weak.

"*Merci, monsieur*," she said, shaking his outstretched hand, and catching another glimpse of his eye color.

"*À bientôt, madame*."

She had lost her breath and did not reply.

He disappeared into a side corridor. Brie stood there, still entranced in the magic and surprises of the Grecian statue. The dashing Frenchman added an aura of mystery.

* * *

That evening, Brie strolled across the street from the hotel to the Café de Flore, another renowned literary café in the *quartier*. The Sixth Arrondissement had been the site of intellectual activity since medieval times. She walked past the Eglise de St. Germain des Prés, named after the bishop of Paris. The historical square gave her a sense of calm.

Brie imagined F. Scott Fitzgerald and Hemingway here, having a passionate discussion about their latest literary projects. Fitzgerald may have created Jay Gatsby and Daisy Buchanan in this very spot. The café and its surrounds came into clearer focus.

Brie felt fortunate to be sitting here, on sabbatical from the university and to have this time following her lengthy medical leave. For the past year, she had worked with doctors, nutritionists, and physical therapists to move her blood count out of the anemic zone. During her surgery, she had suffered major blood loss, which is often the case with open heart surgery. Shifting in her chair at the café, she reflected on a time when she could return to her students, her constant inspiration. Many of them came to visit her during her recovery. Teaching was the one bright spot, her beacon of light, amidst the chaos that had become her life with Jack. Her darker days began after her daughter Chloe moved to California for grad school, then her relationship with husband Jack took a downward turn. Or, perhaps, she took more notice of the shift with Chloe gone.

Chapter 6

A few days passed. Annick telephoned. "How are you feeling? Over your jet lag?"

"Much improved, *mon amie*. I took some long walks, and I was able to clear my head," said Brie. "I'm officially in the Paris time zone."

"We look forward to seeing you. Pierre is with patients until later this afternoon. We want to pick you up tonight and take you for your favorite roasted duck. I made a reservation for half past eight. We can be at your hotel by eight o'clock."

"Oh, that would be lovely. I look forward to seeing you both. I'm in my usual 'Camus' room at the hotel. Jean-Jacques, the hotel manager, will show you upstairs with no problem. I will arrange it with him," she said.

"Kisses! Till tonight!"

"*Bisous!*"

Brie found her black silk dress and chose her vintage red and gold Hermes scarf, a gift from Aunt Françoise when they stayed together in Paris during Brie's time at the university. Her aunt, a staunch Francophile and French speaker, was a major influence in her education of the French culture. Brie added her black Repetto Cendrillon ballet pumps to the ensemble. They made her feel like Brigitte Bardot.

There was a knock at the door and Brie opened it to see the ever – elegant Annick and Pierre, bearing gifts. Pierre handed her a fragrant bouquet of pink roses and a box of Ladurée rose and pistachio flavored macarons. There were the usual three kisses on everyone's cheeks and eyes filled with tears.

Pierre was the first to speak. "So wonderful to see you looking healthy. The last time we saw you, in New York, you were a month out of heart surgery and so pale... so weak."

"I know. I was lying down, drowsy from the medications and I don't remember much. When my sweet sister Lisa brought you in, I heard you all speaking French. I was so honored you'd made the trip," she said.

"We had to come and make sure you were all right," said Pierre.

"I'd forgotten you spoke to Lisa on the phone while I was in the hospital. Did you know she flew down from Montreal to stay with me for two months? She nursed me back to health after my hospital stay," said Brie.

"An aortic aneurysm is no joke. Very dangerous. A silent killer and a congenital condition. It runs in families, mostly northern European lines," Pierre was sounding so much like the doctor he was.

"And now, she's fine," said Annick. "Look at you. You are your beautiful self, again."

The two friends embraced.

Pierre went over and sat down near the window, while Annick and Brie sat on the velvet sofa. She took Brie's hands.

"So, please tell us what's going on now. Why are you suddenly in Paris? And where is Jack?" Annick had a quizzical expression.

Brie's mind darted back to the reason she had left New York in haste, to find respite with her friends. She needed to be far from Jack Taylor, her estranged husband, who, after her diagnosis, began to threaten her emotionally on a daily basis. He criticized her every move. It was worse after her surgery. As a prominent New York attorney, he boasted an Ivy League education. He was well-respected by his law community, with a keen intellect, although his ego could cut glass. A few years into the relationship, Brie discovered he had a mean streak a mile wide. He had a sharp tongue, which is probably why he was such a powerful litigator in the courtroom.

Brie brought her thoughts back to the present. She focused on her friend's question.

"You know how distant he was before, during, and after the surgery?" she asked. "He shocked my family with his coldness, turned secretive, and was gone for days at a time, refusing to give explanations for his whereabouts. He would not respond to my texts." Brie took a deep breath and continued. "After Lisa left to return to Montreal, he became more distant. When I saw him in person, which was rare, he was so angry, yelling at me. He terrified me with his mood swings. I was scared whenever I heard him return to our apartment and I heard the door slam. I felt too weak to do much to care for myself. Then, without a word, he disappeared."

Annick took a breath and spoke after a long silence. "We were shocked that he wasn't there for you when you needed him most. His behavior would be frightening given your fragile state. Some people can only handle the good times. I'm happy you turned to us for support. That you left New York to find safety with us."

"My sister Lisa suggested I come to stay with her in Montreal, but we both agreed it was too close to Jack for comfort," said Brie.

"You're correct in your thinking. He was like a phantom when we were in New York," Pierre added. "Absent in your hour of need. Unforgivable." He shook his head. "Now, he has become a danger to you. You don't know what he will do next. His anger is directed at you for no apparent reason."

"Pierre, we must not dwell on the negative," said Annick looking at Brie. "Let's go to dinner and enjoy the evening together. She is here now. Everything will turn out for the best."

* * *

They took the short walk to the famed bistro. The menu was a creation of Alain Ducasse. The place was busy, filled with Parisians and visitors in the know. The white tablecloths and golden lanterns gave a festive glow to the cozy elegance.

The Maître d' seated them immediately and handed them hand-scrolled menus. Brie's friends knew her preferences since this had been their celebration restaurant for years.

Pierre ordered *les escargots en coquilles* to start.

They all agreed on a Bordeaux rouge wine from St. Emillion.

The waiter poured the wine to one-third full, in each glass, to allow the red wine to breathe. They made a toast.

"*Santé*," they said in unison, making eye contact. Brie added, "I am so grateful to be here with you both."

"Annick tells me that you've been to your usual haunts. You probably have been there more often than we have since we moved out to Neuilly-sur-Seine," Pierre said with a twinkle in his eye.

"Yes, I visited my favorites, including the Winged Victory, today," Brie replied.

"To make sure she hadn't flown away since last time?" Pierre joked. They all laughed.

The waiter brought *le canard aux olives* for three on a rolling cart. The duck glistened with the large Mediterranean green olives. He served the thin, delicate *haricots verts*, French green beans with slivered almonds, with his white gloved hands. The waiter had assured them that the beans were picked fresh this morning while he placed each plate on the table, with grace.

"We insist on knowing when the beans are picked. This is very important to us," said Annick. "We don't like old vegetables."

"We only like old buildings and old wine," said Pierre. They all laughed.

They continued the festivities with dessert— *la patisserie aux fraises avec petits chocolats*. The strawberries were the sweetest Brie had tasted in a long time.

* * *

They said their goodbyes back at the hotel, where they invited Brie to stay at their home.

"Oh, I am fine here in the center of the city," she said.

"She can revisit all of her old friends at the museums," said Pierre, with a wink.

"Well, if you change your mind, we are here," said Annick. "Brie, there is an international literary conference happening next week. I hope you can join me."

"I would very much like that," Brie said.

"So, it's a date," said Annick. "I will text you all the details."

Before leaving, Pierre tapped Brie on the shoulder and talked in a whisper.

"There is a young man in a brown leather jacket, with long dark hair, who seemed to be following us this evening. If you look out the window, you will see him leaning on the Métro railing across near the church, smoking a cigarette."

"Oh, Pierre. You have read too many detective stories," said Annick. "He thinks he is the French Sherlock Holmes. Don't frighten her. Hasn't she been through enough?"

"I'm not worried. Nobody knows I'm here but you two, Lisa, and my daughter Chloe. And now, I have the French Sherlock on the case," she said. "I have no worries."

"In fact, Sherlock was half French. His grandmother was French," said Pierre. "These details are mentioned in *The Memoirs of Sherlock Holmes*."

"Your husband is a knowledgeable man," said Brie to Annick.

Annick kissed Pierre on the cheek.

* * *

Alone in her room, Brie began to reflect on the past. She recalled the time Jack revealed that he loved her and how happy he was for the first time in his life. They were looking up at a full moon on the beach in East Hampton, Long Island. It was a memorable evening for the couple. That was more than ten years ago.

She flashed on the time, before her diagnosis, when she and Jack decided to get away to Nantucket for a long weekend in the early Fall. Nantucket was one of her most beloved islands on the East Coast. The wide expanses of beach, with endless views of the sapphire blue Atlantic and crashing waves gave her a deep sense of freedom and serenity.

As they drove on the highway north, then east toward Hyannis, it was stifling in the car. Brie asked Jack to put on the air-conditioning. He knew how she suffered from heat. Instead, he put on the heater and locked all the windows so she couldn't open hers. When she asked him to turn the heater off, he had put on some loud music that he knew she disliked.

He had a sly smile on his face. She was happy to finally arrive at the boat dock and to board the high-speed catamaran to Nantucket Island. She walked out on deck and let the sea air hit her face, as she viewed the island coming into sharp focus. She decided to fly back to New York City directly from Nantucket after a few days. She made a decision to never get in the car with Jack again.

The exquisite meal she enjoyed tonight began to churn in her stomach and she was nauseated. She sat in a chair by the windows and stared out at the Métro station, reminding herself that she was safe in Paris.

Chapter 7

The sun had not yet risen when her daughter Chloe called from Los Angeles. Brie woke up from a deep sleep. She was drowsy and expected to hear French.

"Mom?" said Chloe.

"How are you, my baby?" She looked at the clock. "It's 6 AM here in Paris."

"I'm so excited, I had to call you. My director invited me to join him at the Cannes Film Festival, so I'll be in France later this month. Maybe we can meet?" Chloe was breathless.

Brie guessed her daughter was taking a run in the Hollywood Hills.

"That's wonderful, sweetie! I'll talk to Annick and her sister Chantal. We can take the train down to Cannes to see you. Chantal refurbished her family villa with multiple bedrooms. Maybe we can all stay there."

"I have to stay at the Carlton with the film entourage, but I hope to have some free time to spend with you," Chloe spoke as she was catching her breath.

Brie's day brightened at the thought of her daughter coming to France. She knew all the hotels on the *Côte d'Azur* would be booked far in advance. The small Riviera town would be packed with film industry people from all over the world. They descended on Cannes every May since 1946. In 1932, the French Minister of National Education had proposed holding the festival, with the support of the British and Americans. The grand prize was the *Palme d'Or*. It was a golden palm frond on a crystal base, created by Chopard Jewelers.

"How are things going on the film?"

"We wrapped in early March. The editors are adding the finishing touches. It's crazy around here," Chloe said.

"Well, that's exciting news. My daughter will be presenting a film at Cannes. Could we ever have dreamed of this?" said Brie.

"It feels like a dream, but it's happening. For my boss. For the actors. For the cinematographer. Not for me," Chloe said.

Brie heard her daughter sipping water.

"You're the assistant director, so don't count yourself out," she said.

"I'm thrilled just to be part of the crew. Some folks don't know me well," said Chloe.

"Behind the scenes is often the best place to be when you are learning," Brie never stopped being a mother.

"I love you, Mom! See you soon!"

"Bye, sweetie. Love you."

Brie then called the reception. She heard Jean-Jacques on the other end of the line.

"Bonjour, madame."

"Bonjour. I'm in need of my *café au lait*."

"You are up early today, madame. Getting used to the time change?"

"My daughter just called from Los Angeles with some exciting news. Her studio will present a film at Cannes this month."

"Bravo! Move over, Spielberg and Louis Malle! You must be so proud."

"My head is spinning," she replied.

"I can imagine," said Jean-Jacques. "I will send up your coffee right away with Claude."

When Brie rose out of bed, she felt dizzy. She sat down on the nearest chair. When she looked out of the windows of the French doors, she thought she saw a man in a brown leather jacket with long hair. She convinced herself she was imagining him.

Chapter 8

Brie was in the garden of the Musée Rodin, opposite the statue of Honoré de Balzac, when she received a text from Annick about the literary conference the following week. She agreed that they would meet at the Palais des Congrès at La Porte Maillot.

She moved to the statue of "The Kiss"— *Le Baiser*. It was surrounded by pink roses in bloom. She followed with another text to Annick about Chloe and her film being presented in Cannes. Annick expressed her excitement and said she would contact her sister Chantal right away. She promised to make train reservations immediately.

Brie remembered the stories about Rodin and his affair with Camille Claudel. She was the sister of the poet Paul Claudel. Rodin had emotionally destroyed his lover because of her talent. He was rumored to have signed his name to his students' multiple works. Rodin believed they should be honored to be recognized by the master. A museum named for Camille Claudel was recently constructed in Nogent-sur-Seine. Claudel's statue "The Waltz" was at last displayed properly in all its brilliance.

She continued on to the Musée d'Orsay, a former train station restored by a female Italian architect. Usually crowded, today there was only a short line to enter.

Brie walked back toward Rodin's "Gates of Hell." On the way, she stopped to revisit Manet's "Luncheon on the Grass" *–Le Déjeuner sur l'Herbe.* The painting had been steeped in controversy at the time it was first presented in 1863, depicting two fully clothed men sitting on a blanket with a nude woman in the foreground. Another nude woman crouched in the background. The nudes gleamed against the dark green and black tones surrounding them. Brie thought about the inequity of the dressed men with the nude women and how inappropriate that would be in today's society.

"The Gates of Hell" had a small group in front of it. She looked up at "The Three Shades— *Les Trois Ombres,"* at the top of the enormous, sculpted doorway. Her eyes followed down to a smaller version of "The Thinker— *Le Penseur."* What was this man thinking about? The figures above him would never know.

At the other end of the corridor, Brie thought she saw a man wearing a brown leather jacket, a gray scarf and cap. His long hair was fastened in a ponytail. She shrugged off her fear. How many Frenchmen were in this city with a similar look?

Brie returned to the hotel and rubbed her feet. French shoes may look elegant, but comfort was not of any importance to the designers. She didn't share the French belief that women could suffer for beauty. Rest was her top priority for the next few days. She amassed some books to read *en français.* She wanted to occupy her mind with thoughts other than of Jack and his whereabouts.

Chapter 9

Brie and Annick entered the convention ballroom filled with about three hundred people, the place abuzz with literary talk. They seated themselves near the front of the enormous room, crystal chandeliers gleaming above their heads.

The speaker approached the podium. The room fell silent. A distinguished man in a well-tailored blue suit was introduced as Monsieur Laurent de Laval from the *Ambassade de France*. He began to speak about French literature and its impact internationally. The printed program stated that he had a doctorate in comparative literature from Oxford University. He authored three books of fiction and five non-fiction works. Brie thought it was unusual that he had studied in England.

Monsieur de Laval began with references to Marguerite Duras, and her novel *Moderato Cantabile*. The Italian words dropped off his tongue like marbles coated in honey. It occurred to Brie that this man looked somewhat familiar.

She whispered to Annick, "That was one of our favorite books, do you remember, my friend?

"Of course, *ma chère*," replied Annick.

The man in the blue suit continued. "The scent of magnolia is so strong in that work it grabs you by the throat and leaves you breathless." He brushed his light brown hair back with his hand, gathering his composure.

Brie realized where she had seen him before. She looked into her purse and found the card he had given her at the Louvre, several days before. "Laurent de Laval, Ambassade de France, Quai d'Orsay, Paris." She showed the card to Annick, who looked back at her with mild shock. Perhaps his description of the magnolia had deeply affected her.

Brie looked up at the stage. Monsieur de Laval's blue-green eyes were focused on her like a panther on its prey.

Annick whispered, "So you are acquainted with him?"

Brie nodded in the affirmative. Her heart fluttered as she fingered her gold necklace.

Monsieur de Laval continued, this time switching the topic to Stendhal's *Le Rouge et Le Noir*—The Red and the Black. Now, he seemed to be losing his train of thought. He crossed his arms in front of his chest and paused. His eyes locked on Brie's, as the audience turned their attention to her. She blushed and looked downward. She felt this flirtation, directed toward her, throughout her body.

"He's very handsome," whispered Annick to her friend. Brie covered her mouth with a handkerchief. She nodded in agreement, leaning forward in her seat, feeling her heartbeat.

He continued to speak of Alain Robbe-Grillet and the novel *Le Voyeur.*

"Mathias is a fascinating character," he said as his voice trailed off.

She could no longer hear what he was saying. After a time, she heard loud applause. She awoke from her reverie.

"Would you like a coffee?" said Annick. "We are at intermission."

"Oh, yes. I think I was in a bit of a trance," Brie said, fanning herself with the program.

They walked toward the reception area to a long table with an elegant white tablecloth, dotted with delicate porcelain cups and silver coffee pots.

Brie felt someone behind her at the table. She assumed it was Annick.

"*Bonjour, Madame*," whispered a man's voice. "I never got your name the other day."

She turned, surprised to see the speaker, the man from the Louvre.

"I'm Brie Taylor," she said and put out her hand. There was the *de rigueur* handshake and eye contact. His turquoise eyes lit up like the planet Venus.

"*Enchanté, Madame Taylor.*"

Brie felt flushed.

"This is my friend, Madame Girard," she said as Annick shook his hand.

"We will talk later," Annick whispered in her friend's ear.

He reached into the chest pocket of his suit and pulled out an oversized white square envelope.

"Please, both of you, do come to our reception at the Embassy tomorrow evening. We have invited authors from Québec and Belgium."

"*Avec plaisir*," said Annick, in a high-pitched voice, adjusting her Tahitian pearls and grasping the envelope. She looked at Brie, who was still in a reverie.

"So, it's all arranged," said Monsieur de Laval, with a confident smile.

"Yes," said Brie, unsure about accepting his invitation. She had grown unused to this attention or the attraction she felt after being ignored for years by her husband.

All three shook hands and Monsieur de Laval disappeared into the crowd.

"You've been keeping secrets," said Annick after the man's departure. "Do you know who he is?" She had a tone in her voice Brie had never heard before. It was deep and probing.

"I have an idea," said Brie, fumbling with her purse.

"Oh, he's important, that one. I will tell you who he is. He can park his car all day in front of the Tour Eiffel and not get towed. He would not get as much as a citation," Annick sighed. She had a dreamy expression on her face.

Brie laughed, rolling her shoulders. The blush on her face was beginning to subside.

Annick became more serious. "He is France, *mon amie*," Annick faced her friend. "This is a coup. *Une* conquête."

A conquest? thought Brie. Now Annick was mixing French with English. She knew her friend mixed languages when she was excited.

Annick rambled on about Napoléon being so proud. "You entered a foreign territory and conquered it."

She continued with more military jargon. Something about seduction as a military skill. It was much like Stendhal's main character Julien Sorel who, at age nineteen, had seduced his boss's wife, who was many years his senior.

"You do know how to move forward from here, correct?" asked Annick.

"I've lived in France. I know the French way," said Brie. "I'm simply not ready for a new man when I am struggling with the old one." She took a few quick breaths, avoiding eye contact with Annick.

"*Au contraire.* Of course, you are!" Annick hugged her friend. "Now what will we wear?"

Chapter 10

The next evening, Brie and Annick took a quick taxi ride from the hotel to the Quai D'Orsay. Pierre stayed at home to allow the ladies an evening out together. When the women arrived at the venue, they could see the vast elegance that surrounded them was dazzling.

"This is like a fancy ball held by King Louis XIV at Versailles," Brie said, her eyes widening as she smoothed her sleeveless black gown.

"You know the kings are all dead," Annick laughed, "but we certainly are in the midst of an impressive event."

Waiters carried silver trays of canapés. A string quartet played Debussy. Most women wore long, elegant gowns. With Annick's coaching, they had chosen the correct attire. Annick loaned her friend a pair of exquisite, pear-shaped emerald drop earrings to complete Brie's ensemble.

Brie wondered where the hosts were. Their invitation was checked by an attendant at the entrance, but she didn't see Monsieur de Laval. "It's like one of Jay Gatsby's parties, where the host never appears."

"This is not at all like *The Great Gatsby*," said a male voice.

Brie shivered and blushed as she recognized the resonant tone.

Both women turned to see Monsieur de Laval in a divine tuxedo, moving closer toward them, while motioning to a waiter to bring flutes of champagne. The bottle of Tattinger was the preferred vintage of the President of France. Another waiter appeared with *foie gras* on tiny toasts.

"We are here to greet our invited guests, not to view them from afar. This is Paris, not Long Island although Long Island is very beautiful," he added, being a diplomat and choosing his words carefully, so as not to offend.

He looked around the room. "I want you to meet one of our colleagues from Québec. Monsieur Roch Carrier," he said introducing his colleague.

Brie shook his hand.

"I've read many of your stories, Monsieur Carrier," she said. "I'm enamored of *The Sweater,* both the book and the film."

"You are a hockey fan?" he questioned her with his strong French–Canadian accent.

"I do enjoy ice hockey. I certainly appreciate the difference between the Toronto Maple Leafs and the Montreal Canadiens," she replied.

"We are arch-rivals," said Roch, "which is connected to one of the themes of my story." He had a ruddy complexion that Brie thought had survived many Canadian winters.

"I'm a New Yorker," she said, offering her hand. "*Je m'appelle Brie.*"

"I'm surprised. Please call me Roch. He looked her up and down, like he was buying a horse. I must admit, from your accent, I thought you were Parisian." He smiled, leaning back on his heels.

Monsieur de Laval chimed in, speaking to Brie. "You surprise me, Madame. I would never have guessed you liked hockey although I agree with Roch that you could very much pass for a *Parisienne.*" He examined her silky dress and her jewelry, placing his hand on Brie's back. She was losing her composure and could feel herself blush. She was usually not one for blushing.

Monsieur de Laval whispered in her ear. "I must leave for Malta early tomorrow, then on to Tunis on assignment. Do you have a card, so I may contact you when I return?" He looked into her eyes. "I gave you mine at the Louvre and I hoped you would contact me."

His rich Dior citrus scent put her in a dream-like state.

Brie hesitated. "I wouldn't call a complete stranger," she said.

"We are no longer strangers, Madame. We bonded over the *Winged Victory*. Then, fate brought us together again at the literary conference, where you accepted my invitation to this reception. We are meeting for the third time." His hand moved further down her back. She could feel his warm breath on her neck.

She considered his reasoning, surprised at his counting and offered him her card. She tried to step back, bumping into Annick, who was watching them both like an *Agent de Police*.

"Are you a Royaliste?" he asked, running his finger over the engraved Fleur de Lys above Brie's name on the card.

"I have been told by a French psychic that I was Marie-Antoinette in a past life," she said.

"It would not surprise me although they say, because she was beheaded, her soul has gone to numerous women." His eyes sparkled.

He reached out and touched the back of her neck, stroking it softly with his finger. She shivered. "You have an indentation here that indicates the guillotine," he added.

She laughed demurely and removed his finger. "You are joking?"

"Not at all," he said, lowering his voice. "We will explore that more fully later."

Monsieur de Laval was approached by another gentleman.

"Excuse me, Mesdames et Messieurs. I must steal Monsieur de Laval from you. His presence is requested by the *Premier Ministre.*"

They said their *aux revoirs* and Monsieur de Laval offered Brie kisses on the cheek. He shook the hands of Monsieur Carrier and Annick.

The kisses did not go unnoticed by Annick or by the Canadian author.

"What was he whispering to you?" asked Annick.

"Oh, something about Marie-Antoinette and Malta," said Brie.

"Our queen was never in Malta, as I recollect," Annick was hungry for information.

"It's just a mild flirtation. I'm not open to anything more," Brie replied. She adjusted her gold necklace and patted her brow.

"You looked very ready to me," said Annick.

"I'm switching to Perrier," said Brie. "I don't want the champagne talking."

"The champagne tells me you have met a very charming man. There are no accidents that you impulsively decided to fly to Paris."

"New York felt stifling to me. So many sad memories."

"I understand," Annick looked at her friend. "You have been through so much. Now, with this year passed, you have a chance to begin again."

"You are a true romantic, *mon amie*," said Brie.

"I am French," she smiled and hugged her friend. "We are born that way."

Chapter 11

The day arrived for their trip to Cannes to see Chloe at the film festival. Brie and Annick boarded the TGV—high speed train—to the *Côte d'Azur*. Pierre had to stay in Paris to care for his cardiac patients.

"I'll sneak away from Paris to join you and Brad Pitt in Cannes at the weekend," Pierre laughed, kissing his wife goodbye. He teased Annick about her Hollywood crush. "I wouldn't miss this chance to visit Chantal and to see Chloe and her film. Keep in touch and I'll do the same."

The women attempted to view the French countryside, but the landscape flew by faster than they could focus on any particular town.

This was the only downside of the high-speed trains. Instead, they napped, ate their baguette sandwiches, drank coffee, and read books.

Soon, they arrived in Avignon, where many of the passengers departed and they switched to a local car. It had been a mere three hours, and they had crossed an expanse the size of Texas. Chloe had always said she wished the Americans had such a train between San Diego, Los Angeles, and San Francisco. She had grown tired of Los Angeles traffic.

"We're so close to Aix-en-Provence," said Annick. "I wish we could get off and go to the street market. It is one of the best in the area, with such a variety of regional spices and cheeses. My sister Chantal likes to serve a cheese board every evening."

"Ah, the cheese!" exclaimed Brie. "A hundred varieties. Plus, I adore all the colorful fabric patterns of Provence, the tablecloths and the pure cotton clothing. We can go to *le marché* in Bandol, right near the sea. As you know, it's not far from Cannes."

"That's true," said Annick, still pining for Aix. "I adore the Cours Mirabeau in Aix and the Café Les Deux Garçons. Do I sound like a tourist in my own country?"

"You are a Parisienne," smiled Brie. "I do the same when I leave New York for a weekend in New England."

"I suppose we can settle for the Bandol Rosé from Domaine Tempier. It is the jewel of the Provençal rose wines," Annick said with a sigh.

"You have good taste," said Brie. "It's a rare find in New York, even in the finest shops and restaurants."

"That's one of the reasons you come here, to the source," laughed Annick.

The train continued along, this time on a local track and at a lower speed. The women could admire the towns and the countryside of southeastern France. Brie thought about Arles, the town where Van Gogh spent much of his time painting in his deep mustard yellow hues and saturated blues. The colors reflected the tones of Provence. She looked at the endless fields of sunflowers and lavender. At this slower speed, the little stone cottages came into view.

At last, they saw the brilliant blue Mediterranean directly in front of them. They both gasped as the watery expanse glittered with a contrasting lighter blue sky above. The sun and the sea were sparkling gems.

The local train stopped at the towns along the way: Cassis, Bandol, Toulon, St. Tropez, and finally Cannes. Brie had explored all of them on many occasions. The south of France was magical to her, and she felt like a contented child. She searched in her purse for her sunglasses, to cut the glare from the sea.

"We have arrived," said Annick, standing up and reaching for the luggage on the rack above them.

On the platform, they were greeted by Annick's grinning sister, Chantal, who waved with joy and ran toward them. There were four kisses, two on each cheek, traditional in the south of France.

It was quite warm, perhaps twenty degrees warmer than in Paris. Chantal wore a white cotton dress with navy espadrilles on her feet. Brie caught the scent of the jasmine and the rose scents of Chantal's perfume.

Chantal led them out to the parking area, carrying Brie's suitcase. Chantal loaded everything into her vintage pastel blue Peugeot convertible.

"How was your train ride, my little *Parisiennes*?" said Chantal.

"Fast and painless," said Annick.

"Beautiful," said Brie.

"Wait until you see our parents' former old crumbling villa. I have been renovating it. Annick has seen it in progress, but you have not, Brie," said Chantal.

"It has quite changed," said Annick. "Here in Provence, the work is not rushed. It has been a lengthy labor of love."

"You have to have patience here," said Chantal. "Not like Parisians."

"I'm very patient when I'm here!" insisted Annick.

Chantal shook her head in disagreement.

Chantal had been promoted to a top executive position at Air France. After their parents and her husband Paul passed away, two years apart, she was filled with grief and needed a project to take her mind off her sudden losses. Her husband was a race car driver, who perished in a fiery crash at the Grand Prix. He left her a sizable nest egg, a common precaution among race drivers to protect their families. Her parents succumbed to old age. Still, it was devastating for both sisters. Chantal was healing and back to her upbeat self.

It was a short drive to the villa. They pulled past two motorized, ornate iron gates into a massive, pebbled courtyard. The outer walls that surrounded the villa were covered in fuchsia-colored bougainvillea. The former crumbling villa, now a large soft beige expanse, with wrought iron balconies, had an immense carved wooden door, which was arched at the top. There were numerous palms that punctuated the entry.

"Welcome to *Villa du Ciel*, 'Villa of the Sky,'" said Chantal. "Your rooms are ready, Mesdames." She smiled.

The women entered a large living room with two cream-colored overstuffed sofas, covered in bright Moroccan pillows of French blue, turquoise, and gold design. There was an antique armoire on the far wall.

They continued to the dining room, with a large oval table and wicker chairs. In the center of the table was a fragrant bouquet of oversized coral roses, mixed with fresh lavender.

Beyond, they saw the Provençal tiled kitchen, in blue and yellow, which reminded Brie of the kitchen at Monet's home in Giverny. On the counter was a huge spread of paté de champagne with cornichons, creamy goat cheese, a large tomato tarte, and marinated artichoke hearts.

"I also have a pot of fresh ratatouille on the stove. The vegetables are from the market today, the spices are from my garden. I hope you are hungry," Chantal said and laughed as she darted at them with two baguettes.

She was certainly in better spirits than the last time they met at the funerals of her parents and then her husband. At that time, Brie thought her friend's tears would never end.

The three friends enjoyed the feast Chantal had lovingly prepared. They sipped Evian water with slices of lime.

"Annick tells me you have a new lover," said Chantal, who was never one to mince words.

"I would hardly call him that," said Brie, almost chocking on her piece of baguette, as she looked over at Annick.

"I did *not* say lover. I said interesting gentleman," Annick defended herself.

"Well, I heard the details, and I don't blame him," said Chantal. "He could not resist the exotic blonde from America, with her full lips, big breasts, and a keen knowledge of fashion." She giggled. Brie was not laughing. Chantal's bluntness had touched a nerve.

"You remember after Paul died. Were you open to a new love?" Brie, asked, flustered. She didn't think of herself as a *femme fatale*.

"It took me years to think of opening myself up to anyone," said Chantal.

"So, you understand where I am?" Brie asked. "I've only heard from Jack once or twice in the past months. I dare not open Pandora's Box. His puzzling anger encourages me to keep my distance. In New York, I would put a safety chain on my door every night before bed. I'd jump when the phone would ring. I couldn't continue to live in that fear and uncertainty."

"I understand, my dear friend. You explained yourself well in your emails. That's why it is wise that you came here," said Chantal. "You had to recover from a twice broken heart, one from the surgery then from that awful man." Chantal's eyes were filled with sympathy.

Brie remembered the surgeon saying to her, before they administered the anesthetic, "I will have your heart in my hands, and I will handle it with care. All of your emotions and the love you now have will remain. I will just repair the damaged part. You will continue to feel everything afterwards. Nothing will be lost. I promise you." He had squeezed her hand as she drifted off.

Brie was brought back to the present when she heard a sharp, high-pitched bark. Loulou, Chantal's tiny Maltese, arrived back from the groomer. The sweet little dog was sporting a grosgrain rose-colored ribbon and jumped up into her lap.

"Do you think Loulou remembers me?" asked Brie, petting the Maltese.

"No doubt," said Chantal, who took the opportunity to give her American friend a hug. "Would you like to give her a lamb treat?"

"Certainly," Brie replied. I have a toy flamingo in my bag that I bought for her at a fancy pet store on the Upper East Side. It is oddly called "The Parisian Pet." When I had my Maltese, Napoléon, I used to spoil him with toys from there."

"Well, this Provençal pup will love it. She likes any kind of stuffed toy with a squeaker inside," said Chantal. Loulou licked Brie's chest, right on her heart.

"Well, I'm ready for a walk on La Croisette," injected Annick. "First, I must change out of these Parisian wools and into something lighter."

"I'm anxious for an up-close view the Mediterranean," said Brie.

"Your wish can be granted. It's a short walk to the sea," said Chantal. "Loulou just told me she is ready for a walk." The fluffy white dog barked in agreement.

* * *

The three women walked down the slight incline to the Mediterranean, whose blue waters shone with shades from light to darker azure blues. The heat was intense for a spring day. They turned left and strolled along La Croisette, past all the designer boutiques. There were a slew of Hollywood types going in and out of the doorways of Chanel, Cartier, and Louis Vuitton.

"I'm channeling Alain Delon and Catherine Deneuve," laughed Annick.

"You are?" asked Chantal. "You know, Alain and Catherine are about to step out in front of you at any moment!"

"Alain, sadly, is no longer with us, but I will never forget his profile in the film *Le Samurai* as the killer for hire, Jef Costello," said Brie.

"I have never rooted for a professional assassin before I saw that film," said Annick. "What a dreamboat, as you say in American."

They walked past the landmark Carlton Hotel and out stepped Chloe.

"*Maman*, Annick, Chantal! I'm so happy to see you!" shouted Chloe.

She ran up to greet them. Loulou jumped up at her, begging to be held. She picked up the white pooch. There were many kisses, as a reunion took place on the Cannes sidewalk.

"You look beautiful, Mom, with that designer scarf. I was just going to call you. I've been so busy working with our publicity department." Chloe was jumping with excitement. She pulled out some items from her purse.

"Here are your guest passes for the film viewing in the morning and for a reserved place near the red carpet tomorrow evening. There's one for Pierre as well."

"*Fantastique!*" They all spoke in unison.

"*Un grand merci!*" said Chantal. "I've never been to the actual Festival before after all my years in Cannes."

"*Avec plaisir,* said Chloe, with a curtsy. "*Eh bien,* I have to rush off to meet with the director. We have so much to do before the opening ceremony tomorrow. Catherine Deneuve is the president of the jury this year."

"Please join us for dinner tonight, if you can. I'm making my grandmother's recipe for bouillabaisse," Chantal said.

"Mmm...I wish I could, but duty calls," said Chloe, breaking into a run.

Chapter 12

When the women returned to *Villa du Ciel*, they were exhausted from walking in the heat. Brie and Annick agreed it was time to relax after their day-long train travel. They were not hungry, so Chantal decided to create the elaborate bouillabaisse another evening, when Pierre was there to enjoy it with them.

The women hugged once more, with *la petite* Loulou wanting to get in on the group-hug. Brie grabbed the dog and lifted her up onto her lap.

"If you don't mind, I am going to lie down," said Brie. She took a bottle of Perrier and the dog with her.

"I'll bring up your suitcase," said Chantal. "Your room is the second one on the right, overlooking the garden. You have a balcony, with a view of the sea."

"I'm in heaven," said Brie. "*Merci.*"

"Our pleasure," said the sisters.

* * *

When Brie awoke, hours later, the room was dark, and the house was quiet. She assumed the others had gone to bed. She decided to set up her laptop to check her mail messages.

She was happy to read a message from her publisher. They had accepted her recent manuscript of her novel.

As she scrolled down, she noticed an unfamiliar address ending in "*Diplomatie.*" It was titled "Malta-Paris." She opened the message. It was from Laurent de Laval.

"Malta would be perfection if you were here with me.

Till we meet again. Laurent"

Brie took a moment to visualize the suave diplomat, who oozed charm.

Warmth filled her body.

Attached were two photos, one of Dwejra on the island of Gozo, off Malta. It was a stunning arched rock formation called the "Azur Window." It was known by the Maltese people and around the world as a "doorway to the sea."

The second photo was of the famous Blue Lagoon, which was inside a rock crater on the island of Comino. The lagoon showed varying shades of turquoise and sapphire.

Brie thought of this Malta setting and the man she knew so little about, for his seductive eyes and his vaguely indiscreet attention toward her at the Embassy *soirée*. She had noticed that the other female guests at the event stared at him with longing, yet his eyes had been focused on her.

She closed the computer screen and looked out at the bright lights of La Croisette. She took to her bed and instantly fell asleep.

Chapter 13

The next morning, the women went to an early screening of Chloe's film. They were impressed with the unique script and superb acting.

"It will be a winner," predicted Chantal.

"I agree," said Chloe's proud mother, Brie.

"Here we are in Cannes, the jewel of the French Riviera. I think it's time for the beach," said Annick.

"My old friend Sven, from Stockholm, runs 'Lido Plage' next to Carlton Hotel Beach. Let's go and see him," said Brie.

"We don't have *chaise* reservations. Can we even find any spots at such a crowded time of the year?" wondered Chantal.

A majority of the Riviera beaches were reserved for hotel guests only or owned privately. They provided all the amenities: chairs, umbrellas, towels. A client needed to only show up with their swimsuit.

As the three women approached the entrance, with the waving flags of France and Sweden, they could see the blue marine and white stripped umbrellas and the *chaises longues* of the venue. They walked down the few steps from La Croisette.

A man with long blond hair, wearing a blue and white striped shirt and a gold chain necklace, waved them away. "*Nous* sommes *complets!*" he said, without looking up at them. "No places," he added in English.

The women had disappointment on their faces.

"Sven, *C'est moi!*" shouted Brie, smiling.

Sven approached her with his own brilliant smile. "Brie, why did you not tell me you were coming to the film festival?" He kissed her on both cheeks.

Annick and Chantal stood there in amazement. Luckily, they had all packed their swimsuits before going to Chloe's film screening.

He gave them each a key to the dressing room. When they appeared in their bathing attire, Sven called to a tanned young man in white shorts and a navy polo, embroidered with the Lido Plage insignia.

"Jean-Luc, show these ladies to the front row!" Sven waved his hand forward. He winked at Brie.

Jean-Luc had a surprised expression on his chiseled face, as he adjusted his fashionable sunglasses. He carefully placed the mattresses— *matelas*—on the *chaises* and handed them each a large blue striped towel. As requested, he adjusted their individual umbrellas to protect them from the blazing Riviera sun.

"I will return to take your order, mesdames," he said.

Chantal turned to Brie. "You have more clout in this town than I do, and I live here. Where do you get all these connections?"

"I met Sven years ago, when I lived in Paris. We've been friends for many years," smiled Brie.

"How friendly?" asked Chantal, probing.

"*Oh là là*, Chantal, where is your mind again?" said Annick, frowning.

They all laughed. At last, Brie was beginning to relax. Her unease disappeared like the wispy clouds in the southern French sky.

"You are back in your habitat, my friend," said Chantal. "Your second home." Brie sat in silent agreement with Chantal's assessment of her present state of mind.

The three women sat three feet away from the sea. Today, the Mediterranean was aquamarine and rippled on the sandy shore.

Chloe ran down to meet them at Lido Plage after receiving a text from her mother. She wore a white cotton lacy Chanel beach shift Brie had bought for her birthday two years before. She kissed her mother, Chantal, and Annick. "So great to see everyone!" Chloe was out of breath, always running.

"Can you at least join us for a little lunch?" asked Brie, as she kissed her stylish daughter.

"I'm surprised you got chairs at the beach today," said Chloe.

"Your mom knows people in high places," laughed Chantal.

Annick nudged her sister on the arm.

Chloe sat at the end of the chaise, looking up at the clear, cloudless sky. She breathed in the salt air. There was a moderate breeze as sea birds flew low over the top of the water.

"I can't stay. I have the final fitting for my gown and then hair and make-up for the red carpet tonight. My assistant will bring me something," said Chloe.

"That's my girl!" said Brie. "I'm so proud of you, sweetie." She hugged her daughter.

Thanks, *Maman*. I know you're always in my corner."

Chloe swirled the delicate gold and diamond band on her middle finger. Her mother understood that her only daughter was jittery and excited for her event.

"*Eh bien*, I'm off to prepare for the biggest night of my life," said Chloe. "The sky is so clear. You know, there could be a green flash tonight. *Le Rayon Vert*. It portends a major life change." She hugged all the women and ran back up to La Croisette.

"She is a little philosopher, your daughter," said Chantal as Chloe departed.

"She's talented," said Brie with a proud expression. "You can surmise she was an undergrad philosophy major before her graduate film studies."

Just then Jean-Luc appeared. "Would you ladies like to take lunch here or at the café?" He pointed to the restaurant in back of the rows of beach *chaises*.

"Oh, I think lunch would be nicer at a table," said Annick. They all nodded in agreement. "This is too much in our laps." Brie knew that the French were more formal for any dining, even at the beach.

The young man showed them to a table with a spectacular view, on the covered, roped off patio. Their bare feet were in the sand, as he handed them each a menu.

"*Bon appétit, mesdames*," said Jean-Luc. He flashed a broad, white smile, projecting a movie star quality.

A waiter soon arrived, with a white shirt and a blue scarf around his neck. The tables were full at the height of the lunch hour, and he appeared rushed.

"*Vous désirez, mesdames?*" he asked, looking around him.

"*Pour moi, la salade niçoise et un Perrier, s'il vous plaît*," said Brie.

"Chantal, you love shrimp."

"Yes, I do. *La salade aux crevettes pour moi*. And a half pitcher of vin rosé." The women spoke *franglais*, half French, half English, alternating between languages.

"*La même chose pour moi*. The same, *merci*," said Annick.

"*Merci, mesdames*," said the waiter, gathering up the menus.

"I've had the shrimp salad here before. You have to peel and clean your own shrimp," said Brie, moving her fingers to demonstrate. "What a mess!"

"That's Riviera style—the whole animal on the plate," said Annick.

"I can't get used to that. I once saw a whole tiny baby octopus in my soup and took it out," said Brie. "All the tentacles. Ooh!"

"And I ate yours, whole! Do you remember?" asked Chantal, laughing.

"How could I forget?" Brie replied.

Annick's phone rang. Brie and Chantal stopped their conversation and listened.

"That was Pierre," said Annick. "He's arriving on the next train. I will go and pick him up after lunch."

"I'll drive her to the station. I don't trust my sister to drive my car," said Chantal, kicking the sand with her bare feet.

"The gears stick and make a funny noise," said Annick with a scowl.

The appealing salads arrived, with butter lettuce, tantalizing tomatoes, and a variety of local olives. Brie had fresh albacore, green beans, and petit potatoes, all dressed with vinaigrette. She had requested the anchovies on the side.

The French women peeled their shrimp effortlessly, with a knife and fork, as Brie looked on with amazement. They sipped their rosé wine and sighed with approval.

Annick directed a question to Brie. "So, will you stay at the beach on your own?"

"Yes. You can't tear me away from here. I'll let Sven know you are leaving," said Brie. "Kiss Pierre for me. I'll see him tonight."

"I will," Annick said and kissed Brie on the cheeks.

"*A ce soir!*" said the sisters, as they waved goodbye.

Brie returned to her *chaise longue*. She was surprised to see the adjoining *chaises* were already taken. Next to her was a stunning young woman in a turquoise and pink flowing caftan with gold trim. Brie wondered who this woman could be, given the small town of Cannes was now overflowing with film people for the film festival. Perhaps an actress? The woman had long, wavy light brown hair with blonde highlights. Her head was partially covered by a matching silk scarf. Her arms were filled with gleaming gold bangles. Long drop gold earrings with substantial emerald gemstones hung from her ears. She wore bright pink lipstick and Chanel sunglasses. The young woman put out her hand to shake Brie's.

"*Bonjour, madame*, I am Layla. So happy to meet you," she spoke French with a strong Arabic accent.

"*Bonjour, je m'appelle Brie.*"

Layla lowered her glasses to make eye contact, and Brie saw the woman had large almond-shaped green eyes. She looked to be in her late twenties.

"Those are my little twins, over there," the woman said pointing to a boy and a girl, perhaps five years old, who played with two women in white uniforms. "My husband is busy presenting his film."

"My daughter is doing the same," said Brie, smiling. She wasn't surprised.

"We are here in a perfect spot on a lovely day. Will you join me for some tea?" said Layla.

"I would like that very much. *Merci!*" said Brie.

The woman raised her hand to a young man in a white uniform.

"Abdul, will you bring us some sweet tea?" said Layla.

The young man bowed to her and hurried away. He soon returned with fresh mint tea in small green glasses with shiny gold rims and a tray of dried fruit sprinkled with pistachios.

"You are my guest today, so just tell me anything you would like. Abdul will bring it for you," said Layla. Then she asked, "So, you are French?" The women were conversing in French.

"No, American, from New York," Brie clarified her own nationality.

"Oh, my husband and I have been to New York several times. We enjoy the city so much. It has such intense energy," said Layla. She threw up her hands to reveal an enormous pear-shaped diamond ring. The glint of the stone in the direct midday sun blinded Brie. She knew that women wore jewelry to the beach on the Riviera, even in their swimsuits, but this young woman looked like a jewelry ad from *Town and Country* magazine.

Brie felt a bit underdressed in her magenta maillot and her grand-mother's vintage ruby ring designed by Van Cleef and Arpels. She added her Dior tortoise shell sunglasses to cut the glare of the increasingly stronger sun. Although they both were covered by sun umbrellas, the light bouncing off the water blurred Brie's vision. The hot tea added to the warmth she felt.

"Would you like to go into the water?" asked Brie.

"That's a splendid idea," said Layla.

Layla got up from her seat and proceeded to walk the few steps to the brilliant turquoise sea. She entered the water in full ensemble, her flowing caftan floating above the water.

Brie entered the sea with her one-piece suit, her hair in a small ponytail. She felt almost naked next to Layla.

Layla walked around in the shallow end, while Brie swam out to the darker blue water. The Mediterranean had such a high salt content that she was buoyant in the tiny waves. After a short time, they were back on the beach, reaching the bamboo mats that created a path for them.

Jean-Luc arrived with buckets of water to wash down their sandy feet.

"You know, I have a new bikini under this caftan," said Layla, with a wistful expression. She flashed the top of the suit to Brie, who smiled at the sight of the fashionable animal print bikini top. Brie understood that in Layla's culture the women had to be covered, even at the beach. The caftan, now soaking wet, would dry in the sun. Brie felt fortunate she could be in a mere swimsuit while she swam.

After a time, there was a loud ruckus behind them. Sven was running after a large group of photographers, who snapped photos of Layla and her children. Sven was frantic to push them aside.

"You must leave immediately," shouted Sven to the photographers. "This is private property. You have no right here. You are disturbing our clients."

Brie, frightened for her new friend, patted Layla on the arm. Layla looked at her with terror on her face. She was shaking.

Sven was effective in herding the paparazzi off the beach. He had obviously had previous experience. Yet, he was happy to have the assistance of Layla's bodyguard, who appeared out of nowhere. He was a gigantic man in tight fitting black pants and a black t-shirt, with arm muscles the size of most men's thighs.

Soon, it became quiet again on Lido Plage.

"I think it's time for us to go," said Layla. "Come on children." She reached for each of their small hands.

She turned to Brie. "So nice to meet you, my new friend." This time she offered kisses.

"Wonderful to meet you. Please take care," said Brie, with a pained expression.

"Sorry for the abrupt interruption," said Layla, as she was escorted by her bodyguard off the beach.

Brie watched as Layla's caftan billowed in the breeze, as she and her entourage disappeared into the soft haze. Then, she stood in silence, looking out at the sea.

Chapter 14

When Brie returned to *Villa du Ciel*, she was covered in a salty white film. She hadn't taken the time to fully rinse off at the shower at Lido Plage. She did stop at La Maison du Chocolat to get some treats for her hosts.

Pierre was at the door to great her. "I see you've been baptized in the Mediterranean," he said. He offered her kisses. "Ah, you're bearing gifts." He noticed the large box of chocolates. "*Merci.*"

"You've gotten some sun today," Annick arrived to greet her. More kisses. "Chantal is in the kitchen preparing her bouillabaisse."

"I'm in here," yelled Chantal, "making you some octopus for tonight!"

She laughed at her own wit. Brie laughed with her.

Brie followed her nose to the large Le Creuset Marseille blue enamel pot on the stove in the kitchen. She caught the heavenly scent of onions, garlic, and fennel.

"Actually, I'm making lobster and mussels tonight," said Chantal, adding a few saffron threads to the broth. "We can all sit down and enjoy, and then take our baths to prepare for Chloe's big night. Pierre is hungry."

Pierre nodded in approval. It seemed to Brie that the French were always either eating or preparing food or talking about what they were going to eat next. For such a svelte group of people, la cuisine was an obsession.

Soon Chantal was ready with her gastronomic creation. She spooned the bouillabaisse into large cobalt blue and green ceramic bowls. The lobster was the star of each portion.

She shouted, *"A table!"* And everyone moved to the dining room table.

Pierre placed one of the large cloth napkins at his neck. His blue-grey eyes sparkled. *"Bon appétit,"* he said.

Loulou jumped up on Chantal's lap. "Somebody is ready for their meal," she said to the little dog. She retrieved Loulou's hand-painted bowl and filled it with Loulou cuisine.

Brie recalled a time in New York when she and Jack decided to rescue a small poodle from a nearby shelter. When they brought the little guy home, he seemed quite willful. She named him Napoléon. He was not good at learning commands, and he jumped up and begged at the table.

Jack had anger issues and lost his temper. Brie was horrified when she saw him kick the little poodle across the room. The dog cried out in pain, and she ran to little Napoléon's rescue. That night, she slept next to the little dog to be sure his was okay. To her chagrin, the next morning, she found the dog unresponsive. Brie rushed him to the vet, where Dr. Gold was able to revive the poodle. Brie had cried with relief and Jack scolded her for overreacting. She had noticed Jack's behavior as an animal abuser as another red flag.

Brie was startled back to the present by Annick. "You're not eating anything," Annick observed. "It's time to get ready for the festival."

"I must be nervous for my daughter," Brie said feeling disoriented. "It's time to celebrate my Chloe." She glowed at the thought.

"Our Chloe," said the friends, noticing Brie's discomfort.

They arrived at the Cannes Palais des Festivals, at their reserved places near the red carpet. Security was tight, the excitement palpable. Bright lights bathed over the massive staircase up to the grand hall.

First to arrive was the ever-elegant Catherine Deneuve, in a stunning golden gown that Brie guessed was created by Christian Dior. Not a hair was out of place. She shone in a dazzling pear-shaped diamond necklace, with bold, matching earrings. She was flanked on one side by the classic actor Gérard Départieu and on the other by the dashing Benoît Magimel. Both men wore impeccably tailored black tuxes. The crowd applauded and photographers swooped in like seagulls.

"I love Benoît," said Chantal, who was almost salivating. "What a man!"

They were followed by female French director Claire Denis, whose films reflected themes of her childhood in West Africa and in France. She was joined by director François Ozon, who had been nominated for the *Palme d'or*.

"I read that François is a Scorpio. Very sexy," said Chantal. Annick gave her sister an impatient look.

"My sister thinks always of sex."

Brie thought about how the sisters contrasted in their style and outlook, yet they were close and loving with each other.

The Americans were next. Brie spotted the director, followed by her daughter Chloe in a black sheath designed by Stella McCartney, and walking with her head held high in her Manolo heels. Brie heard from Chloe about the creation of this gown. Chloe insisted on wearing black. This was a youthful design that followed the lines of her body. She wore her highlighted hair long and carried herself like a star, her smile radiating toward the ever-present photographers, who shouted at her from every direction. She seemed poised and relaxed.

"There's my baby," said Brie to her friends, beaming a smile.

"We see her," said Pierre. "What a beauty!" The women agreed.

"She looks like she's done this a hundred times before. What a pro," said Annick.

Then, on Chloe's arm, they all noticed one of the stars of the film.

It was Brad Pitt, long-haired, in all his glory, in a fitted black tux, black shirt, and tie.

"I think I am going to pass out," said Annick. "But I will die happy. *La Morte Heureuse*, she quoted the title from one of Camus' books.

Pierre took his wife's arm, worried that she could, indeed, faint. This close-up view of Monsieur Pitt was unexpected. Chloe hadn't given them a clue. Annick was not one to be impressed by film stars, but Brad was her one weakness.

Brie and her friends did not enter the Palais des Festivals. The actual event was reserved exclusively for film industry participants. The film viewing passes Chloe had gotten them were a special exception for her family. Chloe would be tied up for several days and Brie was free to continue enjoying the splendid *Côte d'Azur*. She wished she could spend more time with her daughter, yet she was grateful to see her at all, under the circumstances.

Brie and her friends returned to *Villa du Ciel* to relax. They were quite overwhelmed and a bit tired after all the red-carpet excitement.

"That was glorious," said Annick, taking a deep breath. "Brad is even more dashing in person." Pierre gazed at his wife in wonder. He looked at Brie, hoping to change the subject. She picked up on his signal.

"Can we go to *La Verrière de Biot* tomorrow afternoon to visit the glass blowers?" asked Brie. "I have a collection of their glassware at home, and I have always wanted to see their factory."

"What a wonderful idea," said Chantal, nibbling on some cold lobster from the fridge. "I adore their unique bubble glass."

"First, I want to go to the open-air market for fresh vegetables," said Annick. The Brad spell was broken.

"I'm always ready for *le marché*," said Brie.

"I'll stay home and watch the flowers grow," said Pierre. He needed some relaxation time.

The women laughed at Pierre's humor as they sat at the kitchen table, removing their high heels and rubbing their feet.

Brie was amazed how Frenchwomen could wear heels, even walking for miles on the sidewalks of Paris. Louis XIV had taught them that heels allowed for a sexier walk and a more regal posture.

Pierre yawned. *"Bonne nuit à tous,"* he said.

"Good night," said Brie. *"Fais de beaux rêves.* Pleasant dreams."

"Oh, I will," said Annick, who, with a dreamy look in her eyes, seemed back on the red carpet.

Chapter 15

Pierre was the first one at the breakfast table the next morning. He had prepared his coffee. He waved the Nice-Matin newspaper at Brie.

"Take a look! I see that you were lounging with royalty on the beach yesterday," said Pierre. "In full color!"

Brie gaped at the headline and the large photograph below it. There was Layla, in her caftan, with Brie beside her, on Lido Plage. They shared the front page with Catherine Deneuve and Brad Pitt. Annick grabbed the paper and turned to her friend.

"When were you going to share this story with us?" she asked. "Your adventures are astounding."

"I never knew the young woman was a princess, but I am not surprised," said Brie. She had an idea about the identity of Layla, but she preferred to remain discreet.

"We would like to be informed of your breaking news ahead of time," said Chantal. "Not because we are nosy, but we want to share in your experiences. You have a more exotic life than the average person." She grabbed the newspaper to read the article.

"If I shared many of these happenings with most people, they would think I was making them up," said Brie.

"We are not like most people," said Annick. "We believe these stories are true."

"Thanks." Brie felt flushed.

"Let's go to the market before the vegetables get picked over," said Chantal. "We can talk on the way there." Chantal was already planning their next meal.

The Cannes *marché* was swarming with locals who were seeking cheeses, olives, and produce from local farmers. They seemed pleased that the visitors were absent, busy with the film festival.

Brie had learned, long ago, that the customer ought not touch the produce. They must allow the farmers to handle and select the items for the client, whether they are vegetables, garlic, or fresh fruits.

They walked by a stall with locally crafted soaps—*Les savons* de Marseille. The scent of the various soaps stopped Brie in her tracks.

She turned to enter the large alcove and chose her favorite, mixed berry blend—*fruits rouges*—as well as orange blossom and lilac scented bars in bath and hand sizes. The soap maker approached her.

"I would like these," Brie pointed to the soaps that filled her little basket. "*C'est combien*—how much?" Brie asked as she sniffed the soaps.

"They are free—if you take a shower with me!" said the purveyor, smiling.

"What *parfum* are you wearing today, my friend?" whispered Chantal.

Chantal turned to Annick. "She attracts men like flies."

Brie continued. "I prefer to pay in Euros for today," she said to the young man. "But thank you for the offer." She was in *le flirt* mode.

"The offer is always available to you, madame," he said, trying to meet her eyes. She had her head down, so as not to encourage him further.

Annick and Chantal looked at each other, with a knowing glance.

Brie learned that France was a country where *le flirt* rose to an art form. The act of sex itself was often not the goal of the game. Sensuality was everywhere. The French liked to "Celebrate the difference—*Vive la différence!*" She studied the natives and observed their interactions. It was like acting onstage or in film. The difference was the French enjoyed and respected each other.

"Have you heard from the diplomat—Monsieur de Laval— recently?" asked Annick. "You haven't spoken of him since we left Paris."

"I did get a message the other night, from Malta," she said. Brie felt warm thinking of Laurent. "I forgot to mention it."

Her friends rolled their eyes.

* * *

On the way up the winding road to the village of Biot, in the Alpes-Maritimes, Chantal was singing in the car. Her favorite driving tune was *She'll be coming 'round the mountain when she comes in French— Elle déscend de la montagne à cheval.* She sang at the top of her lungs. She wore a red scarf, tied tightly under her chin, to keep her hair from flying in her face. Annick and Brie joined in, holding onto their hats. The old blue convertible still had a lot of power and Chantal raced around the curves with finesse.

The bright blue sky above was filled with puffy clouds. They drove past the town of Mougins, the most famous culinary locale in all of France, if not the world.

"If it wasn't festival time, I would suggest dinner at the *Moulin de Mougins*," said Chantal. "Right now, with the film elite in town, it's impossible to get a reservation."

The Musée Renoir was not far away. Brie thought about suggesting a visit to the museum on the way back to the villa, if time allowed. She enjoyed the breeze and the scents in the provençal air.

They arrived at the fortified medieval village of Biot in the heat of the midday sun. They entered the open workshop, where numerous glassblowers were creating their hand-blown art pieces, as artisans before them had done for centuries. Today, they were blowing quart-sized pitchers in soft blue and pale green bubbled glass. Brie approached the bench of one of the glassblowers. She was mystified by the ancient art form. The heat was intense, and she was wearing a long sleeve blouse to protect her from the sun's rays. She rolled up her sleeves and blotted her brow with a flowered handkerchief. Annick and Chantal watched the artisans at a safe distance, wringing their hands.

Brie moved closer to one of the glassblowers, who had shiny jet-black hair and muscular arms. She was reminded of her estranged husband, Jack Taylor, as both of these men had a bad boy vibe.

Annick caught Brie out of the corner of her eye, and she urged her friend to move backward. Brie heard nothing. She only saw her friend's lips moving. Brie's legs began to shake and an instant later, she was on the ground, blacked out.

The staff and guards of Biot rushed up to Brie, with Annick and Chantal close behind. They kneeled at Brie's side and moved her back, away from the flames. A group of visitors took note of Brie and retreated. A woman, with a gold name plate on her dress, placed a cold compress on Brie's forehead. Brie began to blink and opened her eyes. They carried her to a chair in the shade under a tree. The director of the company provided some cool Evian water and one member of the staff offered to call in their medical team.

"I'm fine," said Brie. "Just a little lightheaded. Thank you."

"Yes, madame, it's unseasonably hot for May this year," said one of the women who attended to her. "You were a little too close to the molten glass."

"I was too close to the heat. My mistake," Brie said and sat back in the chair, listless. She was still groggy, and her throat felt like sandpaper.

"Pierre will examine you at home," said Annick. "My husband is a physician," she added to the attendant.

The ride back to *Villa du Ciel* was not as animated as the drive up.

There was no singing.

*   *   *

They found Pierre lounging in the flower garden at the villa with Loulou when the women returned. Man and dog were both in the white gazebo that offered shade, as the sun had moved to a lower part of the cloud-filled sky.

"Come and look at this patient," said Annick. "Brie passed out in Biot. I'm very worried. Chantal is parking the car."

Pierre jumped up from his spot and came to Brie's side, taking her pulse.

"You look flushed," he said, turning to his wife. "Please bring her some cool water right away."

"I feel much better," said Brie, still feeling dizzy. "I drank a liter of water in Biot. They were so kind," she mumbled.

"I suspect a mild heat stroke," said Pierre. "With your history, I want to do a heart scan today at my friend's cardiology office in town. I'll call him at once." Brie was tired of being the helpless patient, but she went along with Pierre's recommendation.

She breathed a sigh of relief to hear Pierre and his colleague say that all was normal with her heart scan and her blood pressure was back to a safe range. There were no new problems with the heart valves or the aorta, as Pierre had feared. He recommended bed rest, mineral water, and shade.

"No more parties at the beach with princesses, or red-carpet events for a few days," said Pierre, with a stern expression. Annick and Chantal walked Brie to her room. Loulou jumped up on the bed to guard the patient.

Brie's phone rang. On the other end of the line was a very nervous-sounding Chloe. Annick had texted her about the happenings in Biot.

"Mom, I can't leave you alone for a minute! Tell me you're okay."

"I'm fine, sweetie. Thanks. Just some mild heat exhaustion. The climate here is so much different from Paris, combined with this odd heat wave in May." Brie caught her breath, as she lay on the pillow.

"Well, you rest in bed. You're in good hands. I will come to see you as soon as I can," said Chloe.

"Please don't rush. I know you're busy with work."

Chapter 16

Days passed on the French Riviera, while Brie lost count. She continued to rest at the insistence of her hosts and "Doctor" Loulou. She was *en plein forme* as the French say, for good health. Pierre was being extra cautious. She appreciated his concern, as he was the protective big brother she always wished she had. Her own brother had died in infancy, determined by the doctors to have had a congenital cardiac issue.

Brie awoke to hear the voice of her daughter Chloe in the next room.

"I want to see my mom," she said. Brie believed that Chloe had suffered a sort of PTSD after coming close to losing her mother to the heart event last year.

They all followed in a long procession to Brie's bedroom. Loulou barked at them as if they were strangers entering a restricted area. Brie looked up from *Madame Bovary*, the book she was reading.

"*Bonjour, tout le monde*," said Brie, happy to see everyone. "I'm sorry to have caused worry." She was wringing her hands.

Chloe, who carried a bouquet of fresh pink and white roses mixed with jasmine, ran up to kiss her mother. She sat on the bed next to Brie and took her hand. Annick arrived behind her with a vase full of water. She placed the fragrant flowers in water on the round wooden night table.

"You gave us a scare. How are you feeling?" asked Chloe.

"I'm fine, very fine. Thank you," Brie didn't want to cause her daughter any more worry. "I would love to go out for ice cream at my favorite place next to the Hotel Martinez on La Croisette. I don't think ice cream would hurt me, do you?" asked Brie, checking the faces of the group at her bedside. Her energy surged with their emotional support.

They all looked at Pierre, who put his hand on Brie's forehead.

"I suppose it would be fine, if we can wait until the sun sets," he said.

"This is my last night in Cannes," said Chloe. "We fly back to Los Angeles early tomorrow from Nice. Of course, I can wait."

"So, we'll celebrate your accomplishments tonight," said Annick.

"Yes, we will," said Brie, smiling broadly.

Chloe took a bow and they all applauded her.

Chloe's film had not won the Palm d'Or for best film, but they did win an award for directing. All the dedicated work and long hours had been worth it, and Chloe was a big part of that team effort. Of course, the big name and expertise of the director was a major part of the film's success and recognition in Cannes.

When they arrived at La Terrasse, next to the stunning Hotel Martinez, the sun was setting. The café was right in the midst of the action on La Croisette. They viewed chic passersby while they savored the panoramic backdrop of the azure Mediterranean Sea. Brie was content to be out of bed and celebrating with her daughter and their friends.

The group was seated at a large, oblong white table with a superb view of the magenta and golden sky. The sunset was a colorful sorbet of pastels.

"We might see the *rayon vert*—a green flash—tonight. We missed out on the one last week," said Chloe. She elaborated again on the significance of this phenomena and how it brought the viewers' major change in their lives.

"You know, Eric Rohmer did a film about it," she added. *"Le Rayon Vert.* I've seen the film five times, so you can say I'm obsessed."

"Let's hope it brings positive change to Brie, to restore her health," said Annick. They all made a motion to toast and looked to Brie in her Matisse red dress. Brie's eyes sparkled as she blew them all kisses.

The café was packed with film people. Soon, the waiter arrived with the elaborate, illustrated ice cream menus. The list of choices exceeded forty varieties of sundaes.

Pierre ordered his favorite: Café Liégeois, with coffee ice cream, chocolate sauce, whipped cream and shaved chocolate.

The sisters and Chloe chose La Coupe Tutti Frutti—a combination of sorbets with a variety of fresh fruits, fruit syrup, and whipped cream.

Brie chose La Pêche Melba, invented for Nelly Melba, the famous opera singer. It was composed of poached peaches, raspberry sauce, and Tahitian vanilla ice cream. "I like plenty of whipped cream," she said to the waiter.

"Beaucoup de la crème chantilly," said the waiter, giving her a thumbs up.

"Whipped cream is the most perfect food," said Brie. She hadn't eaten any in many months.

When the sundaes arrived at the table, they were quite a sight, with lit sparklers that glowed against the darkened evening sky. The waiter grinned and placed a separate bowl of whipped cream, a foot high, in front of Brie. Everyone laughed, including the patient.

The animated group stayed another hour and a half past sunset, as the crowded café slowly emptied. They were now the only guests at La Terrasse of the Hotel Martinez. Chloe was happy to see her green flash—a clear, bright chartreuse, at the horizon. It was a short blink of light, that disappeared in an instant.

Brie excused herself to freshen her lipstick in the ladies' room. She had learned early on, that French women never apply lipstick at the table or in public. Chantal had told her that women here must be perceived as natural beauties, with no heavy make-up.

"Shall I go with you, *Maman*?" asked Chloe.

"No need. I'll be right back," she replied.

* * *

Brie walked down the long, darkened corridor, at the back of the café. The air was cool and damp. She was startled to hear a familiar, chilling male voice say her name. She froze, her heart pounding in her rib cage. She felt him grab her arm. When she turned, she saw her estranged husband, Jack Taylor, who stared at her, his nostrils flaring.

Her body shook. "Please leave me alone," her voice was a whisper. She attempted to shout, but she couldn't manage it. Her throat was blocked.

Jack's eyes burned on her in the shadows, as he twisted her arm. She tried to break free of his tight grip, but she could not. Jack now had his large hand across her mouth. He pressed his massive, muscular body against her petite frame. She wished she could break loose and return to Chloe and to her friends, to the patio of her contentment and celebration. Why had Jack Taylor followed her here to France, to what she thought was her safe place? How did he know she was in Cannes? She assumed he was in New York. In truth, she had no idea where he had been. He had disappeared after her surgery, without a word.

"I want to talk to you," he said. He was behind her, and she could feel his hot breath on her neck. Her body was pumping with adrenaline, yet it felt limp.

"If you promise not to scream, I'll let you go," he said.

She tried to nod. Then, she attempted to bite his arm.

He turned her around, his penetrating green eyes glaring at her. He slapped her face with a force so intense it made her cheek burn.

"You had me followed?" she choked. "It was you in Paris!"

"Listen to me. I owe dangerous people a lot of money. I left to protect you," he said, loosening his grip.

"I don't trust you anymore," she said, gasping for air.

"I know and you shouldn't. I lied and kept secrets," he said, with menace in his voice. "Then things got out of control. You'll understand one day. One thing I do know is that we are destined to be together. You know that, right?" Then, he let go of her.

She fell to her knees and tried to stand. When she looked around her, he had disappeared. Gone in a flash.

* * *

Brie limped back to the terrace, where her friends and Chloe were involved in lively conversation. They turned to her and saw the terror in her eyes. Her hair was messed, her clothing disheveled. Lipstick smudged all over her mouth.

"What happened, Mom?" asked Chloe.

"Are you feeling ill?" asked Annick. They both rushed to her side.

Brie was out of breath. Pierre jumped up and took her pulse as Chloe put her arm around her mother, protectively.

"He's here in France!" Brie mumbled, with tears in her eyes.

"Who's here?" asked Pierre, with a puzzled look.

"Jack. He's here. In Cannes," she said with a blank stare.

"He's here, now?!" asked Pierre, looking around him.

"He attacked me back there," said Brie, pointing to the empty, dark corridor.

They all gasped, as Pierre moved toward the corridor.

"Don't bother. He's gone." She was sweating profusely, then slumped down in a chair and covered her face with her hands. "He disappeared when the *flic car* drove by, I think."

Chloe began to sob. *"Maman,"* was all she could say as she brushed her mother's blonde hair from her face.

"He was right there," Brie pointed in a shocked state of disbelief.

"Nothing surprises me with that guy," said Chantal.

"Can we call the police?" asked Chloe, her voice shaken.

"No *flics* just yet," said Pierre. "I'll handle him. We'll return tonight to Paris, and you'll not go back to the hotel. Please stay with us. Jack has no idea we've moved out to Neuilly. He may look for you at our old residence."

"I have a good friend, a pilot for Air France, who has his own plane. He can fly you back to Paris," said Chantal. "I'll call him immediately."

"That will be our plan," said Pierre. His demeanor was calm.

"Chloe, you return to the Carlton Hotel and pack for your departure," said Pierre. "You said your plane to Los Angeles leaves in three hours from Nice Airport?"

Chloe nodded and hugged her mother again. "You're in good hands, *Maman,*" she said. "I love you all. *Merci à tous!*" She kissed their friends.

Pierre spoke to Chloe. "After all your mother has been through, we will not let anything more happen to her," he assured her.

"Thank you for taking care of my mom," said Chloe. She kissed Brie on the cheek, noticing the bold redness of the slap, as Brie remained in a state of shock.

* * *

Back at *Villa du Ciel*, Annick packed a bag for Brie and then one for herself and Pierre. Brie was in no state of mind for packing and Pierre appreciated his wife's organizational skills. Chantal made them a snack of baguette with ham and gruyère cheese.

Pierre took out his cell phone. "I'll call my friend and former patient, Detective Thierry Marceau," he said. "He used to be a top homicide detective on the Paris police force. He's retired now, but he takes private clients. He can guard our home and keep Brie safe."

Annick patted her husband on the shoulder and gave him a kiss.

"You are my knight in shining armor, *mon chevalier*," she said.

He kissed his wife on the lips. They gazed at each other with adoration.

"I need all the help I can get," said Brie, with a look of horror on her face, like she had seen a ghost.

There was a knock at the front door. Loulou began to bark. It was Chantal's friend, Luc Fournier, the pilot. He was a tall, strapping man with a capable air.

"*Bonsoir, tout le monde*," he said. "I hear there's an emergency."

Luc and Chantal loaded the suitcases and passengers into his navy SUV with dark tinted windows, and they headed to a private airport near St. Tropez.

When they arrived at the small airport, there was a sudden burst of cool rain. They hurried to an overhang for shelter. At the desk, Luc spoke to another man, with a baseball cap and glasses. He motioned to Luc that the plane was waiting on the tarmac. Their pilot Luc then instructed Brie, Pierre, and Annick to go up the small set of stairs and into the four-seater plane. Chantal would stay behind in Cannes.

The friends embraced. Luc kissed Chantal and whispered something in her ear. They walked up the metal stairs and the pilot closed the doors. They were ready for takeoff.

Brie gazed out the window, at the wet pavement. It reminded her of the final scene in the film *Casablanca*, when Rick's love Elsa and Resistance fighter husband Victor Laslo would be flown to safety.

The pouring rain tapered off to drizzle.

"The sky has cleared. It will be a short flight," said the pilot. The lights of the Riviera soon faded to darkness.

Chapter 17

The Girard home in Neuilly was formal compared to Chantal's provençal villa in Cannes. The large marble entry opened to a back wall of French doors. Brie noticed the lights were on before they entered. The glass doors revealed a large terrace and green area. Persian carpets covered the wood floors. An antique crystal chandelier hung in the dining room and original oil paintings, of impressionist and expressionist style, graced the walls. The high ceilings gave a sense of spaciousness, absent in many Parisian living spaces.

Pierre and Annick's son, Etienne, Brie's godson, appeared. He was a doctor, like his father, with a budding practice in Neuilly. He had been covering for his father since Pierre's extended stay in Cannes. The two Doctors Girard embraced. Annick kissed her son, who in turn, kissed his mother and godmother Brie. Brie had been very close to Etienne since birth, visiting him every year. He was the son she never had.

"I heard about the high drama in Cannes," said Etienne. "And not only in the cinema. More intrigue than at the court of the Palais de

Versailles." He gave Brie an extra-long hug and turned to Pierre. "Your detective is in the guest cottage, setting up surveillance."

"Excellent!" said Pierre. Annick looked on with a relieved expression.

They both made sure Brie was seated on the sofa and drinking Evian.

"Where is *tante* Chantal?" asked Etienne.

"Your aunt is in the south, closing up *Villa du Ciel*. She must return to Toulouse to continue work on an Air France project," said Annick.

"With Luc?" asked Brie. "Our pilot, Luc, looked like more than a friend to her." Brie wasn't the only one leaving out details about men.

"*Eh bien, oui*, those two are close. The first man she has let into her life since Paul died," said Annick.

"Ah, that reminds me," said Etienne. "You sister Lisa called from Montreal. She received your message and asked that you call her in the morning."

"I explained to her in the text that I was in the best of hands," said Brie.

"We will not let you out of our sight until this is resolved," said Pierre.

"I'm lucky to have such loyal friends," Brie smiled at them. "I know I must be careful now that Jack's appeared in France. I had wanted to treat you both to a nice meal at La Maison Epicure or the Jules Verne at *La Tour Eiffel*. Now, we have to wait," said Brie.

"We'll have plenty of time for that," said Pierre.

"How do you think Jack found me?" she shuddered at the thought of him on the loose nearby.

Annick shrugged. She turned to her husband.

"Now you know the French Sherlock Holmes was not overreacting, eh?" said Pierre. "I'm guessing that he was able to track you from your picture on the front page of Nice Matin."

Brie had a terrified look. "You are onto something there."

"Shall I open some wine?" said Annick. "Is anybody hungry? The neighbor left us some fresh eggs. I can make *les omelettes aux fromages.*"

"Not for me," said Brie. "If you don't mind, I'd like to go to bed."

"Of course. What am I thinking?" said Annick. "I will ready your room." She went down the hall.

"I could eat an o*melette,*" said Pierre.

"I'll make us both *omelettes,* Papa," said Etienne. "There's a red Bordeaux breathing in the kitchen."

"Thank you, son," said Pierre, patting Etienne on the back.

Chapter 18

Detective Thierry Marceau entered the kitchen the next morning. He was a tall, solid, well-groomed man with an alert gaze. As a former high-ranking officer with the Paris Police Nationale, he decided working privately after retirement would afford him autonomy and the choice of cases he would accept. He spoke with authority to Brie.

"Madame Taylor, I have made several inquiries into your husband, Jack Taylor. He has some, shall we say, unsavory connections to criminal activity," said Detective Marceau. His probing eyes were fixed on hers.

"What sort of activities?" asked Brie, nervously. She looked to Annick, who had a worried look.

"I'm still investigating him. It's a complex case. I have retained many connections with the Paris Police. I will inform you when I have more detailed information," said the detective. "In the meantime, please be assured you are quite safe here."

Brie noticed a large revolver under his jacket, when the detective reached for his coffee cup on the counter of Annick's kitchen island.

He took a sip of coffee. "I would suggest that you stay indoors, for now, while we get a better perspective on where this case is going. Now that we have full surveillance in place, I will know if anyone approaches this residence. Pierre was right to call on me." He nodded to Pierre. "I'll keep you apprised of new developments." He made a slight bow to the ladies and exited to the back yard.

"Very businesslike," said Annick, taking a deep breath. "Now, we confirm Jack has dangerous secrets."

"The detective is impressive," said Brie. "I feel safer having him here. Pierre was right all along that I was being followed." She wiped away a tear on her cheek. "For so long, I felt this vague undercurrent in our relationship. I never guessed he could be a criminal." Her stomach soured.

"It takes a long time to know someone, and even when we think we know them, we sometimes don't. Am I making sense?" asked Annick.

"Yes, you are," said Brie. She knew Jack had an unpredictable edge.

"I'm lucky with my Pierre," said Annick. "He is my rock." She kissed her husband on the cheek.

"With Jack, I felt an element of danger from the beginning," said Brie.

"Exciting is not always desirable in a man," said Annick. "You don't want to go off the edge of a cliff." She sighed.

"I should have stepped back a long time ago," said Brie. Upon reflection, she had to admit she put herself at risk with Jack on many occasions.

"You didn't know. He was charming," said Annick. "I remember your wedding in French Polynesia. It was breathtaking."

"So glad you and Pierre could come to the wedding. We wanted an intimate beach ceremony. The hotel in Bora Bora arranged it all, so, effortless for me. I was teaching full time at the university, overloaded with work," said Brie. "Jack was swamped with cases at the law firm."

"It was a wise choice," said Annick. "Such a magical destination. A fantasy, on a tropical island in the center of the turquoise Pacific. Enchanting."

"Jack was attentive and loving back then. The wedding was a joyful celebration on every level, wasn't it?" asked Brie. "I thought I was making the right decision, that he would be a good husband."

"He certainly drew me in with his charm," said Annick. "You were a beautiful couple."

Brie thought back to her fragrant headdress of Tahitian gardenias, *Tiare* and all the exotic flowers that surrounded the wedding party on that idyllic beach with the balmy breezes.

"The Tahitian vanilla was hypnotic, and we were under an island spell," said Annick.

"Remember the singing and dancing by the locals at sunset? The divine dinner of lobster and *poisson cru*?" said Brie. She was back in French Polynesia in her mind, to a time when she had been happy.

"We danced to exhaustion with that drumming," Annick laughed. "Pierre learned that Tahitian hip thrust quickly, didn't he?"

Pierre laughed from his belly. "Those Tahitian men are huge. I think that one young man must have been seven feet tall."

"I came up to his waist, remember?" asked Brie.

"Then, the next day, the surfer, Marcel, took us to a reef a mile out, in the outrigger canoe. He fed the barracudas before we entered the water."

"You must watch out for the predators on land as well, my friend," said Annick.

"Yes, my groom became one of those barracudas," said Brie, with a sigh.

"The next day, Pierre saved my life, when I stepped into the sea from the overwater bungalow dock," said Brie.

"You didn't see the stonefish, as it blended in with the rocks," remembered Pierre.

"You would have died within a few minutes," said Annick. "Hard to believe that was ten years ago."

"Pierre is always saving me, somehow," said Brie. "He bought me that book of *Poisonous Fish of the South Seas.* Jack was never protective of me. Just the opposite," she winced. Her muscles tightened.

* * *

Brie placed a call to her sister Lisa in Montreal. She was surprised to hear her sister pick up without the screening from her assistant. Lisa was an attorney at a major Canadian law firm. She met her French-Canadian husband when they were both law students at McGill.

"Hi, honey, this is your big sister calling from Paris," said Brie.

"Great to hear your voice. *Ça va?*" asked Lisa.

"I'll be okay. Pierre and Annick are taking such good care of me," said Brie. "I don't know where I would be without them. I've been in a fog."

"This latest news about Jack is very unsettling, to say the least," said Lisa. "Nothing surprises me about him anymore. I spoke to Etienne who filled me in on the details. This is like something out of a bad movie."

"Yeah. Jack had me followed. *Merde.* He's been involved in illegal activities," said Brie, taking a deep breath. She couldn't imagine what they were, or perhaps didn't dare.

"I must say, I'm not surprised. I always felt he had a distant relationship with the truth. Secretive dude," said Lisa. "People who lie by omission are still liars."

Brie cleared her throat.

"I spoke to Chloe. She told me about the incident in Biot, your fainting spell. You have been under many stressors both physical and emotional. Not good, Sis," said Lisa.

"It's been a blur for the past year. But I am gaining perspective. Now this recent storm has hit," said Brie. She felt a knot in her stomach.

"I want to fly to Paris to see you in person," said Lisa. "My assistant called Air France to inquire about flights. I'm wrapping up a case here. What do you think of that idea?" she asked.

"I can't wait to see you, but don't feel any urgency to come." Said Brie. She continued. "I know you're busy. You were such a great nurse to me for eight weeks, after my heart surgery. I couldn't have made it through without you."

"And that nurse is still around, ready to help. You did the same for me when I needed you. We're sisters. We always have each other's backs, right?" asked Lisa.

"Love you, Lisa."

"Love you more."

*　*　*

Brie checked her messages after her call to Lisa. She noticed a second email from Laurent de Laval. In the midst of all the chaos with Jack, she never replied to his previous message from Malta. Did she want this new man in her life? She wondered about taking a step forward toward the handsome diplomat. What secrets did he carry with him from his past? She pressed her lips together, lost in a daydream. She opened his latest message.

"Bonjour from Tunis. Business is going smoothly. I can see the Avenue Habib Bourguiba from my window. I'm not far from the Mediterranean. I scheduled my return to Paris in mid-June and it is my hope that you will join me for dinner at that time. You are often in my thoughts. Bises, Laurent."

She replied.

"Bonjour from Paris. Your photos from Malta were brilliant. I hope to meet you again in Paris, in June. Brie."

She decided not to add the kisses. Accepting them from him was all she could manage, for now.

Chapter 19

Brie felt imprisoned in Neuilly, although Pierre and Annick did their best to distract her, and she tried to distract herself with reading and writing. They watched films nightly and danced to jazz and blues music in the living room. Annick showcased her culinary talents with a variety of classic and modern French cuisine creations. Her *Lapin au moutard*—rabbit with mustard sauce—was delicate and refined. Her Mediterranean *Mezze* appetizers included six varieties of eggplant dishes, feta in phyllo, marinated garlic lamb, and spiced olives. Such a shame that Brie had lost her appetite.

Annick and Brie had literary discussions, tapping into their vast knowledge of French literature. They dissected Stendhal's *Le Rouge et Le Noir*—*The Red and the Black*—for days. They analyzed the picaresque main character, Julien Sorel, who at age nineteen and as a former student at the seminary, had seduced his boss's wife, a much older woman. *Très français.*

Annick taught Brie to play *Moonlight Sonata* on the piano. Beethoven reminded her of the twinkling stars over Lake Lucerne. Still, Brie was confined indoors for weeks during the investigation and the walls were closing in. She had come to France for freedom, which once again, evaded her.

At last, Detective Marceau had something to report, a month after Brie's incarceration inside the Girard's lovely domicile. He had discovered startling information.

"Madame, we have been informed, by Interpol, that Jack Taylor is heavily involved in an illegal international gambling ring, based at the Casino de Monte Carlo, in the Principality of Monaco. There are criminal charges being brought against him and others, as we speak, by the Monegasque Police. The Las Vegas Police are involved as well. This investigation began about two years ago. At last, they have enough hard evidence to convict the perpetrators."

The French detective placed his hands on his hips, revealing an even larger firearm than the one Brie had noticed when she first met him.

"There was always something about that guy," said Pierre. "He was an iceberg. We saw only the tip of what was lurking below."

Brie agreed with Pierre's iceberg reference. She had felt it on a daily basis, like she was living with a dangerous stranger.

The detective continued. "Monsieur Taylor has been arrested. He is now in custody. You were his Achilles Heel, Madame." He looked directly at Brie. "If he hadn't come to France to find you, as he did, we would never have connected him to this group of criminals, as the kingpin of illegal activities, although I regret, I cannot divulge the details. He forged an impressive cover."

Brie was speechless. She sat down on the couch and rubbed her face with her hands. Annick came to her side and put an arm around her friend. This revelation was beyond what Brie could ever have imagined.

"There's more," said the detective. Brie looked up at him, gritting her teeth. What kind of man was this who had shared her life and her bed?

"Your apartment in New York is considered a crime scene. The FBI has a search warrant, and the contents are being confiscated by them and by the New York City Police. If you have an attorney, I advise you to call him as soon as possible. You, as his wife, do not want to be implicated in any way in this matter," Detective Marceau said, with a stern look.

"I'll call our friend and personal attorney, Jeffrey Klein, in New York," said Brie, "unless Jack has already contacted him." She worried that Jack had been in touch with his former law school classmate and whether Jeff would be willing to help her.

"This is France, Madame. The criminal does not get a phone call. You are guilty until proven innocent here. Not like in America. Make the call right away to Monsieur Klein."

"*Un grand merci, Thierry*," said Pierre. He patted his friend on the back. "You've been thorough in finding this information."

"*A votre service*; anytime my friend," said Detective Marceau.

The two men shook hands.

* * *

Brie felt numb. There was so much to process. In a moment, Jack went from a neglectful, uncaring husband to an international white-collar criminal. She made the call to New York.

Jeffrey Klein and Jack Taylor had been law students together in New York. She wondered if she was making the right choice in calling him.

He picked up on the first ring.

"Hey, Brie, my favorite francophile!" he exclaimed.

"Hi, Jeff," she said. Her voice was monotone, her stomach nauseous.

"Great to hear your voice!" he said. "How are you doing? It's been a long time! Candyce and I were wondering about your recovery from the heart surgery."

"It's been a year-long recovery, but I feel stronger every day," said Brie.

"We were thinking about contacting you," Jeff continued. "Let's set up a dinner date for the four of us soon, if you're up to it?"

"Thanks for the beautiful bouquets and for visiting me in the hospital," said Brie. "I don't remember much from that time. I'm actually calling from Paris." She felt embarrassed to share her unsettling news with him.

"Paris? Are you and Jack on vacation?" asked Jeff. "I haven't heard from him in a while. What a fine place to celebrate."

Brie hadn't shared her sudden departure from New York with any of her friends. Only her immediate family knew of Jack's abandonment of her right after her emergency surgery.

"No, Jeff." Brie's voice was weak. "Jack's been arrested." She was barely able to say the words. Her head was spinning.

There was a gasp and a blank moment at the other end of the line.

"I see," said Jeff, his tone changing. "So, this is not a social call. Is he in French custody?"

She hoped she had his confidence.

She explained the whole scenario with Interpol, the FBI, the French police, the casino in Monaco, and the NYPD. She added details about the French detective, the Cannes episode, and her subsequent confinement at the Parisian home of Pierre and Annick.

"Well, this is quite a story," Jeff took a breath. "My old buddy involved in international white-collar games. Whoosh! The guys on the Law Review always thought of him as a bit of an Ivy League gangster." Another silence. "I admit I can envision him capable of such outrageous behavior." Another pause. "I'm sorry you're going through this mess."

"I'm in shock," Brie continued. Her stomach was churning, but she felt relieved that Jeff may be on her side. "I learned the FBI is at our Manhattan home with a search warrant, gathering evidence. I can't go back there, and I wondered, as his wife, if I have any liability." She struggled to catch her breath.

"That's a good question," said Jeff. "If I remember correctly, you were married in Tahiti, which is legally part of France. Candyce and I were there at your wedding. Since the ceremony was performed on foreign soil, it's therefore not legal in the U.S." He paused. "You have no worries, unless, you had another ceremony in the States that I don't know about."

"No, we did not," she replied and sighed. Her head was pounding less than before. She knew, at the time of the marriage in Bora Bora, they could follow up with a ceremony in New York. She had chosen to only have the Polynesian wedding and Jack never pursued the matter further. They both had been married before.

"So, that leaves you out of this mess, my dear. It's all his problem. My guess is that bankruptcy will be part of this equation, so there may be some financial fallout for you." Jeff hesitated. "I don't deal in international law, and I won't touch this. Jack, if he calls me, will have to find other representation."

Brie felt relieved. "So, you can help me?"

"I'm in your corner," said Jeff. "I would like to talk directly with your French private detective, if you can send me his contact info."

"I will," said Brie, biting her nail. Jeff would be her ally. "Thank you, Jeff. This is such a relief." She took a gulp of water. She was parched. "Jack owns our shared residence outright, but all our other finances have been separate from the beginning, with each having their own bank accounts."

There was nothing in that home she needed or wanted, except for the Renoir painting from her mother. Jack had relegated it to a back bedroom, so she had returned it to her parents for safekeeping. The jewelry she inherited was in her bank vault, in a box under her name. Mementos from Chloe's babyhood, along with childhood treasures, were with her daughter.

"All good news, my dear. You're savvy. I'll delve into this matter right away," said the attorney. "Can I share this with Candyce? She has been quite concerned about you."

"Absolutely," said Brie. "Send her my love." She took another sip of Evian. "It's not a pretty situation, Jeff. I can't believe I didn't notice something strange happening, earlier on."

"Don't fault yourself, Brie. You had enough on your plate, trying to survive," said Jeff. "The undercurrents were subtle."

"He wasn't around much, Jeff. I felt abandoned in my darkest hour," said Brie. Her insides were on a rollercoaster.

"I hear you. Now, you found out what a strong woman you are," said Jeff. "The odds were not with you. Very impressive, my dear."

"Thanks so much, Jeff. I survived for a reason. More will be revealed. You and Candyce are great friends," said Brie.

"Hey, we love you," replied Jeff.

"I love you both. We've known each other for over ten years," said Brie. She had deep affection for those two, more than Jack had, she suspected.

"Have some French pastry for us. I can almost taste those fruit tarts and croissants!" said Jeff. "Don't worry. You'll be fine. Just another bump on life's road. And remember, I'm only a phone call away."

*   *   *

Brie remembered challenges had begun a few years into her marriage with Jack. She recalled a snowy weekend with him in Vermont. It was a bitter cold day, twenty below. The snow on the mountain had turned to glare ice, with brutal winds kicking up without warning. Skiers needed ski masks to prevent frostbite on their faces, but that didn't stop Jack. Brie had been worried about the danger on the slopes and had stayed in the lodge. He had made fun of her choice and left her alone all afternoon.

Another time, in Colorado, Brie enjoyed the powdery conditions on the lower sections of the mountain. She swished down the gentler trails and felt like a bird, flying and free. Jack called her out for staying on "the bunny slopes" and not challenging herself enough.

He preferred the challenging black diamond trails and liked to show off. An accomplished skier, he competed in NASTAR races. He refused to waste his time with his wife on the moderate slopes.

On a particularly stormy day in Vail, Jack insisted on taking Brie to the mountaintop in a gondola. She protested, but then decided to try a new trail. Jack assured her the run would be long, but not steep. He lied.

When they exited the gondola, there were sudden blizzard conditions at the top. Brie could barely see a few inches in front of her. Jack took off on his own, leaving her behind, to fend for herself. She slipped on the steep terrain, rolling down the mountain, and ended up buried in deep snow with gale force winds surrounding her.

It was a stroke of luck that the Vail Ski Patrol was monitoring the trails during these extreme conditions. Two patrolmen discovered Brie, near the top of the mountain, unconscious. They strapped her into a toboggan and took her down to the Vail First Aid Center, six miles below. The doctors revived her and x-rayed her leg. They discovered a severe, spiral oblique break in her right leg. The patrolmen stayed close by, speaking in Norwegian with each other and joking with Brie. They were stereotypical Scandinavians, tall, blond, and handsome. They told her they were from Norway's Olympic ski team and she was relieved to have such competent rescuers.

The Norwegians rolled Brie in a wheelchair to the ski lodge, placing her at a window with a panoramic view of the mountain. The sky was beginning to clear. Her leg was raised up and she was in a cast. The patrollers covered her with a blanket and brought her a cup of hot chocolate.

Jack arrived at the lodge hours later, surprised to notice Brie was not alone. One of the patrolmen told him the story of her accident. Jack laughed and called her a wimp, insisting the weather was not that bad. One of the patrollers, named Henrik, called him a nasty word in Norwegian, and offered to get Brie some dinner. His colleague invited Jack to take a secret run with them on the backside of the mountain, the next day. Jack declined.

Brie thought she had taken risks with Jack that threatened her well-being. She had ignored the red flags.

Chapter 20

Brie spent most of the week in bed, with emotional exhaustion, continuing to process the details of Jack Taylor's arrest and her conversation with Jeff Klein. She slept and vented in her journal. She wrote dark poems to release her fear and disappointment of Jack. She imagined the police going through her belongings in Manhattan, a residence that never seemed like her own. It had been owned and furnished by Jack, in his ultramodern, vacant style. The kitchen reminded her of a chemistry lab, with chrome and shiny cabinets. She was grateful to not be there to see the violation, or to face the prying eyes of her neighbors. She had thankfully left her most precious possessions and childhood treasures in East Hampton with her parents, who had passed away shortly after she married Jack. She read books from Annick's library and hardly ate. Even the Girards' gourmet cuisine, was not appealing. She nibbled on French bread and drank Evian water. She tried to focus on Jeff Klein's assurance that she was clear of any responsibility for Jack Taylor's crimes.

She took time to gather her thoughts and prepared for a long talk with her daughter in Los Angeles. Chloe was initially fraught with anguish.

Brie assured her everything would be fine now that Jack had been arrested and was in custody.

"He was never my favorite person, Mom. He was like an empty shell," her daughter told her.

Brie updated her sister Lisa in Montreal, who was making plans to come to Paris. "He's behind bars, where he belongs," said Lisa.

However menacing the open-ended issues might become, Brie would face those new issues in due course.

* * *

When the dark cloud above Brie's head began to clear, she sensed being cooped up. She was a confined bird, ready to flee her gilded cage and Paris was at her doorstep. All that remained was a long-awaited celebration.

Brie, dressed in dark jeans and a white t-shirt, walked to the kitchen. She caught the eyes of Annick and Pierre, who were preparing dinner.

"Well, the butterfly has emerged from her cocoon," said Pierre, grinning. "How do you feel?"

"It's the weekend. Let's step out," said Brie, more jovial than she had been in a long while.

Annick looked at her with surprise. "Where would you like to go? You've been though an ordeal," She feared Brie was a little off.

Pierre stopped stirring onions in the frying pan. "We've all been through a distressing time." He shook his head. "How about a sail to the Greek Islands, to visit Mykonos and Crete?"

"Are you serious?" asked Annick, wondering about Pierre's comment of going to Greece.

Brie jumped in. "Hey, remember that tiny street off the Boulevard St. Michel, lined with the Greek restaurants?" she asked. "Where we used to go when we were students at the *Faculté*?"

"Oh, yes! Rue de la Huchette. Near the Sorbonne. What a great little walking street!" said Annick. "The Ionesco Theatre is right there, near the restaurants."

"That's an idea. How about tomorrow night?" asked Pierre.

"We can invite Etienne to join us. I'll make reservations," said Annick.

"I'll be ready," said Brie, with a light-hearted expression. "Opa!"

*　*　*

The next evening, at nine o'clock, the four friends entered the animated Greek taverna on Rue de la Huchette. The hosts, the owners, Brie guessed, greeted them with big smiles. Both were broad-shouldered men with booming voices. Three musicians were playing keyboards and bouzoukis. One of them blew a kiss at Brie.

"Welcome, my friends," said a large man with a white apron and a black mustache. He seated them near the dance floor. "We have a very special lamb dish tonight. My grandmother's recipe from the Cyclades." He smiled at Brie.

Pierre ordered saganaki for the hors d'oeuvre. The waiter brought it to the table in a frying pan, to which he added fresh squeezed lemon juice.

The cheese is flambéed at the table in the States. There was no fiery presentation here in Paris, which surprised Brie.

The waiter poured a Greek red pinot wine into tiny glasses. It was *Limniona* from Thessaly.

"The Greek producer of this wine trained in Bordeaux," said the waiter.

Pierre led the toast. The group raised their glasses "to health and freedom—*santé et liberté*." The waiter joined them with his own glass, his eyes focused on Brie.

Horiatiki salads followed, with tomatoes, sliced cucumbers, feta cheese, and olives dressed with lemon and olive oil. The vegetables glistened in the amber light.

The leg of lamb with roasted potatoes, red peppers, and onions followed. The scent of garlic was overwhelming.

"Garlic, to keep away the evil spirits," said Etienne.

They all laughed.

The evening show was about to begin. The lights dimmed. Several men came out of the kitchen and two others from behind the bar. They removed their aprons. They were all dressed in black. They positioned themselves in a circle on the dance floor and one man held a red handkerchief in the air. Another man, with a bottle in his hand, covered the edges of the dance floor with Ouzo. They lit the alcohol on fire, which created a luminous rim. The spotlight came on. The musicians played a familiar Greek tune with animation and the men danced wildly. The women stood behind them and clapped and the diners joined in with the clapping. Then, the men receded and left one of the owners on the dance floor. He wore a black leather jacket, which he placed on the back of a nearby chair. This man picked up a small table in his mouth and held it with his teeth. He danced, knees bending, in the middle of the dance floor. All the Greeks were clapping wildly. The dancer's brother came up and lit the leather jacket on fire. Flames sparked in all directions.

"We always seem to be near the flames with you, *ma petite*," said Pierre to Brie.

"Enough, Papa," said Etienne. "Tonight, is a night of celebration, with no talk of the past." He met the gaze of his godmother, who looked pensive.

The Greek coffee burned on Brie's tongue.

* * *

The evening continued. It was now past midnight. Etienne suggested going down the street to the legendary *Caveau de la Huchette*, a jazz club which had opened in the 1940's. It was next to the Ionesco theatre. Jazzmen like Lionel Hampton, Sacha Distel, Art Blakey and numerous others of distinction had graced the club's stage.

They walked down the steps into the basement venue. It was a large brick room, lighted in reddish tones. The place was jammed with hip clientele. Locals and visitors combined for a contrasting mix of patrons. The ambience was warm, the music cool.

Years before, Brie had been surprised to see the French actually dancing to jazz music. It was a rare sight in New York. The famous club was infused with a boudoir-like atmosphere, and the French dance partners got into a sexy, sultry sway to the music.

She was approached by a young man in a dark blue silk long-sleeved shirt. His jeans were black and fitted. She gave him a wry smile when he asked her to dance. "*Non, merci*," she mouthed softly, shaking her head.

A short time later, Etienne offered his hand to Brie, pointing to the dance floor. To him, she nodded "yes," and he whisked her off to the wooden floor. The skirt of her bias-cut red dress swished with her movements, her blonde hair swirling in the low light. The youngish man, at his own table, glared at them both. They swayed to a Miles Davis tune, *Stella by starlight*. Brie remembered listening to the same tune at the Village Vanguard in New York. Dancing to it, she sensed a whole new layer to the song. The piano player closed his eyes and lifted his head toward the low ceiling. The trumpet player wore silver studded pants, like Miles himself.

Annick and Pierre joined them on the dance floor for the next tune, *Kind of Blue*. The light in the club changed to a soft blue. They clung to each other, looking up to smile into each other's eyes.

The musicians continued with *Blue in green*. The lights faded into a soft blue green, the playlist a Miles marathon. Brie was in her groove, taken off guard by a sudden fantasy that she was dancing with Laurent de

Laval. She wondered if she had a new message from him. She thought he would be a good dancer.

The crowd began to thin. It was past four in the morning, an appropriate time for their night to end. Near dawn, they took a cab back to Neuilly.

Chapter 21

Brie pondered whether she might be overstaying her welcome *chez* les Girards, with such highly charged events. She prepared herself for an exit back to the hotel. She'd heard from Lisa that her sister had booked a flight to Paris.

Brie spoke to her hosts. "I want to tell you both how grateful I am for your support in seeing me through such a difficult time. It's been a long haul. Now that the intensity has subsided, I think you both deserve to have some personal space."

"You are more than welcome to stay as long as you wish," Annick said.

Pierre nodded in agreement. "We love having you here with us and we have plenty of room."

"Thank you so much." She was more than grateful. "My sister Lisa will arrive soon in Paris," said Brie, "and I plan to meet her at the hotel."

"We would love to meet Lisa. Call us," said Annick, smiling. "Let's share a meal together."

They hugged.

* * *

Brie called a cab to take her back to the hotel in St. Germain des Prés. Jean-Jacques, as always, welcomed her and had her room waiting.

"*Bonjour, Madame.* You look well. I hope you enjoyed the Festival in Cannes."

"Wonderful," said Brie. "I had a nice visit with my daughter."

"Happy to hear that," said Jean-Jacques. "Here is your key. I'll call for help with your luggage."

"*Merci bien,*" she said, content to be on her own, although the Girards were close friends and superb hosts.

Brie jumped into the large, comfy bed with the poufy white comforter. It was late afternoon. Pale grayish-blue hues flooded the walls of her room. She closed her eyes and thought about the jazz music of Miles Davis and the lights of *La Cave de la Huchette.* She dozed off.

She awoke to the sudden ringing of her phone. "Allo?" her voice was drowsy.

"Bonjour!" She heard a cheerful male voice on the other end. "Laurent de Laval here. I'm calling to tell you I've arrived back in Paris."

"Ah, bonjour, bonjour!" said Brie. She could feel her face flush. "How was your time in Tunisia?" She remembered the former French colony in North Africa retained some ties with France.

"Fascinating place. Rich history. Currently, with pockets of terrorist activity. We're helping with solutions." He quickly changed the subject. "I would like to see you again." He was direct. "Can you join me for dinner next weekend?"

"That would be lovely," she said, feeling a tinge throughout her body. She tried to sound nonchalant.

"Excellent," he said. "I took the liberty, while still in Tunis, to arrange a reservation at Le Jules Verne at *La Tour Eiffel* for next Saturday. Where can I meet you, to accompany you to the restaurant?" he asked, without the least hesitation.

She gave him her hotel address. She liked this man's confident air. "I look forward to seeing you again." That was an understatement.

"Perfect, I'm dropping off a report at my workplace, *Quai d'Orsay*. I know exactly where you are. Not far at all," he said. "I'll be at your hotel at eight o'clock."

"*A la prochaine.* See you in a few days," she said, with an upbeat voice.

"*Je t'embrasse,*" he said, with his charming intonation.

Brie took a deep breath. She felt a lightness in her chest, though her heart was pounding. This was the first time she'd accepted a man's invitation in a very long time, since her break up. She believed it was a step in the right direction.

She fell into the chair by the window. When she looked out at the passersby on the sidewalks, she saw them in animated conversation. The railing by the métro included children eating ice cream cones. No sign of the long-haired man who had previously followed her.

Chapter 22

The week ambled along as Brie anticipated her dinner with Laurent de Laval. She made a visit to her hairdresser, Babette, at her *Rive Gauche* salon. Babette was an artist of hairstyle, a woman of wisdom, whom Brie had known since her university days. Brie and Babette shared an admiration and trust on many levels.

With the rainy spring weather, Brie spent much of her time indoors, reading novels, writing in her journal, and giving herself a manicure. She had a difficult time concentrating on plot lines, daydreaming of scenarios of her upcoming dinner at the elegant Jules Verne restaurant with her new suitor. It had been over a decade since she felt such a flutter.

When the evening arrived, Brie struggled to decide what dress to wear for her *rendez-vous* with Laurent. At the last moment, after trying on several choices, she decided on her scoop-necked black lace sheath. She added Aunt Françoise's Tahitian pearls with the pear-shaped ruby and diamond pendant. After all, she would be dining with an extraordinary man, and the Jules Verne at *La Tour Eiffel* was one of the most elegant restaurants in Paris.

Her phone beeped at a few minutes past eight o'clock. She read the text. *"I'm downstairs in the lobby. Bises, Kisses, Laurent"*

"I'll be right down," she wrote.

She wasn't ready at all. Her pulse raced as she dabbed a bit more Chanel No.5 on her wrists and in her *décolletage*, her hands shaking. She looked into the full-length mirror and took a deep breath. She decided to put on more mascara, then added a crimson wrap and her Louboutin heels to complete the ensemble. She grabbed her Chanel black quilted leather clutch and descended in the elevator. Her whole body was quivering. She wished Annick was there to offer support.

Jean-Jacques was at the front desk. *"Bonsoir, très* élégante, *Madame Brie.* The gentleman is in the lounge."

He smiled at her.

Brie glided around the corner, waving at Jean-Jacques. Then, she caught a glimpse of Laurent, with his back to her. He was looking at one of the impressionist-style oil paintings.

"Bonsoir," she said in a soft voice.

He turned towards her. *"Bonsoir."* His vibrant blue-green eyes lit up and fixed on her golden brown-amber ones. They were both motionless, hardly breathing.

He sighed. *"Ravissante,"* he said moving toward her, pulling her close. His kiss was soft and lingering.

He wore a black suit with a burgundy silk tie. *Dazzling*, she thought.

"Nice to see you again," was all she could manage.

"My car is just outside. Shall we go?"

"Oui," she said, her voice breathless.

He placed his hand on her back and guided her to the door.

The gleaming sapphire blue Bentley was parked at the curb.

"My driver has the night off," he said, opening the door for her. He helped her inside, moving her wrap toward her shoulder, as he shut the car door.

He was an attentive driver, though he drove at a high speed on the wide boulevards of the City of Light. Her body was cradled in the smooth, dark red leather seat. He held her hand as he drove.

In a few moments, they arrived at the Eiffel Tower. He parked in front. Annick was correct in her assumption that he could park anywhere he wished. Laurent assisted her in exiting his car, taking her arm. They rode the elevator to the second floor.

The Maître d' approached them, eyeing Brie. He greeted Laurent. "Pleasure to see you again, Monsieur de Laval." He showed them to a private table. The interior lighting glittered with the celestial decor. The views of Paris, from the expanse of windows, were panoramic. Portions of the metal structure of the tower itself were visible, framing Paris by night at four hundred feet.

The waiter arrived. Laurent ordered Taittinger champagne. The waiter returned with a silver stand filled with ice. He poured the sparkling liquid into crystal flutes and placed the remainder of the bottle on ice.

Laurent's eyes were focused on Brie's. "So, what brings you to Paris, beyond the Winged Victory and our literature?"

"I'm visiting dear friends from the university. You've met my friend Annick at the literary conference and at your reception."

"Ah, yes. Lovely woman," he said, motioning to the waiter, who brought oversized menus encased in black leather.

Brie continued. "I lived here for four years while I completed my studies. I'm on sabbatical from my professorship in New York, taking some time to revise my novel."

"I do recall," said Laurent. "Let's toast to your return to Paris and to your future book. You grace us with your presence here."

"*Merci.*" she said, laying a hand over her heart.

"Shall we use the '*tu*' form? No need to be so formal this evening," he said smiling.

She nodded in agreement. She knew the French had two forms of address, polite and familiar. At previous events, Laurent was careful to address her as the formal "*vous.*" Tonight, was different.

Their crystal glasses rung in unison. "They say the only bad part of being on the *Tour Eiffel* is not being able to see it," said Laurent, giving her a sly look.

"Oh, I don't mind giving that up for one night," she said, fidgeting in her seat.

"What is the subject of your novel, may I ask?"

"It's about a woman on a quest. Can we explore that later?" she asked, attempting to avoid his penetrating glance.

"Certainly. What are your preferences on the menu?" he asked. "We can choose a variety of courses."

"It all sounds wonderful," she said.

"So, you will permit me to order for us both?" he asked.

"I will," she said, leaning in toward him.

Laurent spoke to the waiter. "We will start with the Scallop with Caviar and the Langoustine with Black Truffle. For the main course, the Venison with Sauce Poivrade. For wine, we will have the Pommard Premier Cru."

Brie perked up at the mention of the wine. "I've stayed at the Pommard vineyard in Beaune. It's my preferred Burgundy wine," she said, wetting her lips.

"So, I have made a good choice of wine," he said. "The venison here is perfection. Please trust me on this."

Soon the waiter returned, and they savored the appetizers, while his eyes focused on her.

When the main course arrived, he leaned across the table and took her hand. "Paris is quite beautiful in the spring, is she not?" he asked.

"It's a feast in any season," she said, meeting his gaze. She thought every item on the menu was an exquisite creation, a culinary delight.

"My daughter Chloe loves France," said Brie. "She presented a film at the Cannes Film Festival this year." She waited to hear if Laurent would talk about any children of his own. He did not offer that information.

"Splendid," he said, motioning her to try the venison.

"My friends and I traveled down to the *Côte d'Azur* a couple of weeks ago," said Brie. "My daughter's film won an award, so we had a cele-bration." (She left out the part about the terrifying encounter with Jack, her estranged husband, and the subsequent sequestering at Pierre and Annick's home in Neuilly.)

"By coincidence, I have a summer house near Cannes, in Mougins. Do you know it?"

"Yes, Mougins, the culinary capital of the south," she said. "Charming village."

"Your daughter has a French name. Does she speak impeccable French like her mother?" he smiled.

Brie blushed. She was taken aback by his compliment of her French once again. She remembered Laurent making a similar comment when they first met at the Louvre, a month before. Usually, the French were anxious to correct foreigners' grammar and pronunciation.

"Yes, Chloe speaks quite well. We often converse in French. She lives in Los Angeles," Brie noticed the formality of her own responses. She had to remind herself that they were alone at dinner and not at an Embassy event with his colleagues.

"She's connected to the film industry, so I'm not surprised she lives in California," he said, taking a morsel of venison into his mouth and blotting his lips with his napkin. "Does she like living there compared to New York?"

"She's very much a beach lover, like her mother," she focused on Laurent's lips.

Brie had not begun to sample her main course although the aroma enticed her palate.

The pair conversed about classic French film directors. Brie knew the preferred topic of the French was their culture.

They contrasted timeless French and American films. Laurent agreed that Americans are more comfortable with happy endings. The French often preferred open-ended stories, as in real life.

"I'm partial to the works of Truffaut and Louis Malle," said Brie. French cinema was one of her loves. "I find Malle's *Au Revoir, les Enfants* deeply moving." She had a faraway look in her eyes.

"It's heart-wrenching," he said. "The Nazi occupation of France was one of the most tragic times in our history." Laurent noticed the sadness on Brie's face. He switched the conversation away from dramas.

"Of the French comedies, do you agree that director Tati was a comic genius?" he asked.

"I've seen *Mon Oncle* three times, with its fish fountain in that ultra-modern house and that wild kitchen scene," said Brie, laughing, her eyes meeting Laurent's.

"It's hilarious, along with his film *Les Vacances de Monsieur Hulot*," Laurent laughed with her.

"Catchy theme song," added Brie, feeling more relaxed.

The waiter approached to pour more champagne. Then, the couple toasted to French and American cinema.

"You have legendary American actors," said Laurent. "Humphrey Bogart is outstanding."

"My preferred Bogie film of all time is *Casablanca*," she said.

"So, you believe in love at first sight? The French call it *Coup de Foudre*," said Laurent, with his dazzling blue-green eyes.

"Yes, I think it can happen," she said, lowering her eyes from his deepening gaze.

"Are you enjoying the venison?" asked Laurent.

Brie nodded.

"Interesting that you were in the south while I was away on assignment," he said. "We were across the Mediterranean from each other, quite close." His look was thoughtful. "I must get down to my vacation home more often. I do enjoy the slower pace of Provence and the sunny *Côte d'Azur.*"

"Are you originally Parisian?" she asked.

"I grew up in Normandy, but my son prefers the north. He studies at Sciences Po and now resides in Paris. I've lived in Paris for many years. I do enjoy the capital and consider it my home base." He said, taking her hand once again. "What I miss most is being close to the sea."

The waiter cleared the table, with a light touch, brushing crumbs off the tablecloth with a silver-handled brush into a silver tray. He returned, moments later, with a petit embossed menu.

"Are you ready for dessert?" asked Laurent.

Brie nodded, sipping the last bit of Pommard.

"Do you like chocolate? It's an aphrodisiac," he smiled into her eyes.

"I'm very fond of chestnuts," she said, "and chocolate."

Laurent spoke to the waiter. "We will have the glazed chestnuts in puff pastry with vanilla cream, as well as the warm chocolate soufflé."

"The soufflé will take twenty minutes, *monsieur,*" said the waiter, departing the table.

Laurent then turned to Brie, continuing eye contact. "I'm feeling especially adventurous tonight." His seduction had begun.

Brie's eyelashes fluttered. "I must confess that I left New York quite suddenly." She ran her hand through her long blonde hair.

"Ah, yes," said Laurent. "Why was that?"

Brie took a breath. "I separated from my husband." Brie felt like a rock was blocking her throat. She hesitated, wondering why she chose to blurt that out at such a time as this.

Laurent reached over and began stroking her arm, sensing her discomfort. She felt a tingle at his touch, down to her toes.

Laurent began. "I divorced five years ago, so I know it is not an easy time." His voice was soft, almost a whisper. "My work takes me away for long periods, which makes relationships challenging."

Brie glanced down toward the tablecloth. "It turns out I wasn't legally married. It's a long story," she said.

"L'amour est compliqué," said Laurent. He was non-judgmental and a good listener, no doubt, two prime qualities of a diplomat.

Brie continued. "I'd been ill with undiagnosed symptoms last year, followed by emergency open heart surgery. The New York doctors saved my life." Why was she confessing to this man?

He took both her hands in his. "Indeed, matters of the heart are complex," he said. "Paris is a place to heal your heart. You are in good hands with us."

She was surprised to feel at ease with him. Laurent showed empathy and shared his own personal details with her. The French were private, so she knew not to ask prying questions, unless information was volunteered.

The desserts arrived on plates with gold rims, decorated with a variety of vanilla and fruit sauces drawn in the shapes of orchids and roses. The scent of the dark chocolate *soufflé* was intoxicating, the flavors multi-leveled.

"Now, it's time to enjoy," said Laurent. He made another toast. *"À nos amours,"* he said, kissing her with his eyes. "Wherever and whenever they may find us."

"To the present and the future," said Brie, her smile returned. *Goodbye to le passé,* she thought.

Espresso followed, then Grand Marnier, as a digestif. Brie was usually not a big drinker. The French paired such beverages with a meal, still she felt light-headed. She took only a small sip of the *digestif.*

"Have you been to the top of this tower?" asked Laurent.

"I have, yes, many times," she said. She thought it must be near midnight.

"Any desire to ride up again?" he said, his eyes still on hers. "It's a captivating, moonlit night, with a clear view of the stars." He took her hand.

* * *

Brie and Laurent rode up in the elevator, to the top floor of the Eiffel Tower. He pulled her close. The lights of Paris became more distant until they were mere shiny dots below.

The doors opened. They exited and the breeze grew stronger. It was near closing time, vacant of others. No guard was in sight.

Laurent led her to the edge of a gated area, facing west. There, they embraced. He kissed her deeply, in the French style. His hand reached to the back of her dress and unzipped it, just enough to pull the dress down around her shoulders. The shining moon revealed her heart scar. He kissed it with a light touch. He unhooked her black lace bra.

"What did you do?" she asked, giggling, feeling flushed.

"Nobody knows more about ladies' lingerie than a Frenchman," he said.

He smiled at her, his blue-green eyes beaming with desire. He kissed her harder until she was breathless.

Brie undid his tie and unbuttoned his white shirt. He pulled her to his muscular chest, then released her, his hands moving to the front, caressing her breasts. Their eyes were on each other like Cartier panthers. She was unsteady on her high-heels and grasped his broad shoulders.

The guard was now in view. When he saw them, he turned and walked away. The tower swayed in the strong wind. Brie and Laurent were on the edge of the railing, his Dior citrus scent filling the air around her. She pulled her dress back into place and he kissed her once more.

Laurent and Brie heard the guard. "We're closing," he said, in distant voice. The couple strolled into the elevator, where the guard joined them. The guard had his head down and was fumbling with the buttons on the elevator panel, attempting to be discreet. No doubt, it wasn't the first time he had witnessed strong emotions at the top of the Eiffel Tower.

Chapter 23

Brie invited Laurent up to her room at her hotel. She knew from her conversation years ago with Annick, that Frenchmen would have expectations with this invitation. Dating, as it was in America, didn't exist here. If you wanted to be with someone, there were no rules of behavior. France was not settled by Puritans, so the couple continued what they began at the top of the Eiffel Tower.

Once behind closed doors, Laurent kissed her in frenzy, on her lips, neck, and the heart scar on her chest. She returned his passion, as he pulled off his suit jacket and tie. She undid his cufflinks. They continued to scatter bits of clothing on the floor around them. They kicked off their shoes, Brie's lips never leaving Laurent's. The Parisian moon flooded through Camus' windows. Laurent's touch was soft, but firm. He knew his way around a woman's body. She allowed his seduction. He was an artist at giving pleasure, and he received pleasure equally, with gratitude. He had seduced her in her mind and body. After so many years of lacking, she welcomed his warmth. French history did not include a prim tradition. Lovers were free to pursue the principal of pleasure to its highest level.

* * *

The morning light of the late spring Sunday highlighted the afterglow of the couple, whose lovemaking lasted throughout the night.

Laurent finished four liters of Evian water, offering Brie several sips. He brushed his hair back from his forehead. She was still drowsy and felt a kind of rebirth of energy within her body and mind. They cradled each other in bed, kissing at intervals. Brie gazed at the light that entered the windows and that danced on the walls and ceiling of the luxurious room.

There was a knock at the door. Laurent pulled on his pants and shirt, then got up to answer it. A young woman, carrying a silver tray, asked to enter with their *petit déjeuner.*

The couple imbibed with appetite. Laurent poured the aromatic, rich French roast coffee from the silver carafe, adding the steamed milk. The croissants, brioche, and pain au chocolat, still warm from the oven, had the perfect flakiness.

"I surprised myself last night," she said. She gave him a dreamy look and fumbled to close her silky mauve robe around her body.

"How so, *ma chérie?*"

"Being with you like this." She had promised herself to keep things light with Laurent.

"Paris is a place of *amour* and healing," he said, grinning and feeding her a croissant.

"I hesitate to rush into anything," she said, chewing on the divine flaky croissant.

"I think it's too late to worry about rushing, don't you?" he smiled. "We can take things slow, as you say, if that is what you wish."

"I'm American," she said. "We tend to second guess our decisions."

"You're not *américaine*," he replied, with a smile. "You're in your own category. A woman of the world."

Brie was jolted by his statement. She took it as a compliment.

They showered together and Brie noticed, in her bare feet, that Laurent was tall. He soaped up the washcloth and followed the curves of her body. She followed his lead and did the same on his chest and shoulders. They rinsed each other playfully with the handheld shower. As they stepped onto the scrolled "M" on the bathmat, Brie noticed two fluffy white robes hanging in the bathroom, instead of one. Perhaps the hotel staff had thought ahead. The couple dressed each other in these robes.

They went back to bed, and Laurent offered her more coffee. "I promised my son, Tristan, that I would play tennis with him later this afternoon," he said, taking his cue from her earlier comments. "Or would you rather I stay with you?"

"You go and be with your son," said Brie. She didn't want too much too soon. She liked that Laurent appeared to be a devoted father.

"Will you go dancing with me next Friday?" he asked, whispering in her ear.

"I'd love that," she sighed. She adored dance in any form and had fantasized dancing with Laurent.

"Excellent. I'll make the arrangements." He trusted his connections would assure them entrance to the trendy, upscale club. "Club Les Bains has reopened with a fresh decor and a new DJ."

"What a wonderful idea," said Brie. She remembered the legendary Les Bains-Douches of the past was a scene for the likes of Mick Jagger, David Bowie and Depeche Mode. It was a similar vibe to Manhattan's Studio 54.

"I look forward to dancing with you," she said, smiling and reaching inside his robe to rub his thigh.

"Haven't we already danced together here and on *La Tour Eiffel*?" he asked, with a dashing smile.

Brie could not reply, though she felt joyful and desired. She grinned into Laurent eyes. He stroked her hair and they held each other until the early afternoon.

* * *

Alone once more, Brie dressed and wandered down the sunny Rue Bonaparte, under a Monet sky, toward the Seine River. She saw groups of families, in Sunday attire, meandering through the narrow streets. Most of the shops were closed. *Dimanche à Paris.* When she reached the river, she drifted along, thinking about Laurent. She felt an exhilarating closeness with him. She pondered never having experienced that same closeness with Jack. Jack had been all consuming, draining. She had lost part of herself in him. She was determined to never let that happen again. Her blithe feelings for Laurent surprised her. She had not come to Paris with the idea of meeting anyone new. It had been the farthest thing from her mind.

As Brie strolled along the Seine, she thought about her family, so far away the States. She began to feel melancholy. She couldn't stay at the hotel forever. It would be her temporary home, as it had been many times before. She walked as far as the Ecole Nationale des Beaux-Arts, where many talented artists had been rejected from entrance into the famous school. Their works were now in the great museums of Paris and around the world. Impressionism had been a dirty word in its time. The idea of artists painting outdoors, in natural light, was thought to be outlandish. Monet's *Impression: Sunrise* was laughed at. Today, it was one of the most valuable paintings of all time, aside from the Mona Lisa, *La Jaconde*, as she was known in French.

Brie drifted past George Sand's home and remembered the writer's legendary nine-year affair with the frail Polish composer, Chopin. Their love became a cerebral, musical one, as Chopin had been afflicted with a debilitating chronic cough caused by a form cystic fibrosis, rather than by tuberculosis, as he was originally diagnosed. Sand had been obsessed and seduced by his melodies. Her novels and lifestyle were considered racy for the time. The female author, who had dressed in men's attire, wrote about women who broke free from the behavioral standards for the wives of nineteenth-century France. Brie admired George Sand for her strength and sense of adventure.

Brie zigzagged across Rue Jacob and Rue de Furstenberg. She bought a few French newspapers and magazines, and then she traversed Saint-André des Arts toward the Café de l'Odéon. She hungered for *steak-frites*, ate them on the *terrasse*, lingering at the café until a light rain started to fall. From the café, she took the short walk back to the hotel, retrieving a small folding umbrella from her purse, prepared for the unpredictable Parisian weather. She wondered if Laurent had played a few sets of tennis with his son before the rain began.

Back in the comfort of her room, Brie removed her wet clothing, put on some yoga pants and a t-shirt. She got into bed with *Le Monde* and *Le Figaro* Sunday editions, reading about some of the complex political issues of France's thirty political parties. She browsed through *Paris Vogue* and wrote about her night at *La Tour Eiffel* with Laurent. His scent remained on her pillows and her body throbbed. More intense rain fell on the windows, offering a calming respite.

Chapter 24

Brie spent the next week writing, talking on the phone with Annick, and messaging her sister Lisa. She decided not to share too much about Laurent, except for details of their sumptuous dinner at the Jules Verne. No need to alert them to her new romance, although she admitted to herself that she thought about Laurent often. She looked forward to their upcoming dancing at Club Les Bains.

She browsed the bookshops along Boulevard St. Germain and "*Boul Mich*" near the Sorbonne, picking up a couple of novels by Marguerite Duras. Brie never tired of walking in Paris or stopping in a café for a coffee with the locals, her preferred *passe-temps*.

* * *

Laurent de Laval arrived at the hotel at nine o'clock in the evening on the following Friday. This time, he came directly to her room.

"*Séduisante*," he said, with a dashing smile, when he saw her in her club attire. She wore a short black skirt and matching silk *décolleté* top. She added a long, delicate gold chain with a pavé diamond key charm around her neck. He kissed her deeply, handing her a Cartier box from his coat pocket.

"What is this?" she asked, surprised and pleased. He was unpredictable, in a good way.

"A token to remember me by," he said, in an adoring tone.

"Are you going somewhere?" she asked, her heart fluttering.

She slowly opened the box to find a glistening yellow and white gold bangle bracelet dotted with small diamonds. She removed it from the box, and he placed the bracelet on her wrist.

"I love this," she kissed him on the lips. "*Merci beaucoup, mon chéri.*"

He drew her to his lips and kissed her deeply. She lost her balance.

"*Hélas,* I must return to Tunisia next week on assignment. I'm not quite sure how long I'll be gone. Perhaps a month," he said as he studied her face for a reaction.

Feeling a pang of unease, she forced a smile. "I'll miss you, but I understand." She avoided eye contact, trusting she could live with the notion of not knowing when he would return.

"I wish I could stay in Paris with you," he said, holding her close.

She felt a sharp twinge that brought a sudden, harsh memory of Jack, who had left her at her time of greatest need. She reminded herself that Laurent was nothing like Jack. Of that, she was certain.

"Alors, *on y va?*" Laurent took her hand. "Les Bains serves a light dinner before the dancing begins."

* * *

When Brie and Laurent arrived at the club, they were guided to the front of the long line. Les Bains had previously been an 1880's restored bathhouse. The new club displayed an exquisite black and gold entry that still had the feel of the old structure, with elaborate, bath-like black and white floor tiles. Elegant, but not ostentatious.

It drew an edgy crowd, like Carla Bruni (former first lady of France), and many other jet setters who frequented the venue in the late 1980s and again in the present.

The Maître d' led them to Roxo Restaurant, with its' black lacquered tables, stylish Scandinavian chairs and Chagall-inspired ruby red decorated ceiling. Huge, luxuriant green palms in brass planters softened the gleaming dark wooden walls. The lighting was golden and subtle.

Brie and Laurent dined on veal ribs and white asparagus. They held hands, looking at each other. Laurent fed her an asparagus, wiping the butter on her lips. She licked his fingers. Brie noticed a door at the back of the restaurant that was slightly ajar. Hanging from the ceiling was a brilliant disco ball, channeling the club's past. Brie remembered Proust's quote here: *"Le Temps Perdu...est retrouvé* — Lost time... is found once again."* Her gold bracelet glittered in the soft light.

The dance music began, as time approached one o'clock in the morning. The chic clientele, who sipped exotic cocktails at the glass Lalique bar, were surrounded by captivating original modern artworks.

Brie and Laurent moved onto the packed dance floor. The DJ played techno music. The crowd undulated to the chill sounds of *Moon Safari* by the French musicians of AIR—Nicolas and Jean-Benoît—who were still as relevant as ever. They remained the "neuroscientists of music."

Brie and Laurent were entranced by the setting and each other's company. They locked eyes as they danced in a heightened, trance-like state, until dawn.

Chapter 25

Brie and Laurent said a long goodbye that would have to last them for at least a month of separation. After his departure, Brie was in a state of melancholic reverie. She recalled a coincidental event from her childhood.

She, too, had a bit of a history with Tunisia, the former French protectorate. When she was ten years old, she had studied the topic of North Africa at school and had read a published letter in her *World Week* newspaper from the Tunisian President, Habib Bourguiba. The President had requested to hear from all his young American readers. Unbeknownst to her parents, she wrote a letter to President Bourguiba, asking for a Tunisian doll to add to her collection of dolls from around the world. A few months later, a delegation from the United Nations appeared at her doorstep with an enormous basket containing gifts of dried figs and dates, a painting of the blue-washed town of Sidi Bou Said and a doll dressed in traditional Tunisian garb. They presented young Brie with a letter, read aloud by the President's personal secretary, in French and English. It was written by the President himself, asking her to accept these gifts on his behalf, as symbols of Tunisia. The basket included an invitation to a *soirée* at the Tunisian Embassy in New York. Brie's parents were stunned and thrilled for their young daughter. They went as a family, with her younger sister, Lisa. The magical evening included live music, North African cuisine, and folk dancing. They would return every year to celebrate at the Tunisian Embassy, as guests of the Tunisian Ambassador.

Brie thought about Laurent landing at Carthage International Airport and wondered what his work there would entail. She dreamed of a visit to the Bardo Museum in Tunis. She imagined Laurent there, taking a private tour with the French and Tunisian delegations.

* * *

Brie met her friend Annick at Le Café Sélect in Montparnasse. They spoke about Brie's night of dancing at Les Bains nightclub.

"You're a *femme fatale,* my friend. Perhaps an accidental one, but one just the same," said Annick.

"I don't know about that," said Brie, remembering that French sexuality was a combination of the sensual and the intellectual.

"You're a temptress, like Diane de Poitiers or Madame Pompadour," added Annick.

Brie laughed. "Hardly. I'm not a courtesan to a king," She fanned herself with the menu. "Baudelaire's poetry did teach me about *volupté.*"

"Voluptuousness was the key lesson," Annick laughed.

"I have one of the poet's quotes in a painting above my bed in New York," said Brie. "*Là, tout n'est qu'ordre et beauté, luxe, calme et volupté.*" The words of the French nineteenth century writer swirled in her head.

"Our literary studies have not been without consequence," added Annick. "You are influenced by those words."

"I am," Brie agreed, nodding.

"Come back to our home; we miss you," said Annick. "With Laurent in Tunis, you might want some company."

"I'll call you in a few days. I'd love to see you both," Brie replied.

Chapter 26

On an unusually hot, humid Parisian morning in June, Brie stood on the balcony of her hotel sipping coffee as she watched the morning rush below. Her phone buzzed. It was her New York attorney friend, Jeff Klein.

"I'm surprised to hear from you, Jeff," said Brie. Her muscles tightened.

"Well, I wish I had better news," he said, clearing his throat.

"What news is that?" She walked inside and began to pace.

"It's about Jack. He was in the process of being extradited from Europe to New York to stand trial and somehow escaped. Bottom line, he's on the loose." The attorney began to cough.

"How could this have happened?" Brie clenched her jaw and sat down on a chair, away from the French doors.

"It seems his police escort lost him while exiting the plane at JFK. Sorry, I don't know the gory details." The attorney, normally articulate, struggled to find his words. "I heard about it from an FBI contact, and then it was in the papers here."

"I don't know what to say," she gasped. "This is terrifying." She felt a pain shoot through her chest.

"You have some kind of French investigator over there, right? Better call him." There was a pause on the other end of the line.

"I only recently began to feel safe," said Brie. She was dizzy.

"Jack could be a danger to you, so this is not good. He's a desperate man and behind the eight ball, as they say. Gambling can be an addiction, you know."

"I don't know," she said, losing her breath. Her heart was pounding out of her chest.

"Try to stay calm. Not the best idea for you to be alone right now."

His advice rang true. "Good thing you are there and not here in New York," he said.

"Thanks for the heads up, Jeff." Her eyes burned, and she could feel the blood rushing to her head, her neck throbbing. Her vision blurred as she stared out the window.

"Fine idea. Contact me anytime, my dear. I've got your back," he said.

With that, Jeff Klein hung up. He had dropped a bomb in Brie's lap.

* * *

Brie hands shook as she swallowed her heart medication. She sat down on her bed, her mind blank, staring at the ceiling for what seemed like more than an hour.

She reached for her cell with a sweaty hand, calling her sister Lisa in Montreal. She would not contact her daughter Chloe, who was on location in Australia, working on a new film. She didn't want to worry her, as

Chloe was prone to overreact. She absolutely must tell Annick and Pierre the sobering news. Later, when she was able to talk.

It was eleven o'clock in the morning Paris time, not too late to call eastern Canada. She would contact Annick and Pierre in the evening, when Pierre returned from his medical office and Annick would be home with him.

"How are you, *ma Parisienne*?" said Lisa, in an upbeat tone.

"Alors, something's happened," said Brie, rubbing the back of her neck.

"You sound awful. What's going on?"

"Jack escaped," Brie gasped, wiping tears from her cheeks.

"What? Oh, *merde*. Where and when?" asked Lisa.

Brie filled her sister in on the details of the alarming call from Jeff Klein.

"I'm scared," said Brie. "Jack is unpredictable. He came after me in Cannes. He would do it again in a heartbeat."

"I agree and I'll arrange to get on a plane to be with you. I assume the authorities have confiscated Jack's passport, so he wouldn't be able to leave the States."

"I don't know. You have to think for the both of us right now. My head is muddled."

"Jack's a slippery character. You can't be too careful," said Lisa.

"I'll call Pierre and Annick later tonight and they can contact the detective."

"Call your doctor in New York and take your meds," said Lisa.

"I took some meds. Pierre's a cardiologist," Brie could feel her blood pressure rising. "Jack owes massive amounts of money to some dangerous people." Brie gasped for breath.

"That's not your problem; it's his. I'm only interested in your safety," Lisa replied.

"When will this nightmare end?" Brie coughed. She closed her eyes. She prayed to the gods of Paris for serenity.

"Let's not fast forward," Lisa was calm. "I'll see you in Paris sometime tomorrow. You've come too far in your survival to give up now and you're not alone."

"Love you, Lisa." Tears rolled down Brie's cheeks.

"Love you, too. Try to be calm. We New York chicks can be tough when we have to be."

* * *

Brie reclined in bed that evening and reached for a Camus' novel *The Happy Death* from the nightstand. She fell asleep with the book open on her chest. Her mind was more fatigued than her body, yet she must have slept for several hours when she thought she heard a message ping on her phone. She fell into a deeper sleep and dreamed about Jay Gatsby, dead in his pool. Many hours passed until the daylight washed the room.

* * *

Brie awoke with a jolt. She thought she heard a knock at her door and looked through the peep hole, her hands trembling. She was relieved to see Lisa. She took a cleansing breath, surprised to see her sister so soon. She had slept through the night and into the next day.

"I'm here," said Lisa. The two sisters hugged.

Brie couldn't speak, but she managed a tiny smile.

"We will figure this out together," said Lisa. "Let's wait until we speak to Pierre and Annick to make any decisions."

Chapter 27

The next evening, Annick and Pierre invited the sisters to their home in Neuilly. They were eager to meet Lisa and anxious to hear more about Jack's recent escape. Brie and Lisa took a cab rather than the métro. Brie never liked the New York subway or the métro, at night and felt more vulnerable with Jack's escape. The sisters stopped at Pierre Hermé, one of the best *chocolatiers* in the city, to get a box of handcrafted chocolates.

"Are you tired?" she asked. "You don't seem to have a trace of jet lag."

"I slept on the plane, so I feel refreshed," said Lisa.

"I never sleep on planes," said Brie, with a sigh.

"We have always been opposites. You're the blonde. I'm the brunette," Lisa replied.

"You're a morning person. I'm a night owl," Brie returned.

"People never guess we're sisters," said Lisa. "That is, until they hear us speak."

"You are the tough one, though," said Brie. "That's why you were the one to go to law school and I studied literature and languages."

"Law is a kind of language," said Lisa.

"One that evades my comprehension," Brie replied, laughing.

"Get ready for tonight's French food frenzy," Brie added.

"That's one area where we agree. Didn't our family train us well when it comes to quality cuisine?" Lisa remarked.

They sisters exchanged knowing nods.

"I never learned those skills," said Brie, with a wistful look. "Cooking has never held my interest. Maybe that will change now that I am back in France."

* * *

Pierre was quick to open the door, with his son Etienne behind him. They went through the *politesse* of introductions and kisses on the cheek. As a family member of their good friend, Lisa was kissed by everyone on the first meeting. She was caught off guard. Brie knew the kissing would last for several minutes. It was a cultural behavior that some visitors found surprising and even tedious.

Annick arrived in her apron to greet her guests. More kisses.

"I need my sous-chef in the kitchen," said Annick to Etienne. "Pierre, will you serve the apéritifs?"

"Dubonnet or Campari," said Pierre.

"I will be like Queen Elizabeth and take the Dubonnet," Lisa said.

"Spoken like a true Canadian," said Pierre.

"I'm a New Yorker, like Brie," said Lisa. "My husband is the Canadian."

"I'll try the Campari with a twist," said Brie.

"Excellent choice," said Pierre.

Annick arrived in the salon, removing her apron, to join in the toast.

"Santé, to our health. Wonderful to meet Brie's sister," she said, smiling at Lisa.

"Wonderful to finally meet you," said Lisa.

"Your sister has told us so much about you over the years. Is it really true that you eat razor blades for breakfast?" asked Pierre, winking.

"Only before a case in court," replied Lisa, with a playful grin.

"We're not serving any blades tonight, so we hope you're not disappointed," said Etienne, laughing.

The talk turned to the upcoming French national holiday, the 14th of July. During July or August, on a staggered schedule, the French enjoyed four weeks of uninterrupted summer vacation. It was a sacred time of relaxation.

"Paris is a ghost town in summer," said Etienne. "We like to get away from the barrage of tourists and go to the seashore."

"Some tourists go to the south of France every year," said Annick. "It's good for the French economy."

They feasted on appetizers of escargot stuffed with mushrooms in garlic butter. The p*lat principal* or main dish was duck à l'orange, with Cointreau flambé, served with potatoes au gratin Dauphinois.

"These potatoes are my mother's secret recipe from Lyon," said Pierre. "*Maman* shared the recipe with Annick after we were married."

"It took me ten years to have success with that complicated recipe," Annick sighed. "Pierre helped me to perfect it. It's his favorite dish." The couple looked at each other with a smile.

"I'm not good in the kitchen," said Brie. "Lisa is the chef in the family."

"I'm sure you have other talents," said Etienne, winking at her. "The French are too much about food all the time."

"You're an accomplished cook," said Lisa to Annick. "Everything is delicious."

"*Merci*. Frenchmen require it," said Annick. "I do enjoy preparing food, although our men are often the chefs in our restaurants or at home. It's not always about the women."

"I appreciate a man who can cook," said Brie.

"*Maman*, shall I prepare the dessert?" asked Etienne, standing up beside her.

"My son's learning," said Annick, with a proud look. "I would hate for him to starve to death, trying to cook on his own."

"Nobody will starve," said Etienne.

Annick dimmed the lights as Etienne arrived with the Crepes Suzettes. "*Voilà*." He flambéed the dish at the table with Grand Marnier.

"Very impressive," said Brie gazing up at her godson with a smile.

"The origin of this dessert is not clear. Some say a woman named Suzette made a mistake by setting the dish aflame, so they named it after her," said Etienne.

"It's said to have happened at the Café de Paris in Monte Carlo," said Lisa. "I know my dessert history."

"Speaking of Monte Carlo, what shall we do with this continuing problem with gambler Jack?'" asked Pierre.

The guests at the table grew silent.

"Chantal has invited us all back to the villa in Cannes for la *Fête Nationale*. You call it Bastille Day in North America," said Annick.

"My detective friend Thierry, whom you met, Brie, will be on holiday down there. I took the liberty to speak to him and he says surveillance will be no problem," said Pierre.

"Can you join us? Both you and Lisa? The villa is so large," said Annick.

"I have to return to Montreal for work. But, Brie, that sounds like a perfect plan for you," said Lisa, looking at her sister.

"I would be delighted," said Brie, without hesitating, "if it's not an imposition."

"Not at all," said Annick. "You know Chantal would love to have you."

"Did Brie tell you about Laurent?" said Annick to Lisa.

"I told you I met someone," Brie blushed.

"You mentioned he's a French diplomat on assignment in Tunis," said Lisa, realizing Brie was sensitive about her new man.

"So not available as a bodyguard for this assignment?" asked Pierre.

"What do you know about him?" said Annick glaring at her husband.

"I heard the phone call," said Pierre.

"*Oh là là, Maman et Papa*, please give Brie a little privacy," said Etienne.

"*Bon*, I will arrange for the flights to Nice. The train seats have already been booked months ago by vacationers," said Annick.

"I can smell the sea air," said Etienne. "My friend has a boat moored off St. Tropez. We will keep you busy, Brie."

"You are all so kind," said Brie. "I'm grateful for such generous, fun-loving friends."

"Our pleasure," said Pierre. "We are grateful for *you*."

"Our specialty in France is a woman in distress," said Etienne. "Coming to the aid of a woman has been a part of French history since the 'Mousquetaires,' if not before."

"American men have a more *blasé* attitude," said Lisa. "Canada is different. I am lucky to be married to a Canadian. In Canada, I live amongst the most polite people on the planet."

"To Canada and to Québec," said Pierre, toasting with his wine.

"*Vive le Canada!*" They all joined in.

* * *

When the sisters returned to the hotel and opened Brie's room door, they saw an incredible sight. There were large vases of red roses gracing the entire room. They gave off an overwhelming sweet fragrance.

Brie's eyes gleamed as she hurried over to read the card. "The flowers are from Laurent," she said smiling, and she held the card to her chest.

"So, I take it that this romance isn't casual?" said Lisa.

Brie was overjoyed. "I guess not."

Chapter 28

Brie pondered the possibility of a lengthy stay in France. She knew she had to set up an account at a French bank and transfer some funds from New York. She had done business with BNP—Banque Nationale de Paris—when she lived here as a graduate student. In addition, she decided to apply for a *Carte de séjour*, which would allow her to stay in France for a year. She would be eligible, having been a student at a French university and with her sabbatical income. She needed official papers and couldn't imagine going back to New York after Jack's recent escape from the police. It wasn't safe.

"Bring Annick with you to BNP," said Lisa.

"Good idea," said Brie. "She and Pierre have an account there. With her assistance, I could avoid the complex discussions with the bank."

She knew doing business in France was not simple and having a French friend simplified the process.

"It would be my pleasure to help you set up your account," said Annick.

"After, let's have lunch at Les Deux Magots," said Brie. "*Je t'invite.*"

* * *

Days later, Brie got a message from her bank in New York with the balances in her American accounts. She was unsure if the amounts were correct. It seemed to her that some of her funds were missing.

"What do you recommend that I do?" Brie asked her sister.

"I was in law school at McGill, so I know Canadian law. I don't remember the laws in the States. In Montreal, there are ways to trace the transactions that go back years. Call your New York attorney friend, Jeff Klein, to be sure," said Lisa.

"I'm dialing him now," said Brie.

"No problem at all, my dear," said Jeff. He was cheery.

"So far, Jack hasn't resurfaced here in France," said Brie. "Still, he's on the loose in the New York area." She bit her nail.

"No news is good news,'" said Jeff. "I have my doubts that he would attempt to leave America. Very risky for him."

"He's a risk-taker," replied Brie, with a sigh.

"Don't worry about the bank transfer. All will be well, my friend. Let's not anticipate problems." Without another word, he hung up.

Brie clenched her jaw, struggling to catch her breath. She knew Lisa had to return to Canada soon. She had to reach down and find her own strength.

Chapter 29

A car arrived at the hotel to transport Brie and Lisa to Charles de Gaulle airport. Brie was flying to Nice for *La Fête Nationale* and Lisa was returning to Montreal.

Jean-Jacques was there to help the women with their luggage.

"I regret to see you go," said Jean-Jacques. "I am used to having you here in residence."

"You know, you're my Parisian home base," said Brie. "I always return."

"*Bien sur*," said Jean-Jacques with a tear in his eye. He patted her on the shoulder and closed the car door. He stood waving on the curb until the car pulled away.

* * *

The two sisters parted, Lisa going to the international terminal for her flight to Montreal, and Brie meeting Annick and Pierre at the Commuter Terminal for a short ninety-minute flight to Nice.

"Be sure to give me weekly updates," said Lisa.

"I wish you didn't have to go," said Brie, with a sigh.

They hugged each other with an embrace that lasted several minutes.

"This Trans-Atlantic flight is nothing for me," said Lisa. "I could be in Paris or Nice on short notice." They were both in tears. "Enjoy the holiday and forget about Jack. I know you'll have a great time."

"*Bon voyage, ma soeur.*"

Brie arrived at the gate marked Nice. She found Annick, Pierre, and Etienne waiting, coffees in hand. There were kisses all around.

Brie hadn't been in an airport in the more than two months since her sudden New York departure. This smallish commuter terminal smelled like Europe, with tobacco and enticing baked goods. Her life was shifting in a new direction once again.

"Please take my coffee, and I'll get another," said Etienne, handing her his cup.

"*Mais non*, I had one at the hotel," said Brie. "You know me and French coffee. A little is enough to last me all day."

"We must build up your tolerance," said Pierre, laughing.

"Is Lisa on her way back to Montreal?" asked Annick, noticing her friend's sad expression. "Won't she join us in Nice?"

"She has a lot of work for an upcoming case," said Brie. "Then, she and her husband have a trip planned to Australia in August. They want to visit Down Under in the cooler season."

"That's a long flight!" said Pierre. "Canadians don't like hot weather. It's 93 degrees Fahrenheit in Nice right now. Sunscreen required."

"The humidity will kill me," said Annick. "My hair is already too curly."

"The fireworks in Cannes on the fourteenth are the most spectacular on the *Côte d'Azur*," said Etienne. "Do you remember last time, Brie?"

"How could I forget?" she said, her eyes shining. "You took my picture with your fancy camera, and silver stars were exploding above my head."

* * *

They expected to see Chantal's welcoming face at the Aéroport de Nice.

Instead, Annick received a long text from her sister.

"I'm detained in Toulouse. There's a crisis at Air France, with a threatened holiday strike by employees. Please take a car to Cannes. My next-door neighbor, Madame Fifi, will have the key for you. She's looking after Loulou, the pooch, who will want to go home to the villa with you. Sorry for the delay. I'll be back as soon as possible.

Bises, Chantal."

Madame Fifi was the eccentric neighbor, who owned a well-known art gallery in the chic village of St. Paul de Vence. She had a slew of artist friends throughout Provence. She was waiting at the *Villa du Ciel* with Loulou in tow. The little white dog was barking with excitement. Fifi wore a bright orange dress and a headscarf with red and yellow flowers. Her oversized gold hoop earrings shone in the midday sun. She had several gold bangles on each arm that clanged as she approached the car.

"Bonjour, bonjour!" said Fifi, waving. "You are smart to arrive here before the big crowds." She was tanned and sported white and gold espadrilles on her feet. Her scent was "Rose des Roses" by Dior.

"Bonjour, Madame," said Brie. "I'm happy to meet you."

"Moi aussi," said Fifi, kissing Brie on both cheeks. "I've heard your name many times from my friends here. You are the mystery New Yorker."

"Lovely to see you, Fifi," said Annick. "You remember my husband Pierre and my son Etienne." More kisses.

"Please join us for dinner this evening, Fifi," said Pierre.

"*Merci*, but I must meet some friends in St. Paul tonight to organize our weekend opening of my new show at the gallery. I'll be sure to send you an invitation," Fifi replied.

"Perhaps another night?" added Annick, "after Chantal has returned?"

"That would be my pleasure," said Fifi. "In the meantime, please feel free to pick some peaches from my tree." Loulou barked in agreement.

"You know where to find your room," said Annick to Brie.

"I do, *merci*," said Brie.

"I'll prepare an Italian antipasto for lunch. Chantal told me she left some cheeses, salami, olives, and marinated vegetables in the fridge. We have canned smoked trout. Pierre, will you or Etienne please pick up a baguette before they sell out?"

"We'll take a little walk together to the *boulangerie*," said Pierre to Etienne, putting his arm around his son.

*   *   *

Brie unpacked. She noticed she had very few items of summer clothing. She would have to pick up a cotton dress or two, and sandals to add to her wardrobe before the holiday season began. When the upcoming swarm of tourists arrived in mid-July, they would descend like locusts on the local boutiques. Cannes was a beach city—casual by day, dressier by night, and always in the height of fashion.

Brie's phone rang. She assumed it would be her daughter Chloe. Brie didn't recognize the caller's number.

"Chérie!" It was Laurent's voice on the other end.

"Laurent! Are you still in Tunis?" asked Brie, her heart beating fast. There was interference on the line, and she was having difficulty hearing him.

"I am," said Laurent. Brie heard what sounded like gunfire on the other end.

"Are you safe?" She worried about possible unrest in Tunis.

"Mostly safe. *Et toi?*" His voice sounded anxious, and he was quick to change the subject.

"Good to hear your voice,' she said. "The roses were magnificent. *Merci beaucoup*," she added, trying to downplay her excitement. "I'm here in Cannes for *le quatorze juillet*. Very happy you enjoyed the flowers and remembered me." *He is unforgettable, she thought to herself.*

He continued. "My plan is to spend the holiday at my cottage near Cannes, in Mougins so we can be together."

"That's wonderful news," she said.

"*Parfait.* I'll fly from Tunis to Nice in the next few days," said Laurent. "I'll call you when I arrive."

Brie looked down at the gold bracelet he had gifted her. How could he think she would forget him? She would soon introduce him to her French friends. Annick met him briefly. Now, he would meet the entire Girard clan.

"Kisses," they both said together.

"*A bientôt, ma chérie*," said Laurent.

"*A la prochaine*," Brie said feeling her heartbeat quicken.

Chapter 30

After lunch, in the heat of the mid-afternoon on the *Côte d'Azur*, Brie and Annick visited the fashionable Cannes clothing boutiques. Laurent and Pierre stayed behind at the villa to take their siestas. Brie told Annick that Laurent would be arriving for the fourteenth of July, so Annick encouraged her friend to make new clothing purchases.

"You must look your best. We will welcome him with open arms," said Annick.

As they strolled the boutique streets on Rue d'Antibes, behind La Croisette, Brie noticed the mounting number of tourists wearing their vacation chic. Even the men were well-groomed and stylish. She counted twenty shoe shops in a row, with dress shops on the traversing streets. La Croisette itself housed the top French and Italian designers that few could afford. Brie was a fan of their handbags, scarves, and sunglasses. She often preferred the lesser-known, upcoming designers. Haute couture was very structured, full of buttons and zippers, and elaborate, hand-sewn linings. They were beautiful, but not comfortable, not easy to wear and they required special care.

The women entered a boutique with an Italian name—Luca Giovanni Fratelli. An attractive man, appearing to be in his late twenties, approached them. He wore a finely tailored khaki summer suit and a yellow patterned silk tie.

"Good afternoon, *mesdames*," said the tanned young man. "May I assist you?" He looked Brie up and down, with a smile.

"I would like to see some summer dresses," said Brie, flipping her blonde hair.

"Of course," said the man. "Please follow me. I am Luca. My brother Giovanni and I design these clothes. We have a nice array of summer dresses in cotton that wash well. Practical and chic."

Brie caught the scent of Italian cologne and espresso. An elegant, older woman arrived from the back room with an armful of dresses. "*Bienvenuta*." She said when she saw the women.

"Mama, perfect timing," Luca waved her over.

"I was just about to put these on the rack," said the woman, who was dressed in an orange ensemble. Annick viewed her with interest.

The young man eyed Brie, seeming to take her measurements. "Look, madame, these are in your size."

It amazed Brie that European men could be so accurate in assessing a woman's body.

Luca led Brie to a dressing room in the rear of the shop. "Please, madame, take off your blouse," he said, with a gleaming smile, staring at her breasts.

"I will, when you leave the room," she said, looking away.

"I must assist you, my beauty," he said in Italian-accented French. "This is how we do it in Roma."

"In New York, we give privacy to a client," said Brie, in a flat tone.

"So sorry. I will wait outside," said Luca, bowing, and walking backward.

Brie modeled a few dresses for Annick. Luca and his mother nodded with approval. Brie decided on two dresses. One, an ultramarine blue sleeveless sheathe and a second white eyelet A-line with shell buttons.

Annick stood near the register, fingering an oversized cotton scarf with streaks of rich blues and turquoise. "Very Italian," she said.

Brie added the scarf to her choices as a special gift for her friend.

"I want to buy you a little present," said Brie.

"Not necessary," said Annick, "only if you borrow it as well."

"It would be rude not to accept your friend's offer," said Luca's mother. Annick agreed and *Mama* wrapped it in a lavender box, tying it with a light blue ribbon.

"I hope you will return to see us again, madame," said Luca, kissing Brie's hand.

"*Merci, monsieur,*" said Brie, exiting the shop. "*Bonne Journée.*"

The women walked a few blocks, stopping at an elegant shoe shop with a flowery display. Brie and Annick both decided on bright red sandals, in differing styles.

"We'll be wearing the colors of the French flag on the fourteenth," said Annick, with a smile.

"So patriotic," said Brie, grinning. "*Vive la France!*"

* * *

"What would you like for dinner tonight?" asked Annick, on the walk back to the villa. They were talking again about food.

"I can make my Moroccan chicken in a clay pot for dinner, if we buy a fresh chicken and some spices," offered Brie.

"I thought you didn't cook?" Annick has a quizzical look.

"I know a few simple recipes," said Brie, pointing to a *supermarché* down the block.

"Chantal has tons of lemons on her tree and olives in the pantry," said Annick. "The men will love your dish and so will I."

The women walked, arm in arm, toward a small shop at the end of the street. Brie noticed the beginning of the onslaught of Parisians and French tourists from other regions of France. Their accents indicated their origins. In addition, she heard Russian, Spanish, Italian, and English being spoken. Cannes was a world class resort town. The vibe in July was much different from the Hollywood atmosphere during the Cannes Film Festival in May. Less Catherine Deneuve and more holiday relaxed, but still crowded and lively. Brie was happy to have the *Villa du Ciel* to return to, as a respite.

* * *

After dinner, Pierre served an exotic violet gelato for dessert. He and Etienne bought some at the corner store for dessert. They agreed it was smooth and flavorful, like violet flowers. The rich color was divine. It complimented the Moroccan spiced dinner.

"I've been in contact with Detective Thierry Marceau. He was here this afternoon while you ladies were shopping. All the surveillance cameras have been installed inside and outside the villa," said Pierre.

Brie sighed with relief at this news.

"*Tante* Chantal has three different sizes of ladders," said Etienne. "The tool shed was stocked with everything we needed for the installation."

"Chantal is the French Martha Stewart," said Brie, with a laugh.

"I thought you decided to both take naps?" asked Annick.

"We wanted to be ready before the festivities of the fourteenth, when everything will be closed," said Pierre. "Etienne made the suggestion."

"I knew the detective would be busy with his family in Nice and I didn't want to take any chances," said Etienne. "We have a precious guest, whose safety we must insure."

He smiled at Brie, his green eyes sparkling.

"I have the French Sherlock and Watson here with me, so nothing bad can happen," said Brie. She patted both men on the shoulders.

"I'm impressed that you've set up the security," said Annick, with a sigh. "Now, we can concentrate on enjoying our summer celebration."

* * *

A few hours after dinner, when the house was dark and quiet, Brie pulled her bathrobe around herself and entered the salon. She was unable to sleep but still exhausted from a full day in Cannes. She looked out of the back windows, then tip-toed to the kitchen to pour herself some Perrier. She wondered if the security cameras were recording her. She heard a sound from down the hall that startled her. It was Etienne, wearing shorts and an unbuttoned shirt, walking in her direction.

"I couldn't sleep either," he said. "Would you like an *omelette*?"

"*No, merci*. I have my Perrier." She raised her glass.

"How about some cognac?" he asked, taking a bottle and two small glasses from the cabinet.

"My grandfather thought cognac was a solution for every problem," said Brie. "Including colds, flu, and heartbreak."

"Like the English and their tea," said Etienne, smiling.

"*Alors*, I will join you in some cognac," said Brie. She took a sip and flinched at the strength of the drink. The alcohol burned her lips, so she followed it with some water. "Strong stuff."

"Would you like to walk in the garden?" asked Etienne, taking her hand and moving toward the French doors at the back of the living room.

"Are we covered by the cameras?" asked Brie, looking around.

"Not an inch of this villa is without coverage," said Etienne. "You're being filmed, so watch out. I don't think they can hear us, though."

Brie and Etienne stepped into the moonlit garden, walking carefully in their bare feet. Brie pulled her robe more tightly over her pink nightgown. They stopped at a darkened corner of the yard and looked up at the stars. Venus and Saturn were bright and close together in the summer sky.

Etienne turned to her with a serious look on his face. "Have you ever thought of taking a younger man as a lover?" His eyes beamed on hers.

"I have been with a younger man, before I met Jack," she said, taken aback and uncomfortable having this conversation with her godson.

He took a step closer toward her, his naked, muscular chest revealed by his open shirt. "I mean with me," said Etienne. He was inches from her now, stroking her hair.

Brie pulled away, in shock. "Dear Etienne, you're my godson." She looked at him directly. "I held you as a baby."

"Maybe you noticed, I'm not a baby anymore," said Etienne, firmly.

"You're a handsome, young doctor. You can have your pick of any woman on the Riviera." She caught her breath.

"The truth is, I want *you*," he said. His eyes blazed on hers.

"That can never happen," she looked away. "You must know that. I love you as a son and your parents are my closest friends."

"I understand, but I can't help my feelings. I'll always be your friend, but I could be so much more," he said, sulking.

Brie thought she saw tears in his eyes. She slugged down her cognac, in an attempt to calm herself.

"Let's go inside," she said. "It's damp out here."

Etienne stood silent. He looked like a child whose dog had died. "You'll meet somebody wonderful at the upcoming celebrations. You're a catch." She hugged him. Then, she bolted toward the French doors.

"*Bonne nuit, mon fils*," said Brie, looking back at him. "Let's go back to sleep."

"Good night," said Etienne, not looking up to meet her gaze.

Brie was aware that young Frenchmen were often attracted to older women. She was surprised, but not angry with her godson for his inappropriate advances. She hoped she took enough care not to hurt him.

Chapter 31

In the early afternoon of the next day, Chantal returned to the *Villa du Ciel* in time for the national holiday. She roared into the driveway in her light blue Peugeot. Her employer, Air France, had averted a strike. She found everyone in the garden. Loulou ran up to her in a flash and she picked up the little dog, Loulou licking Chantal's face.

"Did I miss anything?" said Chantal. "The roads from Toulouse are packed with tourists coming here from the southwest. They have their expanse of beach in Biarritz. Why don't they stay at their own ocean-front?" she added.

"They want to leave the big waves to the surfers at this time of year," said Pierre. The swimmers don't want to get hit by a surfboard." He changed the subject. "We do have the surveillance cameras up and running."

"That's great. We don't want any gangsters trying to break in here," said Chantal, with a laugh.

"Other than that, no news, nothing happening," said Annick.

Etienne looked at Brie, who coughed. She wore a big straw sunhat and oversized black sunglasses.

"We were waiting for you," said Brie. "Now, the party can begin."

"You're quiet," said Chantal to Etienne, studying her nephew's morose face.

"I'm meeting a friend from med school for tennis this afternoon," he said.

"He's in a bad mood," said Chantal.

"You'll be meeting Brie's new beau on the thirteenth. He's coming here for dinner," said Annick.

"That's big news," Chantal smiled at Brie. "I'll make my famous bouillabaisse. No man can resist that recipe."

"I have to go," said Etienne.

"What a downer," said Chantal. "He needs an attitude change."

"He works hard," said Annick. "He will feel better once he has had time to relax."

"And he has had a woman," Chantal grinned.

Nobody said a word.

Chapter 32

Laurent de Laval arrived at the *Villa du Ciel* on the evening of July thirteenth with a huge bouquet of multicolored roses in hand. He wore a crisp, light blue shirt and finely tailored, straw-colored linen pants. His light tanned complexion set off his exotic blue-green eyes.

Brie responded to his knock at the door. She wore her new white eyelet dress and her favorite grey pearl drop earrings. She rediscovered Laurent's penetrating kiss and felt a jolt through her whole body. She couldn't speak.

"*Entrez, entrez,*" said Annick, who stood behind Brie, smiling.

"Pleasure to see you again," said Laurent, who kissed Annick on both cheeks.

"This is my husband, Pierre," said Annick.

"Pleasure to meet you, Doctor Girard," said Laurent.

"Enchanté. Please call me Pierre. And may I present another Doctor Girard, my son Etienne?"

Etienne stepped forward and the men shook hands. Etienne examined Laurent like he was a virus under a microscope.

Chantal entered the foyer. "I'm the sister, Chantal. Welcome to my home," she kissed Laurent and gave Brie an approving nod.

They all sat in the spacious living room and Pierre opened the champagne rosé. They made a toast, à *notre santé*, glasses clinking.

"Your home is beautiful, like the pages from a magazine," said Laurent, looking at the high ceilings. "So much open space." He raised up his hands.

"*Merci*. I have a small talent for décor," she said.

"Exceptional talent," said Laurent. Chantal beamed.

"*Eh bien*, Monsieur de Laval, is this region your home?" said Annick, checking with Brie for direction.

"Please, call me Laurent," he said, switching from polite French to the familiar form, after confirming with his hosts that they were comfortable with the change of pronouns. "My origins are Normand and Parisian. My most recent assignment, as Brie may have shared with you, is in Tunis."

"We vacationed in Tunisia a few years ago, near Djerba," said Pierre. "It's spectacular, with whitewashed buildings and pristine beaches."

"The North African sun is strong, although I don't have much time to spend at the beach. My Embassy work schedule is full," said Laurent.

"Certainly not, Monsieur Laurent," said Annick. She had difficulty to call him by his first name.

"I prefer the French coastline here," said Etienne, looking at Brie. "This is not a desert."

"There's no comparison," said Annick, with a tone of annoyance directed toward her son. "Both have their beauty."

Chantal returned to the kitchen.

Laurent talked about the history of Carthage, an ancient Phoenician capital. "It has been the wealthiest of historic capitals with its trade and commerce. Today, few of the riches remain," said Laurent, wistfully.

Chantal called them to dinner. "*A table, s'il vous plaît.* Please come and sit. My bouillabaisse is ready and must not be kept waiting." She turned to Laurent. "Monsieur de Laval, I hope you like seafood?"

"Of course, I do. I'm a Frenchman," replied Laurent, with a jovial laugh.

"France has two thousand miles of coastline," added Pierre. "We are a bunch of fishermen."

They all laughed.

"And farmers," said Laurent, looking at Brie. She thought the French were sophisticated purveyors of land and sea.

Etienne stared at the couple with a troubled look. He had chosen a seat opposite Laurent, watching him with intensity.

Throughout the meal, the group discussed literature, while sipping Bandol rosé wine. A soft, floral scented breeze entered from the garden through the French doors.

Annick directed a question to Laurent, who sat next to her. "I take it you are enjoying your Tunisian assignment?"

"Tunis is fascinating. Spending time on the North African coast, I now understand more about Camus' adoration of Algiers and Oran and other towns bordering the Mediterranean Sea." His voice drifted off.

"Camus was never a fan of Paris or New York, believing Paris to be gray and overrun with pigeons," said Chantal.

"Bandol is the best of our provençal rosé wines, don't you agree?" said Pierre to his guest. "I wonder if Camus was a fan of rosé wine."

"This is my preferred rosé," said Laurent, raising his glass.

Etienne looked at them with mild disgust. "Give me a Bordeaux white wine instead." They all looked at him with dismay.

"Your bouillabaisse is marvelous," said Laurent to Chantal.

"I'm so pleased you like it," said Chantal. "I added extra saffron in your honor, Monsieur."

"*Merci*, Chantal," said Laurent, shifting the conversation back to literature. "You know, it's tragic that we lost Camus at such a young age. He was only forty-six when he died in that car crash, as few years after winning the Nobel Prize."

"I can only imagine what brilliant literature he would have continued to write," Annick remarked.

"His publisher, Gaillmard, was driving when the car hit a tree," said Laurent. "Ironic that the driver walked away without a scratch."

"Brie's favorite hotel room in Paris is where Camus completed the final chapters of *L'Étranger*," said Etienne, joining the conversation.

"Yes, it is," said Brie. "I can channel his vibe. He was wrongly labeled as an existentialist, due to his friendship with Sartre."

"Camus is a humanist. His philosophy says each day is precious and must be celebrated," said Laurent, giving Brie a kiss on the cheek.

"Now that we have solved the pressing philosophical questions, let's toast to summer and to life," said Pierre.

Etienne opened another bottle of wine. "Has Brie told you to watch out for our surveillance cameras?"

Laurent gave Brie a concerned look.

"I'll explain later" whispered Brie to Laurent.

Annick glared at her son. "Etienne, can you please assist in the kitchen for a moment?" She took her son aside. "Why would you make such a comment to Monsieur de Laval?" Her voice was stern.

"I don't like the guy. He's pompous," said Etienne.

"He certainly is not. Why would you purposely try to embarrass Brie?"

"You hardly know him," said Chantal to Etienne. "He represents our country abroad. He's educated and charming."

"I think he's too slick," said Etienne.

"I regret giving you an extra portion of my bouillabaisse," said Chantal. "You sound jealous."

"I'm not jealous. He doesn't impress me. I know his pretty boy type," said Etienne, almost dropping the bowl he was carrying.

The sisters looked at each other in disbelief.

"We'll be serving dessert," said Chantal. "Etienne, if you can't be nice to our guest, please leave the table."

"After all that Brie has endured, she deserves this happiness," said Annick. "Do not create such drama."

"She has such a glow on her face around Laurent," said Chantal with a dreamy look.

"I'm not hungry for dessert," said Etienne. He turned on his heels and left the room.

*   *   *

Brie helped Annick serve the chocolate raspberry cake she bought at the legendary Lenôtre bakery in Cannes.

"This is a most delicious cake," said Laurent.

"Good choice," said Pierre. "Where is Etienne? This is his favorite."

"He decided to skip dessert tonight," said Annick. "I think he is meeting a friend."

"Etienne believes chocolate is an aphrodisiac," said Chantal.

"It's known to be a powerful one," said Laurent. He whispered something in Brie's ear, and she blushed.

The group returned to the living room, where Annick served coffee.

"Thank you, once again, for the memorable meal and for the delightful company," said Laurent.

"It is our pleasure," said Chantal.

"Brie has agreed to accompany me to my summer home in Mougins this evening," said Laurent. He looked at her adoringly.

"We can meet tomorrow in the early evening to ensure a good viewing spot for the holiday fireworks display," said Brie. "I spoke to my friend Sven, who has reserved *chaises* for us at Lido Plage."

"My man Luc from Toulouse will join us," said Chantal.

"*Excellent!*" said Pierre. "*A demain.*"

Chapter 33

Brie and Laurent drove up the hill to Mougins, just north of Cannes.

They parked in the driveway of a large stone cottage with mature trees in front and walked up the stone path to the carved wood front door. Brie noticed a brass Maltese door knocker just below the arched window on the oversized door.

When Brie stepped inside, she was surprised by the contrast of the old stone exterior with a more modern interior. The kitchen was updated, and the colors were blues, grays, and whites. The open feel was masculine, clean and very Laurent.

They sat on the stylish sofa, covered with varying shades and sizes of blue accent pillows. The lighting was soft and welcoming.

"This cottage belonged to my grandparents. I used to come here as a child," said Laurent.

"You must have many memories of those days," said Brie, looking at the family photos on the walls.

"Here is my grandfather in the garden and this photo is my grandmother in the kitchen," said Laurent.

Brie saw a handsome, tall gray-haired man standing amongst a variety of vegetables with little porcelain signs hand-written with the names of the plants. The woman in the kitchen wore a traditional provençal print cotton apron. She had a faint smile on her face. The images were faded black and white.

Brie noticed a little light-haired boy in shorts standing in the sun, carrying a basket of fruits and vegetables, with fruit trees in the background.

"Is this you?" She asked, pointing to the picture.

"Yes, the young farmer," said Laurent. "I was about six years old in that photo."

Laurent put his arm around Brie's waist and pulled her toward him.

He kissed her hungrily. She returned his kiss with an equal fervor.

"Would you like a drink?" asked Laurent, his eyes sparkling.

"How about some Perrier with a slice of lemon? I'm so dry from this heat," said Brie.

Laurent took out two large bottles from the fridge and cut up some lemons that were in a ceramic bowl on the counter. He poured the bubbly water into pale blue Biot hand-blown glasses. Their eyes locked as he poured.

"Shall we continue the tour? Would you like to see my bedroom?" asked Laurent, pressing his lips together.

"I would, yes," said Brie, her heart pounding.

They walked down the hallway to enter a spacious bedroom, with a high ceiling, supported by huge brown wood beams. Moonlight from the skylight above illuminated the oversized bed. The bed was covered with a white comforter and a variety of white pillows. Laurent lit a candle inside a clear glass lantern on the nightstand.

He returned to her side, looking into her eyes, and putting her hand to his chest. *"Déshabille-moi.* Undress me," he said, his face beaming with desire.

Brie was in the midst of an adrenalin rush and proceeded to unbutton his shirt. He moved his arms backward to allow his shirt to fall to the ground.

He was in a hurry to unbutton the front of her white eyelet dress. It slid past her shoulders and onto the floor. She stepped out of the dress and Laurent brushed it aside with his foot. Brie stood seductively in her French pink lace bra and panties. She leaned down and unzipped his linen trousers.

He threw her onto the pillowy bedding and kicked off his loafers. She stepped out of her red sandals, as he undid her bra, with one movement, then reached for her panties.

"Did you miss me?" he asked, without giving her a chance to answer. His lips were on hers. They devoured each other with passion.

* * *

After hours of lovemaking, he collapsed at her side. "I've missed you," she said, pushing back her long blonde hair.

He turned on his side, facing her in silence. He stroked her body from her neck to her thighs. She rubbed his massive shoulders and muscular abs. His skin was soft and enticingly smooth.

Laurent sat up in bed and removed his gold watch with the brown lizard band. He opened a drawer on the nightstand and took out a small black box with a pink bow. "I've missed you, too," he said, giving her the box.

She was lying down, her head on the pillow. When she saw the box, she sat up. "What's this?" she asked, smiling at him.

"A small token of my affection, *chérie*," said Laurent. "From Tunisia."

"How thoughtful," said Brie. "I must ask, did I hear gunfire in the background when you called me?"

"Nothing to worry about. Bullets bounce off me," said Laurent, with a sly smile.

She pulled the sheet up to her chest, covering her breasts. She undid the ribbon on the box. Inside, she found an old coin rimmed in gold on a golden chain. "Did you find this at an archeological dig?" she asked.

"I don't usually rob sacred, historic sites," he said with a laugh. "But for you, I made an exception. Just don't ever wear this around a Tunisian."

Brie giggled and kissed him on the lips, lingering for several moments.

She took the necklace out of the box, and he fastened it around her neck.

Then, she decided to tell him the story of her childhood times at the Tunisian Embassy in New York, and about the letter she wrote to the Tunisian President.

"Our meeting was *kismet*,'" said Laurent. "It was fate. First at the Louvre, with the *Winged Victory* and then at the literature conference. Now, we have Tunisia in common. There are no coincidences."

"I feel it, too," she said. The coin necklace fell just above her heart scar. "It's the perfect length," she added and touched her gold bracelet from Laurent. "I'll never take this off."

He looked down and touched her chest and then her wrist, kissing her in both places. Every one of Brie's senses reached a heightened state. She reveled in them with delight. She inhaled Laurent's citrus scent and lay back on the pillow in his arms. She, too, believed in fate.

* * *

The next morning, Brie heard Laurent in the kitchen. She showered in the adjoining bathroom, with walls covered in an elaborate Moroccan tile design of blue and white. The soap carried Laurent's scent and filled the steamy shower.

When she entered the kitchen, Laurent was shirtless and in shorts.

"Come in, my darling. Your *brioche* is waiting. I will pour your *café au lait*," he said.

"Happy fourteenth of July," said Brie, approaching him.

"Happy fourteenth," he said, kissing her with his tongue. Brie could taste his coffee and the sweetness of the *brioche*.

"Do you have a large celebration for your fourth of July in America?" he asked.

"We usually have a big family picnic at the beach. This year, I'm in France, so the date passed by unnoticed," she said.

They sat down near the French doors, at a small, circular Moroccan mosaic table with two blue painted wooden chairs. The warm breeze, with an aroma of lavender, filled the air.

"I like all these Moroccan accents throughout your house," said Brie.

"Souvenirs from my assignments in the Maghreb," said Laurent. "It reminds me of times spent in that culture. The bathrooms were tiled by Moroccan artisans my grandparents met in Marseille years ago."

"I enjoy surrounding myself with artifacts from my travels," said Brie. "I like living with the good memories and making new ones."

"It's already noon," he said. "I wonder why we are both *très fatigués?*" They snuggled together.

The couple drank their *café au lait* from oversized, hand-painted ceramic cups. Laurent's had his name on it. Brie's cup had the name *Catherine* on hers.

"That was my grandmother's cup," said Laurent. "She had them inscribed for our family one year before *Nöel* in the town of Quimper, on the coast of Brittany."

"I've spent memorable times on the northern coast of France. The cliffs are spectacular," said Brie.

"I wish I'd known you then," said Laurent. "You've spent many times here before we met."

"Our timing now is auspicious," said Brie, touching his arm.

"Will you please enlighten me?" Asked Laurent. "What was the comment from Etienne last night about the surveillance cameras?"

Brie paused before speaking. She wished Laurent had forgotten Etienne's indiscreet remark. It was not a topic she wanted to discuss. "I had an incident with my ex-husband in Cannes after the film festival. Pierre thought it best to install cameras."

"You had an incident with your ex, in France? He was here?" asked Laurent, with his piercing blue-green eyes on hers.

"Yes, two months ago, when I was with the Girards and my daughter in Cannes. It turned out that he was having me followed," said Brie. Her eyes were in a downward glance, as she rubbed her pink lipstick stain off the rim of her coffee cup.

"For what reason did he follow you?" asked Laurent.

"For an unknown reason," said Brie. She wished Laurent would stop his questioning.

"You haven't seen him again, have you?" he asked.

"No sign of him," she sighed, rubbing her hands. "We heard he has returned to New York."

She had a knot in her chest, thinking of Jack Taylor on the loose.

"That is my hope. You know, I will guard you with my life," said Laurent, placing his arm around her shoulders.

"I know," she said, closing her eyes. "Thank you."

* * *

Later that evening, on the fourteenth of July, Brie and Laurent stopped by the *Villa du Ciel*. Brie changed into her new blue dress for the occasion. She added a spray of her Dior rose perfume. The Girards were in the garden, sipping Bandol rosé.

When the couple entered, everyone stood up to greet them, including Luc, the Air France pilot and friend of Chantal's from Toulouse. They approached and offered kisses. Etienne was noticeably absent.

"Etienne sends his regrets. He says he cannot join us tonight." Said Pierre. He mentioned his preference to view the fireworks off-shore and will join his friend on their yacht near St. Tropez."

Brie knew that Etienne's favorite fireworks viewing spot had always been in Cannes, at the beach, but she kept this to herself.

She thought about what had transpired between Etienne and herself in the garden, a few nights before, when Etienne confessed his feelings to her. Brie felt uncomfortable harboring this secret about her godson. She questioned why she hadn't noticed Etienne's crush on her. Perhaps, he had hidden this, even from himself. Her affection for him ran deep, but it was a mother's love.

* * *

When the group arrived at Lido Plage, they found Sven dressed head to toe in blue, white, and red, the colors of the French flag. His dog Cary wore festive *tricolore* attire. (Brie recalled that Sven had named his dog after his favorite actor, Cary Grant.)

Sven showed them to the front row of lounge chairs, where Brie had spent the afternoon with the Arabic princess, two months prior.

"Someone has big connections," said Luc, who hugged Chantal.

"Not me," said Chantal, pointing to Brie. The comment did not go unnoticed by Laurent, who looked at Brie with an expression of surprise.

It was close to eleven at night when classical music began, played by a full, live orchestra on the beach side of La Croisette.

"Handel's Water Music," said Laurent.

"How appropriate with us being right near the water," said Pierre. "Unfortunately, not a French composer."

The air was warm and humid, with a balmy floral-scented breeze. Annick wore her new blue Italian scarf and Brie complemented her friend on the stunning look. "*Très chic*," she said. Annick blew her a kiss.

Pierre hugged his wife.

The pyrotechnics, created by a famous Italian group, started with an elegant display of gigantic silver and gold freeform snowflake patterns. They sparkled all the way down to the water. The crowds cheered in unison, with the musical accompaniment in a crescendo. The revelers who strolled along La Croisette started to dance. Some did the minuet, recalling the dances from the times of the French kings.

Pierre noticed the dancers. "We're supposed to be celebrating the end of the monarchy tonight," he said.

"Some of those beheaded might have been my ancestors. Did you know that Brie could have been a relative of Marie-Antoinette?" asked Laurent, laughing. Pierre looked over at her with surprise.

Each explosion of changing colors was unique and titillating to the audience. The Bay of Cannes was lit up, as if by ten thousand moons, surpassing the spectacular show of "Sound and Light" held at the Château de Chambord in the Loire Valley each summer.

Much of the time, Brie and Laurent had their eyes focused on each other. "The show is over there, *mes amis*," said Chantal, with a smile.

"My favorites are the mauves and pinks," said Brie, her eyes glistening.

"To match your lingerie," Laurent whispered in her ear. She touched his face and looked longingly at him.

The fireworks lasted almost two hours with a grand finale of non-stop explosions.

"That was like great sex," said Chantal. "I feel so satisfied."

Luc gave her a kiss on the cheek. Annick blushed.

After the fireworks display, a local children's chorus sang the French national anthem: "La Marseillaise." The crowd joined in, many of them wearing their blue, white, and red clothing and waving French flags.

Numerous bands and trios lined the streets of Cannes along the beach. There were jazz bands, blues trios, and some rock and roll. A band from Moscow played songs by the Rolling Stones and The Beatles, singing the lyrics with strong Russian accents, "You can't always get vat you vant."

French teens did American dances from the 1950s, including lindy and swing. Groups of French nationals, international visitors, couples of all ages, and children danced wildly till the wee hours of the morning. Pierre and Annick joined Chantal and Luc with Brie and Laurent in front of the Russian band. That particular band had an array of talented musicians and singers. The lead singer was a dead ringer for a Russian Mick Jagger.

By the time the group sauntered back to the *Villa du Ciel*, the sun was starting to come up.

Chapter 34

Pierre was the only one, on July fifteenth to see the light of day after the night of celebration. He was alone in the kitchen, preparing his *omelette* in the late afternoon. He read the local papers and perused the photos, noticing an article on the front page of *Nice Matin* of a drug bust on a private yacht off the coast of St. Tropez. He thought he recognized his son's picture as one of those in handcuffs, but the photo was not clear. He decided to hide the newspaper until he could confirm the reporting. Any hint of drug use would ruin his only son's medical career for life.

* * *

In the early evening, the rest of the partygoers from the fourteenth of July filtered into the large kitchen. Furry Loulou was the second to arrive, nose alert to any food preparation. Luc opened the French doors to let the dog out to the garden. The pooch had been afraid of the sound of fireworks since she was a puppy.

"I'm not cooking today," announced Chantal. "I'm too tired."

Brie and Laurent stumbled in, yawning. "I can prepare a North African dish, if you like. I do need a few ingredients," offered Laurent.

"He cooks, too?" whispered Chantal to Brie. Both women laughed.

"What is the joke?" asked Pierre.

"Nothing," said Chantal. "Just female talk."

"Do you like pastilla?" asked Laurent. "I can make the North African pie with some chicken and phyllo dough."

"Sounds delicious. I've tasted the dish in Moroccan restaurants," said Chantal. "I have some chicken and phyllo dough in the freezer, spices in the pantry."

"You freeze chicken?" asked Annick.

Laurent busied himself with his culinary creation. It was a long process that took more than three hours. Brie was at his side, learning his techniques and offering assistance. She cut up some carrots to marinate in Moroccan spices, as a side dish, watching him in amazement.

"In the meantime, we have fruits from the trees and Pierre's croissants," said Annick. "Nobody will go hungry in this house."

"Who would like coffee?" asked Pierre.

"I need a liter of coffee myself," said Luc. The massive man approached with his cup, wearing an Air France t-shirt.

Loulou busied herself ripping paper in the corner and peeing all over *Nice Matin. My newspaper photo problem is now resolved*, thought Pierre to himself.

Chantal looked over at her petite pooch. "She's recovering from the fireworks," said Chantal. "Poor baby." She went over to comfort the dog.

Annick entered the kitchen. "Those were the most spectacular fireworks I have ever seen in Cannes."

"The colors were extraordinary. So unique to see violet and fuchsia," said Brie. She felt lucky to be on the Côte d'Azur, celebrating summer, French-style.

* * *

The clock in the hall rang midnight when Pierre got a call on his private line. He walked away from the others to the opposite end of the room.

"If you were involved in what I suspect, you will have to figure this one out for yourself. You're a grown man and a doctor. It is your responsibility," said Pierre, raising his voice in anger.

"Who were you talking to?" asked Annick from the living room, where she was watching a film on television.

Pierre reentered the living room. "We'll talk later, *mon amour*," he said to Annick. She looked at her husband with concern. "Let's go to bed. We can discuss it in the morning."

* * *

The next afternoon, Laurent drove up to his cottage in Mougins, leaving an exhausted Brie at *Villa du Ciel*, as she requested. Chantal's friend Luc went back to Toulouse and the villa returned to normalcy, although Etienne was still absent.

"Laurent asked me to stay with him in Mougins for the next few weeks," Brie said.

"What have you decided?" asked Chantal. "You know you always have a home here with me, my friend." The women smiled at each other.

Brie pondered the question. "It seems premature to move in with Laurent during the summer holiday. His son will be arriving from Paris for a visit. If I stay here with you," she looked at Chantal, "I plan to contribute to the household."

"Please stay here," said Chantal. "You can look after the villa and Loulou when I'm in Toulouse. It would be a great help to me, and we can be housemates sharing occasional grocery expenses."

"What a good idea!" said Annick.

Chantal continued, "My neighbor, Madame Fifi, will be busy all summer with her gallery in St. Paul, so I can't count on her. If you would stay, it would be a perfect solution."

"That's a tempting plan," said Brie.

"Please, *ma chère*, we want you to stay here. Your New York residence has been completely disrupted," said Annick. "You don't want to risk anything with *you know who*.'"

Brie shivered at the thought of another encounter with Jack. She knew a return to New York at this time was not a choice for her.

"So, it seems that my wife and sister-in-law have figured out your life for you," said Pierre to Brie. "At least we know we have surveillance here and you will be safe."

"Thank you, my friends," said Brie. "So, it's decided. I'll call Chloe and my sister Lisa to give them both an update."

The friends cheered and Pierre brought a bottle of champagne from the fridge. "To the French–American alliance," he said, laughing.

"I have something promising with Laurent," said Brie, "although he goes overboard with the gift-giving." She showed her friends the coin necklace from Tunisia on the gold chain.

"Did he rob a museum to impress you?" asked Pierre.

"Stop it, Pierre. We adore Laurent," said Annick. "He's attentive and generous because he's smitten."

"I'm not used to this much attention," Brie said, looking pensive. She felt a cold shot of hurt blast through her heart. She touched her chest.

"Laurent is handsome, intelligent and he cooks," said Chantal. "Great combination!"

"He's a worthy Frenchman who appreciates you," added Pierre, with a grin. "We approve."

"Now, where is my son, Etienne?" asked Annick. "He's disappeared."

She looked at her husband with a worried expression.

"The phone call I got late last night was from him. He has been detained by the local police," said Pierre.

"What?" screamed Annick, her face ashen. Brie and Chantal looked on, in shock.

"The yacht party he attended last night had drug users onboard. There was a drug bust by the police," said Pierre. "The owner is a doctor friend of Etienne's. He allowed his guests to partake in illegal substances. Etienne will have to find a good attorney who can do some smooth talking to clear him."

"*Mon dieu*, can't you do something?" asked Annick, covering her mouth.

"He's a grown man. He must face his own consequences," said Pierre.

"I agree," said Chantal. "What was he thinking? Or, not thinking?"

"What a sad situation," said Brie. She felt somewhat guilty for causing Etienne pain by rejecting his advances. She knew French law and how the French had a horror of drug users. The penalties would be severe.

"I'll not let this ruin my vacation," said Chantal, in disgust.

"I feel devastated for my son," said Annick. She turned to Brie, who hugged her friend. "Is there never a dull moment in this house?"

"Maybe they'll send him to the dungeon of the Chateau d'If, for his punishment," said Chantal.

"This is not a joking matter," said Annick, beginning to weep.

"I'm sorry," said Chantal. "It's a horrible situation for my nephew."

The atmosphere turned quiet and pensive at the *Villa du Ciel*. The celebratory times had come to a jarring halt. Loulou groaned in the corner, reflecting the change in mood.

Chapter 35

Laurent's son, Tristan arrived from Paris the following week. Laurent called Brie to tell her of his son's request to play tennis with his father in the mornings and spend afternoons at the beach. Tristan would soon meet up with his Italian girlfriend and her family, who were vacationing in Sardinia.

"I hope you can return here to join me for dinner at Le Moulin de Mougins, after Tristan's departure. I have a table reserved," said Laurent. Brie agreed, thinking how much she missed Laurent, allowing herself to feel this joy at the prospect of seeing him again.

* * *

The week passed, without a word from Etienne. Then one morning, when the friends were preparing to go to the beach, they heard a knock at the front door. Pierre responded and he discovered a disheveled version of his son Etienne, standing with his head down, in wrinkled clothing, bleary – eyed and with a seven-day growth of beard.

Annick peered over and looked at her son in horror. "Oh, look at you! Come in and tell us everything," she said, as she embraced her son, her whole body shaking.

Etienne pulled up a chair and slumped down. "I was in the wrong place at the wrong time," he said, looking at his father. "Do you think I would knowingly get on a boat and sail out to sea with a bunch of drug-gies, risking my medical career?" He took a deep breath.

His father glared at him.

He glanced at his mother. "Can I have a coffee?"

Annick poured a cup of hot espresso from a thermos and handed it to her son.

Etienne continued to explain, his voice was raspy. "By some miracle, they believed my story, after days of questioning by two detectives, who asked me the same questions over and over. The lockup was not pleasant. I barely slept. They took blood and urine samples and did a series of lab tests. I must have been exonerated by the negatives results." He sipped the coffee and rubbed his forehead. "I was lucky to have a talented lawyer friend to represent me."

Annick gritted her teeth. "Thank God."

Pierre looked at his son with disbelief. "Next time, you ask a few questions and get to know the people you're with, before you socialize on a boat out in the Mediterranean." He was still furious. "Use your head, man."

Chantal listened to her nephew in silence. Brie felt a pang in her chest.

She looked at Annick who was distraught, her face pale. They would save the beach for another day. Loulou whimpered on her dog bed and closed her eyes.

Chapter 36

Brie contacted Chloe that morning. Her daughter was back in Los Angeles, hard at work on her next film. Brie invited Chloe to join her once more, in Cannes.

"Sorry, Maman. I'll be shooting over the summer months. We lost valuable time during the hiatus to celebrate in May at Cannes. In the film industry, even one day missed costs a fortune," Chloe said. "I won't have time off until late fall."

"I know film budgets are similar to those of small countries," said Brie. "The main thing is to enjoy the process. Can you tell me about the new film?"

"It's a drama. A murder mystery with some grizzly scenes. A woman is killed, with the prime suspect being her estranged husband. The bad guy is an expert at gaslighting and covering his tracks. Very Hitchcock, with a touch of Claude Chabrol," said Chloe.

Brie shivered at the thought of such a plot line. She fought back a sudden wave of nausea and terrifying memories of her ex, Jack. It crossed her mind that he could be capable of killing. Why had she stayed with such a duplicitous man? She realized she had been in denial about his character.

"Sounds like you may be honored in Cannes again, next year," said Brie. "I can imagine shadows and staircases as prime visuals." She thought to herself that she wouldn't choose to see such a film. It crept too close to her present state of mind.

* * *

Brie called her sister Lisa, who was wrapping up a court case in Montreal. Lisa was anxious to prepare for her upcoming adventure to Cairns and The Great Barrier Reef of Australia with her husband.

"The best time to go is during our summer and their winter, otherwise, it's too hot," said Lisa. "The diving and whale-watching will be exceptional." Lisa, a trained scuba diver, was an outdoor lover like her Canadian husband.

"I know you adore the undersea landscape. Enjoy!" said Brie.

"What's new in France?" asked Lisa.

"Some craziness with Etienne," Brie explained about her godson's arrest and subsequent positive resolution. She struggled to find the right words, leaving out the part about Etienne's confessed love for her.

"How about you?" asked Lisa. There was a pause at the end of the line.

Brie caught her breath. "I feel happy and relaxed for the first time in ten years," she said. "Laurent is a fine man."

"I'm glad," said Lisa. "You deserve this happiness."

Brie continued, "My sabbatical from the university came at a perfect time." She told Lisa about her plan to stay with Chantal at the *Villa du Ciel*.

"I wouldn't be running back to New York either if I was in your situation," said Lisa. "I'll text you from the reef. Love you."

"*Bon voyage*," said Brie. "Love you."

Chapter 37

In the blazing hot afternoon, sunlight flashed on a white envelope as Chantal handed a letter to Brie from the mailbox. It was addressed to Mrs. Brie Taylor at the *Villa du Ciel*, Cannes—written in smeared pencil. The dirty, crumpled envelope arrived, with a series of stamps that were partially unglued. The postmark indicated it was from New York, with an illegible date. Brie hesitated before opening it. She had a sinking feeling about its origin. Chantal stood by her friend, perhaps thinking a similar thought. Inside was a hand-printed note in black ink, on lined paper, which looked like it had been written by a child.

"Happy Anniversary to you, my distant love. July is our special month. I know where you are, and we will be together soon. You can never escape me. You have my promise. It's not over."

The note was unsigned, but Brie had no doubt it was from Jack. She felt weakness in her legs, as she tried to catch her breath. She showed the letter to Chantal.

"How could Jack have known your exact location?" said Chantal. When Chantal looked over, she saw her friend Brie had collapsed on the floor.

Etienne, who was in the dining room, heard the thud and came running. He scooped Brie up into his arms, taking her pulse. He asked Chantal to bring a cool, wet cloth and some water. Chantal complied, and in a few minutes, Brie had regained consciousness. Pierre and Annick, hearing the clamor, rushed to her side. They passed around the crumpled note.

"Where will this end?" asked Annick in a wavering voice.

"I'll alert the detective right away," said Pierre. "He hasn't contacted me with updated information in a week."

"The detective is on holiday," said Annick wringing her hands.

"We shouldn't have gotten complacent with Jack Taylor," said Etienne. "He could be anywhere. We were warned about his recent escape."

Brie's vision was blurred. "Is he here now?" she asked, looking around her. Her thoughts were numb, her body limp. "Was he having me followed?"

Pierre left the room and reappeared with a stethoscope. He spent several minutes listening to Brie's heart and breathing pattern. "You are fine," he said with a smile. She made an effort to smile back at him.

"I received a message from Detective Marceau. The authorities have no confirmation that Jack ever left America. *Hélas*, they haven't been able to locate him. Yet," said Pierre. "The detective will be here later in the afternoon to examine the letter and speak to us."

"My fault. I let my guard down," said Brie in a soft voice, still light-headed. "How could I ever have gotten involved with such a frightful man? I'll forever question my judgement."

"He's a liar; he kept secrets. Don't blame yourself for not knowing what was hidden from you," said Chantal.

"Come and lie down in bed," said Annick. "I'll sit with you."

"I'll let you know when Detective Marceau arrives and we can listen to his recommendations," said Pierre. "Let's put this back in the hands of the professionals."

* * *

Detective Thierry Marceau turned up at the *Villa du Ciel* in the fading, late afternoon sunlight. He wore khaki shorts and a bright red Lacoste polo shirt. He sported a suntan and aviator sunglasses. Brie had forgotten how huge a presence he was. She felt relieved to see him.

"*Bonne après-midi*, Thierry," said Pierre to his friend. They shook hands. Chantal remarked that he had "a grip like a vise."

"Thank you for interrupting your holiday," said Annick.

"No problem," he said stoically. "Where's the letter?"

Brie brought it to him. He took a moment to read it, with an expressionless face. "May I take this with me?" he asked. Without waiting for a response, he placed the letter in a plastic bag he pulled from his pocket.

"Shall we call the police?" asked Chantal, moving closer to the detective.

"I am the police," he said, looking at her with distaste. Chantal stared back at him with an expression of intimidation on her face.

He continued, "We checked your surveillance cameras, and nobody has been on your property with the exceptions of your neighbor Fifi, a gentleman named Luc from Air France, and a man we have identified as Laurent de Laval. He is an esteemed member of the French Diplomatic Corps. Now, the mail is a different story. Please don't open any future suspicious mailings without contacting me first. Understood?"

They all nodded as if they were students obeying a strict teacher. Brie was relieved she had such a conscientious detective looking out for her well-being, along with her loyal friends. She sat on the sofa with a glazed look.

"The moment we begin to relax, there's another crisis," said Etienne.

The detective turned to Etienne. "I'm pleased everything worked out with that little mishap on the boat. Things could have taken an unpleasant turn," he said.

Etienne and his parents looked at each other with dismay and surprise.

Pierre's eyebrows arched. "Thank you very much for all you have done to help my family," he said to the detective.

Thierry patted his friend on the back. "We take care of our friends," he said, dryly. "We want to keep them out of trouble." He winked at Etienne.

* * *

In the evening, after everyone had gone to bed, Brie stayed up in the living room with Loulou at her side. She needed to process the events of the day, by writing in her journal. She was interrupted by Etienne, who entered the living room in a bathrobe. Brie jumped up from the sofa when she saw him, her heart pounding.

"Please, don't worry," he said, reassuring her. He realized he had startled her. "I came to check on you and to apologize for my behavior toward you last week. I had no right to say what I said to you, my god-mother. I was not thinking clearly. Can you please forgive me?" he asked, his eyes pleading.

Brie took a deep breath. "Your words took me off guard, but you were being honest. I can't fault you for that," she said, shaking her head.

"So, you can forgive me?" asked Etienne in a gentle tone.

"If you never cross that line again," said Brie. "I must believe I'm living in a safe place, and I can trust you."

"I'm so sorry. I was a disgrace to you, to my family, and to my culture," said Etienne. He looked down at his feet.

"We will not speak of this again, I hope?" asked Brie, glaring at him.

"We will not, but I can't promise you my feelings for you will subside, if I am honest," he said, his eyes on hers.

"This must remain between us," said Brie, looking into his sad eyes. She believed he had learned a harsh lesson and respected her boundaries.

"I would never dream of adding to your stress," he said. "Please know that I want what is best for you, always." His look was soft. Then he hugged her, turned away, and left the room.

Brie continued to write in her journal. She decided to tell Laurent about the interlude, without elaborating on too many details to give him cause for major concern. She wanted Jack in her past, where he belonged. She wondered if she would ever write a book about her life. If she did, she would write it as a work of fiction.

Chapter 38

Chantal's neighbor, Madame Fifi, came to visit and handed her an invitation for all of them to come to an art opening at her gallery in St. Paul de Vence. It was a big event she held every year in late July, highlighting the top artists of the area. Her paintings were often amongst those featured.

Fifi was known for her Expressionist style and bold use of color. A Parisian, she had relocated to Provence in her later years. She followed the tradition of other French artists who moved south as they got up in years and craved more favorable weather.

Picasso had been one of the artists who came to the southern coast of France. He had abandoned his native Spain and then his adopted city, Paris. He moved to Antibes and the Musée Picasso then opened, containing only his work, including his many ceramics. Picasso himself spent much time at that location.

Brie recalled a chance meeting she had with Picasso at his museum in Antibes when she was nineteen and he was in his seventies. She had noticed him on the back veranda with a backdrop of the blue

Mediterranean. He was hard to miss, wearing all black, his bald head gleaming in the sun. Her aunt Françoise encouraged her to go up to greet the artist. Picasso offered to give Brie and Françoise a tour of the museum and they were thrilled. After two hours with the artist, he invited Brie to come to his home, on her own, to have dinner with him. Her aunt whispered to her niece of Picasso's infamous reputation with women. He had offered to gift her a piece of art, if she accepted. Brie reflected on his lurid depiction of women in his art and was quick to decline his invitation.

The poster announcing Madame Fifi's art exhibit hung in many shop windows in Cannes, Nice, and beyond. This year's poster featured an abstract painting in oranges and purples, reminiscent of Rothko and Matisse. Only a select group of members from the art community were invited to the actual opening reception to meet and mingle with the artists. The hors d'oeuvres and wine were catered by a well-known restaurant. Brie put in a request to invite Laurent. Fifi informed Brie that she was acquainted with Monsieur de Laval and that he was already on the list. He had purchased art from her in the past and she considered him to be a VIP client.

* * *

The group met Laurent at the gallery. He looked rested and tanned in his natural linen ensemble. He noticed Brie across the room and moved directly toward her. Brie and Laurent greeted each other with a lingering kiss, as if the gallery was empty and they were the only ones in the room.

Madame Fifi appeared with her big hair and intense, color-blocked dress. She looked like a painting in motion, wearing bright purple, lemon yellow, and crimson. She and Laurent nodded to each other from afar. Fifi kept her distance as she watched another kiss between Laurent and Brie, and as Laurent placed his hand on Brie's lower back. Brie wore a black and white geometric dress that clung tastefully to her curvy frame. Her shining blonde hair was styled in loose waves and her lips were bright Chanel red, matching her berry red heels.

The gallery buzzed with a Who's Who of the art world. The invited guests were a well-dressed group, who drank champagne and chatted about the art that hung on the bright white walls surrounding them. The lighting was impeccable, enhancing each work. The clientele carried catalogues, making notes inside. Several paintings had red dots, indicating they were already sold.

Annick and Chantal sampled the smoked salmon and capers hors d'oeuvre. Pierre and Etienne raved about the local shrimp. They watched Brie and Laurent from a distance, then moved in to greet Laurent with kisses all around. Etienne and Laurent shook hands. Etienne had a morose expression. When Chantal asked him if he was enjoying the art, he replied "*Comme-çi, comme – ça*," which indicated he was not enthralled with being there. Brie knew it was not the art that disturbed him, and she tried to lighten the mood.

"Madame Fifi matches her clothes to her gallery, it seems," Brie said with a smile. "I wonder if her ensemble is for sale." She exchanged looks with Laurent.

"Not too many women can pull off that dress she's wearing," said Chantal, with a laugh. "She looks like she had a collision with a wet Picasso painting."

"Or a Matisse Odalisque in progress," said Annick, smiling.

Brie admired a multilayered, mixed-media piece by a Latvian artist who now lived near Lubéron. It resembled the cubist style of Braque, only in strong, richer colors. The depth of the layers attracted her and Laurent agreed that it was a unique, colorful work.

A string quintet of local musicians played Andalusian music, which complimented the art.

Brie walked toward the powder room with Chantal, where she noticed a young man with a ponytail leaning on a back wall. She feared she recognized him as the man from Paris.

"Do you know him?" asked Chantal.

"All these artsy types look similar," she said, laughing it off. She felt a sudden flutter in her heart and a sour taste in her stomach.

She decided to approach the man. "Do we know each other?" said Brie, looking him directly in the eyes."

Chantal was shocked to witness her friend confronting this stranger and tried to pull her away.

"No," said the man. "You confuse me with someone else, madame." His voice was high-pitched, his accent pronounced. It did not fit his appearance. He was, perhaps, eastern European.

Meanwhile, Pierre noticed the man and alerted Annick in a lowered voice. "Isn't that the guy from Paris with the ponytail, over there?"

"Oh, Pierre, really?" she questioned.

"He's a dead ringer," said Pierre.

"Please don't spoil the evening for Brie," said Annick. "I'll ask Madame Fifi for the guest list tomorrow and we can turn the names over to our detective. He told us to be alert and not panic."

"Good plan," said Pierre. He had an idea to take a photo of the man, pretending to be photographing the art. But when he looked to the corner a few minutes later, the man had vanished.

* * *

The crowd began to disperse on that steamy summer evening in late July. Laurent told Brie they had dinner reservations in Mougins, and the couple said their goodbyes. Madame Fifi accompanied them to the front door. She informed Brie and Laurent that her August event would be an exhibit called "Erotic Art and Fashion." She would be sending out invitations. Laurent responded that he was intrigued. Brie wanted to get into the cooler breeze outside. She had trouble adjusting to the French lack of air-conditioning in some venues during the hot summer months.

They walked onto the cobblestone street, past the fountain in the center of the village of St. Paul de Vence. Brie was relieved to feel the droplets of water from the fountain that the breeze blew in her direction.

Laurent's sports car was parked in a darkened alley, away from the gallery. The couple sat on the hood of his car looking up at the star-filled sky, both breathing in the fragrant air from the surrounding provençal countryside. The sky was like the stars in a Van Gogh painting, with swirling light above them. The metal hood on the car was still warm from the day's heat.

"Are you hungry?" asked Laurent, looking into her golden brown-amber eyes.

"I'm starved," said Brie.

Their passion took over, as they kissed on the car hood, hidden from view. The couple made love in the shadows, thrusting against the metal hood, amid the distance voices coming from the gallery guests, who were now departing. The clientele flowed onto the street.

"Shall we go, *mon amour*?" asked Laurent, stroking her hair.

"Yes, let's get in the car," said Brie. Her voice was barely audible.

Laurent drove the short sprint toward Mougins like a cheetah on the run. His driving technique was effortless on the narrow, winding country roads.

Brie was covered in moonlight. She reflected on their frenzy of heat and touch in the alleyway. Her mind was a calm, glimmering sea.

Laurent turned off the car ignition in front of the restaurant in Mougins. They combed their hair with their fingers and Brie reapplied her lipstick, clearing the smudges off Laurent's mouth. They sat looking at each other for several minutes.

"I feel serene when I'm with you. I don't want this to end," said Brie, breathless.

"Why would it end?" asked Laurent. "I'm here to stay." He took her arm and helped her out of the car.

*   *   *

Once inside, the Maître d' greeted Laurent. "*Bonsoir*, Monsieur de Laval. Your table is waiting." Laurent nodded. He looked at Brie. "*Bonsoir*, *madame*. Right this way."

They feasted on caviar and duck foie gras from the Dordogne with fresh almonds and peaches, and then Mediterranean tuna with crab meat ravioli.

The dessert was apricots with melted butter and rosemary. The flavors were rich, yet delicate.

The lovers hardly spoke. They had eyes on each other, both lost in a dream-like state. Laurent stroked Brie's arm with his fingertips.

*   *   *

Laurent's stone cottage glowed in the light of a full moon. The couple went for a swim in his free form pool in the garden. He lowered the lights so they could enjoy watching the stars above. The scent of lavender filled the air. They swam nude, wrapping their arms and legs around each other. The air was balmy and covered them in a blanket of ecstasy. Brie never imagined she would know the level of happiness she felt on this night.

Later, they moved to the bedroom. Brie awoke in the arms of Laurent, who was in a deep sleep. She peered out the window to see the glorious moon. She reflected on author Michel Houllebecq's belief: By allowing ourselves to be overcome with great passion, we make ourselves vulnerable. The higher the joy, the more it has the potential to cause pain. Caring for someone, connecting with them on the deep level, is risky. It was at that moment, Brie decided she was willing to take that risk with Laurent.

Chapter 39

Brie and Laurent wandered into his kitchen for *café au lait* and toast with butter and red fruits jam. It was a sizzling summer day, as August began, the most sacred month of leisure in France. Paris was *en vacances.*

Brie sipped her *café au lait* out of the oversized cup, as she told Laurent about the letter she had received. She spoke about the detective friend of Pierre's and the surveillance in place. She mentioned the man with the ponytail, who appeared to be following her in Paris and then again at Madame Fifi's gallery the night before.

"Are you sure it was the same man?" asked Laurent, with concern in his voice.

"It was the first time I heard the ponytail man speak, but yes, I do," said Brie. "I confronted him." Brie wondered if it was the right thing to do.

"That was brave and direct," said Laurent. "I wouldn't want you to endanger yourself." He poured himself another cup of black coffee.

"I was in a room filled with people. I didn't want to cower in fear," said Brie. "I can't live my life in worry. It's not good for my heart." Brie placed her hands in the middle of her chest.

"Jack didn't appreciate you. Now he tries to get you back in this ridiculous manner, by having you followed. Can't he see that he's too late for that?" Laurent asked, looking disgusted. He turned to Brie, touched her heart area and kissed it. Then, he kissed her lips.

"I'm not a perfect man, but I do know what I have with you," he said. "I live the life of a diplomat, so I am living out of a suitcase much of the time. I'll try hard to be present and open with you and never take you for granted."

Brie inhaled his appreciation of her. "You're a good man," she said. She reflected on this man she met at the Louvre and then in his official capacity as a representative of France. She contrasted his public formality with the private man, who showed a relaxed charm. He retained his aesthetic tastes, with an endearing, seductive sentimentality. Even the most formal Parisians could let their guard down, she thought.

Laurent continued, "I have cameras in place here, outside the cottage. I put them there a couple of years ago. As you know, I am gone for long periods of time and my son Tristan thought it would be a good idea." He added, reassuring her, "I'll check the recent footage to see if we find the mystery stalker."

"I feel safe when I'm with you," she said, running her fingers through his hair. They lingered over a kiss and enjoyed the rest of their *petit déjeuner*.

Laurent licked the red fruits jam from his finger. "This is homemade by a woman in the area who grows her own red fruits—strawberries and raspberries and sells the jam at the Mougins market," he said.

"Delicious!" said Brie, looking into his eyes.

* * *

Brie received a call from Annick, while on a walk with Laurent around Mougins village. Annick said she was calling on behalf of Etienne, who stood by her side. She extended a sailing invitation from Etienne and his friend. *Was Etienne uncomfortable speaking directly to her?*

"I get *mal de mer* on boats," said Annick, "so Pierre and I will stay at the villa."

"I remember that on the *Bateaux-Mouches* in Paris," said Brie. "The Seine has strong currents."

"Chantal was summoned back to Toulouse for an Air France emergency," said Annick. She has to handle the chaos of a pilot threatening to walk off the job."

"Let me check with Laurent," said Brie.

"*Salut*, Brie." She heard Etienne's upbeat voice. "Please join us this afternoon for a sail," he said.

There was silence on the other end of the line.

Etienne continued. "Of course, it's not the former friend from the infamous July fourteenth fiasco. This family has a sleek, forty-eight foot sailboat in Cannes harbor. We're preparing an Italian picnic. Can you and Laurent meet us at two o'clock, when the wind picks up?"

There was another pause, while Brie discussed the sailing opportunity with Laurent. He nodded his head in approval.

"We'll be there," said Brie. She heard a sigh of relief from Etienne, who was obviously trying to repair his relationship with his godmother.

* * *

Brie and Laurent approached the dock and were greeted by Etienne, who was dressed in white shorts and a white polo. He looked like a handsome tennis player. He unlocked the gate for them to enter, kissed Brie and shook hands with Laurent.

Etienne guided them to a boat named *La Sirène*—The Mermaid. The flags onboard were Italian and French. Under the name was scrolled

"Capri, Italia." It was an impressive vessel with freshly oiled teak through-out and included a large interior cabin. The sails were at half-mast.

A young, lively blondish woman, in her mid-twenties, appeared from below deck. She wore a tiny, sun yellow bikini. The petite woman's bouncy breasts were popping out of her string bikini top. In contrast, Brie wore a turquoise caftan embroidered in gold, with a one-piece matching bathing suit underneath. Brie slid her oversized sunglasses down her nose to take another look at the young woman, who cooed to Etienne. "So, these are your friends, darling?" She cuddled up to him.

Brie was surprised that Etienne had never mentioned this woman, who he called "Sofia." There were introductions all around.

"My parents couldn't be here today. They're entertaining our family from Italy. It will only be the four of us," said Sofia. "We will have plenty of room." She was friendly.

She looked at Etienne. "Darling, could you make our friends some drinks?"

Then, she turned to Brie, eying her with interest. "So, you are the famous godmother? You don't look like you could be his mother at all."

Sofia motioned for them to sit down, rubbing Laurent's arm. "Are you the husband?" she asked.

"We are together," said Laurent, who sized up the woman in front of him. Sofia bounced close to him and threw her body about, as he drew Brie to his side.

Sofia continued her attentions toward Laurent. "Haven't I seen your picture in the newspapers?" she asked, twisting her torso.

"I don't know, have you?" replied Laurent, drily. He seemed offended by Sofia's familiarity.

Etienne arrived carrying a tray of blended drinks with fresh pine-apple and cherries.

"Sit down, Sofia, so our guests can get comfortable," he said.

They toasted "to the sun gods," and Brie took a long swig of the rum drink. "Very good," she said to Etienne. "I taste coconut."

Sofia hopped out onto the dock to untie the lines, as Etienne started the motor.

"Once we get out of the harbor, we'll pull up the sails and *La Sirène* will be on autopilot." She shouted. "Our work will be done, and we can have our picnic." She smiled at her guests and jumped back into the boat.

Brie put on her wide-brimmed straw sunhat with turquoise band that she tied under her chin. Laurent placed his arm around Brie and pulled her close to him as they sailed out of Cannes harbor.

Etienne was at the helm, steering the boat. Sofia ran toward the boom and appeared to press a button that lifted the sails to catch the wind. They were in the open, aqua blue ocean, sailing at a brisk speed.

"The computer will do the rest. We are on course," said Sofia.

She arrived with a can of spray-on sunscreen. She sprayed Laurent, Brie, and herself, lifting Brie's caftan to spray her feet and legs, taking care to avoid the golden straps of Brie's sandals.

"The sun and wind are a harsh combination. We must be protected," Sofia said.

Laurent tried to explain that they were already wearing sun protection, but she bobbed off toward the helm.

Sofia sprayed Etienne's arms, legs, and face and kissed him on the lips. Etienne wiped his lips with a little scowl. He looked like the little boy Brie remembered, taking sailing lessons every summer in Cannes, from the age of ten. He loved the ocean. It was evident that sailing remained one of his passions.

They all sat aft and looked out to watch dolphins jumping in the sea, accompanying the boat at a distance. Etienne breathed in the salt-filled air and hugged Brie.

"Thank you for coming," he said. Laurent patted him on the back.

"This is beautiful," said Brie, thinking the coast of the Riviera was a grand sight.

Brie addressed Sofia. "Where did you meet Etienne?" she asked.

"Oh, in Paris. I was at the university for a short time. I decided it wasn't for me, so I dropped out to join my father in his import/export business. My father is Venetian and Florentine. He deals in leathers. We vacation in Cannes as a family each summer," she said, smiling at Etienne. "Right, darling?" Etienne was staring out at the dolphins.

"Italian leathers are superior. My sandals are from Capri," said Brie.

"I guessed they were," said Sofia, reaching down to touch them.

"When your father watches *le football*, is he in favor of Venice or Florence?" asked Laurent, watching Sofia rearrange her bikini top, that had slipped to one side, in danger of revealing her breast.

"He's in favor of Italy. My mother is French," replied Sofia.

The men discussed the Paris St. Germain team. Sofia suggested they serve the picnic and Brie followed her into the galley.

The women returned on deck with two trays of food. There was prosciutto wrapped melon, Genoa salami with provolone cheese, Castelvetrano green olives and marinated artichoke hearts. Etienne poured the rosé wine. They ate with appetite. There were peaches and raspberries for dessert.

"I get hungry out at sea," said Etienne.

"Yes, he does," said Sofia, with a laugh. "Very hungry."

"Very good," said Laurent, as he placed a white cloth hat on his head. "The south of France is a natural mix of French and Italian cultures. We have many similarities."

Sofia offered Laurent a breadstick, by placing it in his mouth.

"I'm a big boy. No need to feed me," he said, taking the breadstick in his own hand.

Etienne looked at Sofia, who arranged her bikini top and went over to sit in Etienne's lap.

Brie removed her hat and caftan in one swope and she revealed her curvaceous body, as if in a magic act. Etienne watched her every movement, as did Laurent.

"Shall we go out to the bow?" Laurent asked to Brie, pointing forward. He removed his polo shirt. His muscular, tanned chest shone in the bright sun.

"*Oui, mon amour,*" she answered.

Laurent turned to Sofia and Etienne. "Thank you for a delightful picnic. It's time for our siesta."

"I'll bring the mattresses," said Etienne, watching Brie.

"The wind is picking up and the sails are full," said Laurent.

Etienne arrived with two blue and white covered mattresses. He placed them apart. Laurent put them together and looked up at Etienne.

"Thank you, my friend," he hugged Etienne. "You remind me of my son."

"You have thought of everything, Etienne," said Brie, smiling at him.

Brie and Laurent rubbed more sunscreen on each other. Brie took out the Lancaster crème she had in her straw bag and smoothed it on Laurent's expansive shoulders. He, in turn, covered her arms and décolletage. Brie liked the feel of Laurent's hands. They were strong, yet soft. They fell asleep in each other's arms, while the soft sea breeze caressed their bodies.

* * *

Brie awoke to a sudden chill. The sails had lost their fullness and the sailboat appeared to be drifting off course.

Etienne came running from the cabin below deck, adjusting his swim shorts. Sofia followed, her hair in disarray, wearing only her bikini bottom.

"The computers are not always perfect," she said with a concerned look.

"Get dressed, Sofia. I'll handle this mishap," said Etienne.

In a matter of minutes, Etienne had the sailboat back on course.

"We need to be heading back to the harbor, anyhow," he said.

Sofia returned, wearing a red and green t-shirt that read "Viva Italia." "Don't worry. Etienne knows this boat as well as my father does," she said.

"We're not worried," said Laurent. "I know my way around a sailboat. It's not safe to leave the boat unattended, even with the computer."

Etienne had a sheepish look on his face. "I got distracted."

"How about some music?" asked Sofia.

"Music for the return is a great idea," said Brie.

Julien Doré's *Le Lac* began to play on the boat's sound system. A playlist of French and Italian tunes guided *La Sirène,* sailing back to Cannes harbor. Pulling into the slip, the group noticed the seafood restaurants preparing for their evening clients on the outdoor *terrasses*.

"The hours fly by out at sea. It's almost dinner time," said Brie.

Laurent assisted Sofia in tying the sailboat to the dock. "How do you like my gondola?" she asked Laurent with a smile.

"She's very seaworthy," said Laurent, who helped Brie off *La Sirène,* kissing her hand in the process.

Etienne stored the sails with the automatic system, then hosed down the deck. He looked professional with his boat shoes and gloves.

"I hope you will join us again," said Etienne to Laurent and Brie.

"Maybe I can encourage my parents to come next time. I'll offer my mother some medication, so she won't suffer from seasickness."

"Some people prefer to stay on land. Even a whiff of sea air can cause them discomfort," said Laurent.

Sofia chimed in. "Well, Etienne's mother raised a sailor son. He can't get enough, right, darling?"

Etienne kissed Brie and shook hands with Laurent.

"I had a spectacular day out at sea with you," said Brie to Etienne.

"Thank you." His eyes shone brightly on hers.

Chapter 40

Detective Thierry Marceau informed Brie, Pierre, and Annick that he checked the guest list from the art reception and did not find any irregularities in the group. Nothing suspicious. The man in the ponytail, he concluded, must have slipped through the open back door, where clients were smoking in the rear of the venue. His associates checked the security cameras, and could not locate the intruder, who seemed to know where to stand to avoid the cameras. After speaking with Madame Fifi, he discovered that she didn't know of any guest fitting the man's description. The detective had no doubts that Brie and others saw the intruder in person.

Detective Marceau continued, speaking about the letter Brie received from New York. He determined the postmark was from upstate New York, near the town of Poughkeepsie, in the Hudson Valley, about an hour north of New York City. He would keep investigating through his

New York connections. Brie confirmed that the detective had attorney Jeff Klein's phone number.

* * *

Annick suggested a short trip to the flower market in Nice, as a diversion for Brie from all this intrigue. Pierre had an afternoon planned with Etienne, for a father–son outing. Laurent had some business calls to make and then some tennis with his neighbor, who was a poet from Belgium.

"I'll drive Chantal's car," said Annick. "It's been sitting there, driverless, for over a week."

"I can drive back," said Brie. "I do feel tentative around these drivers, but Nice is not far."

"If you expect the unexpected, and drive defensively, we'll be okay," said Annick. "Drivers will cut you off, speed, and yell or gesture out of windows in a variety of languages. These tourists are the worst."

Brie decided it best to not comment about European drivers. They thought Americans drove like the elderly.

The women were lucky to find an open parking spot near Old Nice, called *Vieux Nice* by the locals. They walked to the open-air market. Annick bought a variety of fresh vegetables and fruits and placed them in her basket. She was excited about the enormous peaches.

They continued on to the famous Nice Flower Market, with its astonishing array of blooms, including roses of every size and color. Brie stopped to sniff them, along with the lilacs and tuberose. Annick inhaled the fragrance of the orange blossoms. They decided to purchase the flowers at the end of their stroll, so the blooms would not wilt in the heat.

Brie recalled the Nice Flower Parade she had attended a few years back. The floats had been covered with floral arrangements. The participants threw flowers from vases to the spectators along the route, so everyone went home with a large bouquet to enjoy. It was unlike the Rose Parade in Pasadena, California on New Years' Day, where the flowers were left to die on the floats. She thought the French approach was an excellent way to recycle flowers.

The friends continued, arm in arm, down the narrow, winding cobblestone Medieval streets. Brie was partial to the colorful facades of the buildings and the red tile roofs. Compared to New York, it was like a fairyland of pastel colors. Rose pinks, yellows, and rich salmons, with soft green and white shutters.

Annick suggested they stop for gelato at the famed Fenocchio Glacier. Brie pointed out the exotic olive-flavored gelato with basil. She had her usual, rose and violet combo. Annick chose chocolate orange. They found a table in the shade, where they enjoyed the frozen treats. It was a crowded area, with tourists from around the world.

Brie noticed a man in a dark blue New York Yankees baseball cap with a ponytail, leaning against the wall of an old building, far away from the crowd. He appeared to be glaring at her. She alerted Annick, who suggested they start walking back to the car.

"Is that our man?" said Annick.

"I now perceive every man with a ponytail and his look as our man," said Brie. She snapped a photo.

"Well, we can't be too careful. I'll call Pierre and let him know, so he can talk to the detective," said Annick.

The women left Nice without purchasing any flowers. Annick drove back to Cannes, allowing Brie to process the afternoon's event. They drove west along the Boulevard des Anglais, past the Hôtel Negresco with its pink dome and Belle Epoque style, along the Baie des Anges—Bay of Angels. The Mediterranean was a dark blue and the sky was full of clouds. Their day had been cut short in Nice.

* * *

217

Detective Marceau was waiting for the women in the living room at *Villa du Ciel*, along with Pierre, Etienne, and Laurent. The detective recited his updates on the case to the gathering.

"We ran the photo of the suspect Pierre took at the gallery opening through our facial recognition. No match. It appears he's not in our system."

Brie, who was startled to see this group all together on her behalf, found her way to the sofa and sat down next to Laurent, who grasped her hand.

"I took another photo of him in Nice today. I can tell you he had an Eastern European accent, perhaps Hungarian or Czech. He spoke very few words to me at the gallery," said Brie.

"I don't recommend confronting a suspect," said the detective. "If he meant you physical harm, he probably would have made a move by now. It's been three months, but his motives are still unknown."

"Do you think I'm in physical danger?" said Brie, her eyes widening. The others looked on with concern. "I can't live with a constant cloud over my head." Her stomach was churning.

"We don't know his employer and he's not working alone. We suspect he is employed by your ex, Jack Taylor, or by those to whom Mr. Taylor owes money. He has had plenty of opportunities to approach or hurt Mrs. Taylor, if that was his plan. He has been bold and out in the open. He is not trying to hide his presence, so he thinks he is untraceable."

"Would you suggest we keep Brie sequestered here now, like we did in Paris?" asked Etienne. He looked at his godmother with worry.

"Is that necessary?" asked Laurent, turning toward Etienne.

The detective continued, "Neither the NYPD nor the FBI know the whereabouts of Mr. Taylor at this time. He's clever and well-hidden and he's not making any mistakes, except for sending that letter to Mrs. Taylor. The authorities are investigating upstate New York. We have no indication that he is here in France."

Brie hated being called "Mrs. Taylor." Her emotions were caught up in her throat. She couldn't speak.

"My recommendation is that we follow the ponytail suspect, by following Mrs. Taylor. Pierre told me the man sometimes wears his hair long. He could change his appearance." He turned to Brie. "We will be with you from now on, but discreetly, in unmarked cars and in tourist attire. You will go about your normal activities without any particular or predictable routine. To apprehend this fellow would move us closer to bringing Mr. Taylor back into custody and to keeping Mrs. Taylor safe."

"Please call me Brie," she said to the detective. "I'm no longer Mrs. Taylor." She thought about going back to her birth name, Brie Beaumont.

"Brie can stay with me in Mougins. We haven't had any incidents there," offered Laurent. She smiled at him, feeling warmth in her body.

"That would be an option," said the detective.

Brie thanked the Girards for their continuing support. There was a group hug, New York-style.

"Go and stay with Laurent. They seem to be watching this house and we want you to be as safe as possible," said Annick.

"We are in the midst of a kind of American thriller," said Pierre. He turned to his wife and put his arm around her. "Don't worry. Those usually have a happy ending."

*　*　*

Brie sent messages to her daughter Chloe and her sister Lisa, taking care not to alarm them. They were both far away, Chloe in Los Angeles and Lisa in Australia. Lisa was enjoying perfect scuba conditions at the Great Barrier Reef. They didn't need to worry about Brie.

Chloe's film was in crisis. They had to replace the lead actor due to a family emergency, so the script had to be partially rewritten. The director was at a crucial scene in the film when the husband attempts to murder his wife.

Brie kept her comments upbeat and focused on her contentment with Laurent. She decided to spend the next two weeks with him in Mougins.

Chapter 41

Laurent suggested they go to Lido Plage. In summer, the Côte d'Azur sunset was hours later in the evening than in New York. Sven was there to welcome them and show the couple to the front row of *chaises longues*. They chose the double chaise. Jean-Luc brought towels, Evian water, and arranged their umbrellas.

High heat and humidity characterize the French Riviera during the summer months. Brie and Laurent decided to take a swim in the turquoise waters, which matched his eyes. They swam in tandem toward the deep blue, cooler water. Brie wrapped her legs around Laurent, and he held her close.

"We're like sea horses mating," he said. Brie laughed. She felt warmth swimming next to Laurent, even in the cool water.

The Mediterranean, known for its high salt content, gave them buoyancy in the gentle swells. They felt the current draw them further out to sea. Laurent noticed the pull, suggesting they swim back to shore.

"The Mediterranean can be dangerous," he said, drawing her to his body.

With little effort, they reached the lighter-colored aqua waters, then the sand and they were soon back on their *chaises*.

"I feel refreshed," said Brie, drying her hair with a towel. "That was like a baptism."

"The sea is a healer. I often turn to the ocean when I'm facing stress in my life," said Laurent. He kissed her wet cheek. "No harm will come to you when I'm around."

They both fell asleep on the *grande chaise* in the warmth of the sun, their bodies glowing.

* * *

Brie awoke from a nightmare on the beach. Sweaty and out of breath, she remembered being in the Hamptons on Long Island with Jack. He had taken her for a swim at sunset and left her alone in the waves of the mighty Atlantic Ocean. She was caught in a powerful rip current. The lifeguards, who were closing up for the day, noticed her in distress. She was bobbing up and down, waving her hands frantically. They were able to rescue her and asked if she had been swimming alone. She said she had been with her husband, but he had disappeared.

When the lifeguards accompanied her back to Jack and Brie's summer house, Jack was there with his buddies, smoking cigars and playing poker. He laughed when he saw her and said he knew she would find her way back. The lifeguards were not amused.

The next day, Jack apologized and promised he would never do anything like that again. He agreed with her that he had been neglectful. He had been on his college swim team and knew Brie was not a strong swimmer. Brie had wondered if she should ever trust this man again. Now, she was certain she could not.

* * *

Laurent returned from the showers at Lido Plage. He became concerned when he saw Brie in tears. "You were crying out in your sleep, *ma chérie*. Were you having a nightmare?"

"*Oui*, a bad remembrance," she said. "I'm processing, letting go of negative memories. They'll pass."

"Your subconscious is at work."

"It's unsettling to relive a scary experience," she said, taking deep breaths and staring at the soft ripples of the Mediterranean.

"How about a distraction tonight?" he said.

Brie thought for a moment. "Let's go dancing. There's a little impromptu outdoor club on the sand at Point de la Croisette."

"Perfect plan. That's been on my agenda," said Laurent and kissed her on the lips.

*   *   *

The couple arrived at Laurent's stone cottage in Mougins.

"I'll make us dinner," he announced. "I bought some fresh filet of sole at the fish market this morning. I want to prepare it *provençal*-style, with olives and tomatoes."

"I've never tried it that way," said Brie. She watched his hands, noticing his effortless skill, similar to the way he touched her, with delicacy and grace. She thought it seductive to observe some men in the kitchen, the ones who knew what they were doing. He created a side dish of baked artichoke hearts with parmesan in a lemon sauce.

"Where did you learn to cook?" she asked, kissing him on the cheek.

"I'm self-taught. When I'm away on assignment, I enjoy preparing meals for myself and sometimes for my colleagues," he said.

Brie felt a tinge of jealousy and wondered if those colleagues included women. She didn't want to imagine those aqua eyes fixed on anyone else. She wanted his sweet caresses only for her.

"I like variety in cuisine and to experiment with spices," he said.

"You're certainly accomplished with seafood," she said, with a grin.

"It is easy to overcook *les fruits de mer*, so I've learned to prepare them with a gentle touch."

They sat in the dining room, at the large, round wooden table. A fragrant summer breeze entered through the open windows. At one end of the table, there were place settings for two, with bright blue placemats and matching cloth napkins.

"I took the liberty of selecting a Sancerre Blanc from the Loire Valley. It is supposed to have some pear notes. Will you taste?" he asked.

"With pleasure," she said, watching his hands open the bottle.

Laurent poured the white wine in her glass. He continued, "It goes well with fish and it's not as heavy as Chardonnay. I usually choose a local rosé when I'm in the south, but I found this intriguing one in a nearby wine shop."

"Your sole is so flavorful, and I love the grilled tomatoes. The wine has a lovely, complex finish," Brie said.

"*Merci, ma chérie,*" he said, smiling. "I like complexity in my wine and in my woman."

Brie fanned herself with the napkin.

They ate with appetite, gazing at each other. They were hungry after their swim.

Laurent returned to the kitchen to prepare the dessert. "I have a raspberry and peach compote. The peaches are from the trees outside this window. My grandfather planted them many years ago."

Brie thought the fruits were ripe and sweet, admiring the idea that the peaches had a history on the property.

"Come, *ma chérie*. I'll serve you coffee in the living room," he said.

"I need a shower first, *chéri*," she said, smiling. "I'm so salty and I only rinsed off at the beach. Then you were so quick to cook the fish."

"I'll take a bite of you now, if you're not careful," he said, embracing her.

* * *

When Brie entered the large salon in her pink caftan, Laurent had candles lit on the coffee table. A song by Francis Cabrel was playing in the background. *C'est écrit – It Is Written.* They sat on the cushy sofa, and he handed her a small blue velvet box.

"For you," he said, his eyes fixed on her.

"Thank you, *mon amour*," she said, with a broad smile. "There's no need." Brie's voice trailed off as he took her hand.

"As you know," he said, "I must leave at the end of August to return to my post in Tunis. This is so you won't forget us."

"I would never forget you," she said, with a sigh. *This man is unforgettable,* she thought.

She opened the box and was surprised at its contents. It was an exquisite ring. She recognized the large oval center stone as a rare Paraiba tourmaline, the stone of empathy, known to have curative powers. The exotic blue-green color matched the color of Laurent's eyes. The Paraiba was surrounded by delicate diamonds.

"Breathtaking," she said, kissing him on the lips.

"The stone is from Brazil. Will you try it on?" he said.

"Yes," she placed it on the ring finger of her right hand. "Perfect fit."

"I took a lucky guess," he said.

She kissed him with fervor, and they fell back on the sofa together, lost in a passionate embrace. Brie was able to stay in the moment, as Camus had taught. No thoughts invaded from the past, no worries of the future.

"I hope you will not tire of my absences," he said, brushing back her hair with his fingers. "I knew my work would take me away when I chose my career." He wrinkled his brow.

225

Brie's face was hopeful. "I live in the present, these days," she said. "I promised myself, after my heart surgery, that I would be thankful for every day." She had tears in her eyes, grateful that she met him that morning at the Louvre. He wiped the tears from her cheek with his finger.

"The situation with your ex-husband is looming," he said. "That's why I hesitate to leave you, but I must." His expression grew pensive.

"Don't worry about me. I'm not the woman who left New York four months ago. I didn't tell you, but I plan to start a self-defense class next week, taught by Detective Marceau's associate," she said.

"Not a bad idea," he said, kissing the ring and her hand and then her lips. "I'm happy the Girards will be here with you."

*   *   *

It was in the wee hours of the morning when the couple arrived at the open-air club on the beach at the Point de la Croisette in Cannes. The dance venue only existed on the sand during the summer months.

The guard at the entrance nodded for Laurent and Brie to enter. Most of the clientele were dressed in white or beige tones. Many were barefoot.

"I've never danced in sand at night before. It's cool and damp," said Laurent, kicking off his sandals. Brie was already barefoot.

The live musicians played the music of Antonio Carlos Jobim, the master jazz composer from Brazil. They swayed to the Bossa Nova. "*O grand amor.*" Laurent was singing the lyrics in Portuguese in Brie's ear. He held her close to him.

"This reminds me of my assignment in Brazil a few years ago," he said. "Rich culture and hypnotic music."

"I love Rio," said Brie. "There are traveling musicians on the beach at Copacabana and Ipanema, with music and dance everywhere."

"The Brazilians are enamored of the French culture. Some of their poets write in French. It was gratifying for me to spend time there," he said.

Stars shone above, covering the sky like a painting.

During their slow dance, they bumped into a large man and a petite woman on the "dance floor." It was Detective Marceau and his wife. The detective flashed them a grin, motioning for them to carry on. It was rare to see the detective smiling.

Brie danced with joy. She was in her element, summering on the French Riviera, with a man she cared for deeply. She soaked in this new life, a stark contrast to her existence with Jack during the previous ten years, when she held her breath, anticipating another crisis. Now, she was beginning to breathe.

Chapter 42

Brie and Annick arranged to meet at the self-defense class recommended by Detective Marceau. A short, slender female police officer was the teacher. She wore a pixie haircut and black yoga pants with a white t-shirt. The class was made up of ten women, of all sizes and ages.

"It's ironic that all those years I lived in New York, I never felt the need to take a defense class," said Brie.

"I think it's important for all women to know how to defend themselves, no matter what their age," said Annick. "I took a class in Paris, years ago, but it's good to have a refresher."

The instructor modeled the first move with a male officer, who posed as an attacker. They were both seated. When the man grabbed her, she demonstrated poking at his eyes and then pushing in his nose.

"These are delicate areas of the face," she explained. "You must use force. Don't be a wimp. Be decisive. You can stomp on the attacker's insteps, grab his hand, and pull back his little finger. Try it on each other. But watch out, it's very painful."

The women practiced with their partners, taking care not to cause harm. A few participants, who had been too forceful with each other, reacted with pain.

The next move included a man approaching. The officer instructed the students to pull the attacker toward them and demonstrated kneeing him heartily in the groin.

"Disarm him with this surprise move. He won't like this."

"I'm sure he wouldn't," said Annick to Brie, laughing. "Should I try it on Pierre later?" Brie shook her head, indicating it was a bad idea.

"Then, you must run quickly in the opposite direction," said the instructor, in a loud voice. "Don't forget about yelling 'NO!' This will alert those who might hear you that you are in distress. Make noise. Don't stay silent."

The women all yelled "*Non, non, non*" in French, at the top of their lungs. Brie had a hard time screaming. In situations of distress, she was like a clam. Shut down.

"Try to avoid getting in a vehicle with an attacker. If he forces you inside, grab the steering wheel and try to crash the car." The instructor continued. "If you're ordered to drive, crash the car. The airbags will save you."

The female officer asked for questions from the group.

"What about carrying a gun?" asked Annick.

"I don't recommend weapons such as those. They can be used against you," said the officer. "It's best to use the defenses I have shown you against any would-be attacker."

"I hope we never have to use these techniques," said Annick.

"They are good to know," said Brie, breathing deeply. She wondered if she would be able to take such actions in a dangerous situation.

The women continued their practice. The officers assisted them with the various postures. It was a grueling workout, and the women blotted their faces with the towels provided.

* * *

After class, Annick and Brie decided to go for coffee. Even though they were sweaty, they needed some caffeine. When they were seated opposite each other, Annick noticed her friend was wearing a new piece of jewelry. "That ring you're wearing is quite impressive, my friend," she said. "When did you get it?"

"It's from Laurent. An 'au revoir' gift," said Brie.

"Goodbye?" mused Annick. "That's a stunning gift for any reason."

"That it is," Brie looked down at her hand. "He reminded me that he will be returning to Tunis in a couple of weeks."

"And you'll remain in France, so not far away, n'est-ce pas?" Annick asked. "Chantal will be here with you."

"Another change in my life," said Brie, with a distant glance.

"But a good change," said Annick. "Meeting Laurent was not an accident."

"I never thought I could have feelings like this for any man again," said Brie, her eyes tearing up.

"Madame Fifi has been asking about you. She wants to read your tarot cards," said Annick.

"Do you believe in those readings?" asked Brie.

"*Believe* is a strong word, but I find tarot fascinating," Annick replied.

"Madame Fifi's hard at work, preparing for her next gallery show. She's installed major air-conditioning and plans to lock the back door to the gallery. She doesn't want another mishap like last time, with the uninvited ponytail intruder finding his way inside her private party. She's hired guards for the front door, including some of Detective Marceau's esteemed colleagues."

"That does put my mind at ease," said Brie. "And we are now armed with our defensive moves." Brie shivered at the thought, hoping she would never have to use these moves she learned in class.

"Yes, we're ready. Bring on the rogues," said Annick, laughing. "Did you know that Chantal has taken years of Karate classes? She has a brown belt, I think."

"Chantal is *Wonder Woman*," laughed Brie. "She's tough."

"Nobody messes with my sister," said Annick, grinning.

"Or mine," said Brie. "Lisa can take care of business."

Chapter 43

The big night of Madame Fifi's *Bal Masqué* arrived in mid-August. She called it a Masquerade and Erotic Art Display. It would be a hot night, in many ways, in the small village of St. Paul de Vence. Fifi promised her new air-conditioning installation would be ready and at full blast, unusual in France. Europeans in general were not big fans of air-conditioning, preferring natural breezes. Such breezes were rare during the summer months in sun-drenched Provence.

The invited men were asked to wear formal black attire. The women were given free rein in their costumes.

Brie wore a clingy burgundy satin slip dress that followed the curves of her body and accentuated her breasts. She had a matching sequined mask. The Tunisian gold coin from Laurent hung at her throat, on a black velvet ribbon.

Laurent, who named Brie his "seductress," was in a fitted black Dior tux with a black shirt, unbuttoned, revealing his chiseled chest. He had a burgundy silk handkerchief in his breast pocket and carried a black velvet Venetian molded mask on a carved wood handle.

The couple met Pierre and Annick at the door. The security included armed guards. All guests had to show their printed invitations and identification to the guards and be checked off a list of names. Chantal and Luc, who had returned from Toulouse to continue their holiday, talked with Etienne and Sofia toward the back of the line.

Pierre was dashing in his Armani tux. Annick surprised them all, in her black leather miniskirt, thigh high boots and flowing black silk organza blouse. She had a delicate gold and diamond chain around her neck. Pierre couldn't take his eyes off her.

Sofia was in a scanty see-through black lace top, skin-tight black leather pants and shiny blazing red pumps. She wore a black leather mask and carried a small whip. She clung to Etienne, who was shirtless, in his black tux

They entered the expansive room to a raised model's runway, anchored at the ends by Michelangelo-styled statues of nude men. The rosy and violet lights were dimmed, as the music of *Thievery Corporation* played in the background. Scents of vanilla and musk filled the air.

All guests were directed to view the artwork around the perimeter of the gallery. Several of Picasso's erotic drawings were on display, with placards naming them from private collections. Velvet ropes kept the guests at a safe distance.

Brie reflected again on that chance meeting with Picasso in Antibes at his museum. She shared this recollection with Laurent, who was relieved to hear that she hadn't dined alone with the art world's infamous womanizer, when she was an ingénue.

Brie and Laurent noted that Detective Marceau and his wife were among the guests. The detective scanned the room, his work made more challenging by the majority of guests wearing masks.

Madame Fifi made her entrance in full Italian courtesan attire. Her scarlet satin dress had a fitted bodice, revealing her massive cleavage. She wore an oversized matching velvet hat with wide brim and multiple shades of red feathers. Her mask had eyelashes painted on the outside, and her arms were covered with her signature gold bangle bracelets. Fifi swayed as she walked, with her gloved hands in the air. The crowd cheered for their dazzling hostess.

Fifi was followed by waiters in white gloves carrying trays with champagne flutes, containing Dom Pérignon with strawberries and pitted cherries.

The guests continued to view the artwork. Laurent's favorite of the photographs was a color image Brigitte Bardot in St. Tropez, eating a strawberry fed to her by an unknown admirer. Beyond the photographs were a series of Matisse's *Odalisques* from the artist's Moroccan period, part of another private collection. Brie and Laurent, both admirers of Moroccan culture and décor, spent additional time admiring these works.

Brie preferred the illustrated version of the French poet Baudelaire's *Invitation au Voyage*, written for his exotic Haitian mistress, Jeanne Duval. Brie had analyzed Baudelaire's poetry in depth and recited her favorite quotation to Laurent, who recited it back to her. "*Là, Tout n'est qu'ordre et beauté, luxe, calm et volupté.*" This juxtaposition of images enthralled them both and they embraced in front of the illustration.

Laurent examined the illustrations of the poet Verlaine's love poems, as well as quotes from Flaubert's *Madame Bovary*. He thought these were brilliantly drawn. He recalled Flaubert's journal written about a voyage to Egypt. Brie agreed that Flaubert's *journal de bord* gave intriguing details of his travels.

The lights dimmed and the focus became a spotlight on the runway stage in the center of the gallery. "King Louis the XIV" the Sun King, appeared in his elaborate purple and golden robes, gold tights and high heels. He posed with his mistress, the "Marquise de Montespan." She wore lavender French lace lingerie and was coiled around the King like a seductive snake. Brie felt her skin tingle.

The "Marquis de Sade" ushered in men and women, some with devilish tattoos and harsh make-up, clad in scanty black leather attire. He swung around his red-lined cape, slapped his followers, unzipped some of their garments and laughed menacingly toward the audience. He reminded Brie of her ex, Jack, who had been sadistic and dominating. She shivered at this memory and grabbed Laurent's arm. The crowd booed as the Marquis exited.

The tiny "Toulouse-Lautrec" led *cancan* dancers from the Moulin Rouge. The women, some topless, lifted their numerous petticoats, their make-up, clown-like and chalky white, exaggerated their flaming red lips. One such dancer represented *La Gouloue* in Lautrec's paintings. Brie touched her throat. The music of Jacques Offenbach played, and the audience danced along with the tune.

A troupe of undulating belly dancers entered the hall, to the haunting oriental music of Turkish clarinets and drums. Their fuchsia silk flowing skirts, topped with rich silver and gold beaded bras and belts, glittered in the intense spotlight. The dancers played their brass finger cymbals, called *zills*. The women tilted their breasts and moved their hips in figure eights. Their eyes, rimmed in bold black eyeliner with ultramarine shadow above, flashed their long black lashes at the viewers. The women in the crowd joined in the movements with the dancers on stage. Brie had studied belly dance in Istanbul and Cairo. She grooved in front of Laurent, with hands above her head. He was mesmerized by her skillful gyrations, pulling her by the waist and kissing her on the lips. A Turkish drummer approached for a solo with one of the dancers. Her belly rippled in time to the drums. Another dancer balanced a candelabra, lit with candles, on her head, while another balanced a curved sword on hers as she shimmied. The belly dancers received an outpouring of applause and took deep bows.

A coquettish "Brigitte Bardot" bounced onto the runway, wearing her signature St. Tropez white bikini, blonde curls flowing. She was followed by a sultry "Sophia Loren" in black silk lingerie with gleaming red lips. Both women joined hands and bowed to the audience, who went wild for these two icons of European cinema.

"Marilyn Monroe" was next to appear, in the legendary filmy dress she had worn to sing an alluring "Happy Birthday" to the American President, John F. Kennedy. She cooed and sashayed around the stage, throwing kisses to the ecstatic crowd. Brie threw a kiss back at her.

The male statues of Michelangelo came alive at the ends of the runway, as the nudes, in loin cloths, were followed by Donatello's "David." They displayed their idealized male bodies to the onlookers. Women and men applauded with delight.

Next came the Egyptian Queen, "Cleopatra," who rolled onto the runway in a gleaming golden chariot. "Cleopatra" shimmered in the spotlight and embraced her lover, "Mark Antony," who was seated next to her. They had a prolonged kiss, encouraged by an appreciative audience.

The grand finale, a group of Italian counts, were accompanied by their lusty courtesans. They surrounded Madame Fifi, who was now in a bright green satin and lace gown with defined bodice. She sat in a regal position, in a mock, motorized black Venetian gondola. Her skirts billowed as she strolled. She was drenched in enormous emeralds – a bold necklace, elongated earrings with diamonds, a triple-rowed emerald bracelet and a giant oval emerald and diamond ring. The live orchestra played Vivaldi's *Four Seasons*.

They were upstaged by a surprise visit from the "Emperor Napoléon," on wooden horseback, in full military dress with his signature two-cornered hat. He dismounted and took the arm of his "Empress Josephine," haughty in her cream-colored floaty gown of Empire finery, punctuated by an enormous glittering diamond necklace and crown. The couple appeared more regal than the Sun King.

"The Empress" was pushed aside by Madame Fifi, as she approached the "Emperor Napoleon," who kissed Fifi's hand. The crowd began to spontaneously sing "La Marseillaise." "The Empress," not to be upstaged, rejoined her beloved "Napoleon," giving Madame Fifi a ferocious look. It was a spectacle. Brie and Laurent locked eyes on each other as they sang the French anthem.

Waiters appeared once more, this time with silver trays covered with chocolates of all flavors and fillings. Dance music played, as the guests continued their celebration of the five senses. Brie and Laurent moved together like a couple in love, their perfumes intertwining. Chantal fed Luc a few chocolates, kissing him on the lips after each one. Pierre embraced Annick and commented, "Madame Fifi never disappoints."

* * *

Later that evening, in the arms of Laurent, Brie thought how eventful and almost carefree her summer had been on the French Riviera. She knew that real life would intervene when autumn and the Mistral winds arrived on the Blue Coast. She wanted to hold onto every bit of summer that remained, and to what she had with Laurent. She luxuriated in the French *Joie de vivre*.

Chapter 44

After another week at *Villa du Ciel*, on a bright summer afternoon on the *Côte d'Azur*, the Girards held their annual August picnic. They invited a select group of neighbors and friends from Cannes and the surrounding area. Annick and Chantal spent days preparing hors d'oeuvres, along with Laurent and Brie as sous-chefs. Etienne selected forty varieties of cheese at *le marché*.

Madame Fifi, draped in a golden caftan, read tarot for the guests under an enormous platane tree in the back yard. Her bracelets jangled as she mixed the deck. Brie awaited her fate, as she selected her cards. The reading of Brie's past included the Ten of Swords, indicating her strife with Jack. Her present indicated the Emperor and Empress, and the Two of Cups, which Fifi identified as Brie and Laurent's happy relationship. The future part of the reading revealed the disturbing cards of the Tower and the Death card. Brie rustled in her chair as she looked over at Laurent, who was talking with Pierre and Etienne. Brie's mouth and throat felt dry.

"Death does not mean an actual death," clarified Madame Fifi. "It brings change and transformation. The Tower represents major upheaval."

"Put those cards away," said Chantal. "You're bringing negative energy to our party."

"The cards don't lie," insisted Fifi. "Believe what you like." Fifi shook her head in dismay, as Brie wrinkled her brow.

Detective Marceau had joined the group of men. Loulou, pooch on the loose in the yard, jumped up at him. The detective lifted the little dog in his muscular arms and petted her with a soft touch, still scanning the party through his dark aviator sunglasses. The man with the ponytail hadn't resurfaced since Nice. Still, the detective remained vigilant.

Brie recalled the time, a year ago, when she had awakened in her hospital bed after her surgery. She was surrounded by attentive nurses, caring doctors, dear friends, and family. She remembered seeing Jack appear, just once, in her hospital room, after she was moved from intensive care. He sat in the background, while her family and friends brought cards and flowers. They were with Brie on her bed, telling her how happy they were that her surgery was a success. They encouraged her during her twelve-day hospital stay and visited her during her subsequent year-long recovery at home, bringing prepared food and cheerful conversation.

Jack was rarely present during her six months of learning to carefully move to protect her incision, to dress herself and to walk short distances. Brie would tire easily after limited exertion. Her sister Lisa assisted Brie with her daily shower, which was a challenge that left the patient exhausted. Lisa drove her sister to follow-up doctors' appointments. After "Nurse Lisa" returned to Montreal to her law practice, visiting nurses checked in on Brie at home twice a week, as did physical therapists, who helped her regain her strength. Jack was noticeably absent.

Jack never told her that he loved her during that long expanse of time, nor that he was thankful for her survival. At one point, he disappeared and did not reply to phone calls or texts. Nobody from his law office kept in touch with Brie or offered any information on Jack's whereabouts.

* * *

The sky above *Villa du Ciel* darkened to a richer blue, as the guests began to depart from the gathering. They thanked the Girards, including Laurent and Brie, who, it seemed, were now part of the extended family.

Madame Fifi, who finished her final tarot reading with the last of the guests, put her deck of Art Nouveau cards in a purple velvet pouch. She walked over to Brie, who was still in a dazed state.

"Don't worry, my dear," said Fifi, looking into Brie's eyes. "The cards can tell many stories, and my readings vary day by day. If you take one reading to heart, you will lose your way. Everything happens for your highest good. You are protected and you know you are a survivor."

Brie nodded, "Thank you, dear Fifi. I'll keep an open mind." Brie's pulse raced as Loulou ran to her side, barking loudly. The dog sensed when Brie needed comforting.

"Call on me anytime, said Fifi. "I'm not just your neighbor, I'm your friend. We French don't take friendship lightly. You know that."

Brie and Fifi gave each other departing kisses on the cheek. Brie's mouth quivered as she managed to give Fifi a smile.

Chapter 45

As the end of August approached, Laurent suggested to Brie that they attend a summer festival at Le Château de La Coste, near Lubéron. He had arranged for tickets, awaiting Brie's consent. They could attend the Lavender Festival by day, and the ballet with a live orchestra at night.

The couple viewed a panorama of stunning landscape en route, with fields of lavender that went on for miles. The strong floral scent and lavender color soothed them both. Brie felt at home in France, and she couldn't imagine a more nurturing place. She leaned back in the car seat and looked at Laurent's tanned, serene face as he drove.

When they arrived at their destination, they found shade, and watched the "Lavender Parade," complete with elaborate floats. Participants were dressed for the floral occasion. Venders sold lavender in all forms, including lavender ice cream. For years, in coming to the south, Brie had bought sachets. She used to keep them in her lingerie drawer. Then she noted how the scent attracted bees. When one flew into her car window and stung her under her skirt while she was driving, she decided to use the dried lavender only for display or for scenting a room. It made the New York apartment smell and feel like the south of France.

* * *

In the evening, they approached the ballet stage, with a backdrop of Roman ruins. Laurent had chosen seats close to the front. The dancers, in flesh-colored tights and creamy white costumes moved in precision in the balmy air. The ballerinas wore long, filmy skirts, except for the prima ballerina in her soft pink tutu. Their bodies blended with the ancient stone columns behind them. The stars were a backdrop for the dancers and the indigo sky served as a canopy.

While they watched the performance, Brie thought about her relationship with Laurent as a kind of fantasy. From the time they met, by chance, at the Louvre, and during their holidays in southern France, she had felt a calm. No strife, no cross words, just a flow of contentment between them. With the newness, there were no bumps, as in real life. Absent was the mundane.

As the lights faded on stage, Laurent embraced Brie. The lovers gazed at each other. She thought of him as a gift from the heavens, with the stars in alignment. She never wanted their time together to end. Laurent was the first man in Brie's life with whom she felt such intimacy and she could feel her broken heart healing.

* * *

During the drive home, Laurent posed a question.

"*Ma chérie*, what were you thinking about during the ballet? You had a faraway look in your eyes," he sounded deeply concerned.

Brie hesitated. "I don't want these moments to end." She had a morose tone, as she looked down at her lap.

"This is certainly not an ending," said Laurent, taking a breath. "I can assure you of that."

"You'll soon be leaving to return to your post," she said. "I fear the feelings we now share may change."

Brie thought back to the numerous times in her life when she had been let down by her former husband. All the secrets he kept and how often he had cut her off in mid-sentence, when she tried to speak or to ask him a question.

"Change is not an ending," Laurent continued, gazing at Brie. "Please have faith and trust in me. My life's work has been to bring harmony to circumstances."

"I've lived through enough drama for ten lifetimes," she sighed.

"We'll write to each other, and talk. I often have long nights alone, after working all day. I spend those hours writing and reflecting. It is a solitude I embrace, although I do get lonely," he said.

Brie remembered the reception at the Embassy, when he was surrounded by fascinating people, men and women, who vied for his attention.

She continued, "My struggle has been with uncertainty and demons from my past. Life is unpredictable. Not my comfort zone."

"We all have demons that belong in the past," he said, seeming to read her mind. "We can continue a relationship that includes a temporary hiatus. My favorite example is Napoléon and his Josephine. The emperor spent much time away in battle. The couple endured long periods of separation. Perhaps some distance is the key to happiness?" he said. "Longing for your lover can be as enticing as being with them, *n'est-ce pas?*"

Brie thought it was a very French point of view. Then she remembered that Napoléon had divorced Josephine because she could not bear him an heir.

"So, tell me your fantasies, when you are alone," she said, holding her breath.

"That, *mon amour*, you will discover in my writings to you," he said.

"I must confess, *mon chéri,* that when we met the first few times, I thought you were arrogant," said Brie. "You gave me your card and asked me to call *you.* We used the formal 'vous' in public and you seemed aloof, yet flirty."

"And now, what do you think? You know me better," he squeezed her hand.

"I think you are a romantic. A dreamer, like me," she said, glancing at his profile.

"So, we are the same," he said. "Let's go with the current and see where we go. Can you do that?"

"Yes, I can," she said, pushing her blonde hair out of her face. *We will see,* she thought.

Chapter 46

The couple spent their final August night celebrating with Annick, Pierre, Etienne, and Chantal. The men would be leaving the next day to return to work. Annick would not start back at the university until October, so she would remain in Cannes during most of September. Chantal had some additional vacation time, having worked most of August. French citizens were guaranteed a minimum of five weeks of vacation each year. Few major employers dared to tamper with this guaranteed leisure time off.

The sky reflected the setting sun, as the six of them strolled along La Croisette, parallel to the beach in Cannes. The juxtaposition of a blazing pink hue above and a deep aqua sea brought strong emotions to Brie. Sunsets sometimes made her pensive and she disliked endings.

The group stopped for dinner at an elegant seafood restaurant facing the shore. They sat for a long time in silence, staring out at the Mediterranean. The mood was heavier than the August humidity.

Brie and Laurent were lost in each other.

"It's been a beautiful time here in Cannes," said Annick, with tears in her eyes. She looked at Etienne, who blew his mother a kiss.

"We're grateful Chantal worked hard to complete the renovations on the ancestral home, so we could all gather together here," said Pierre.

Chantal smiled at him.

"Yes, it's been splendid to be together. Thank you all for being my anchors during the roughest time in my life," said Brie, closing her eyes, trying not to focus on the negative. Laurent put his arm around her.

"You're not going anywhere, my friend," said Chantal, winking at Brie. "We plan to be housemates for the foreseeable future, *n'est-ce pas?*"

"I have so much gratitude to have found a refuge with you in France," said Brie. "With Jack Taylor on the loose, it's not safe for me to return to New York. The city holds haunting memories of him."

She thought about New York, her childhood home, filled with joyous times at the skating rink in Rockefeller Center, family celebrations at Tavern on the Green, lengthy visits to the Metropolitan Museum of Art with her grandmother, and lunch at the Museum of Modern Art with Aunt Françoise. She wanted that New York City back, the city that had been stolen from her by a heartless man. She hoped to return one day, to reclaim her roots.

* * *

The following morning was busy at *L' Aéroport de Nice.* The end of summer brought throngs of people returning for *La Rentrée* to school and work. The crowded lines to the Paris flights meandered in front of the security gate, allowing time for long goodbyes. Pierre held his wife in his arms as they whispered to each other. Chantal kissed Etienne, as did Loulou, who was a willful pup and insisted on being along for the *au revoirs.* Brie embraced Laurent, who wore his beige summer suit. He seemed quiet, deep in thought. He had become the French diplomat again. Yesterday, he was simply Laurent, her lover, with his sultry, seductive eyes.

Brie accompanied Laurent to his Tunis departure gate, feeling morose, yet attempting a smile and wanting to appear upbeat. This gate had fewer passengers than those bound for Paris. The flight to Paris was a short hour and a half from Nice. Nice to Tunis was over five hours of travel. Brie thought the distance equivalent to her flights from New York to California, to visit her daughter Chloe.

"This is a difficult day for me. I don't want to leave," said Laurent, hugging Brie who became tearful and choked up when she heard his words. She remembered them making love for the last time, the night before. His touch was as arousing for her as their first night together at the Eiffel Tower.

"It's comforting that the French say, 'until I we meet again' instead of goodbye," she said. "*Au Revoir, mon chéri.*" She felt that rock in her throat.

"Wait for my messages. I promise you won't be disappointed," said Laurent, caressing her long blonde hair. She wondered if he wrote such messages to his former wife, and whether long separations had destroyed their marriage.

"Will you sign your messages from Napoléon?" Brie laughed, thinking of his explanation of how the emperor had kept in touch with his empress.

"To Josephine," he smiled.

His final lingering kiss was meant to last them both for several months. It shot electricity throughout her body in a most heart-stirring way. She thought about touching his naked body last night, his skin smooth. Brie would recall this moment during his absence.

As Brie watched Laurent board the plane, Chantal stood with her friend. Chantal, who carried Loulou, had used her Air France clout and badge to accompany them directly to the boarding area. Laurent walked onto the ramp leading to the plane, looking back at Brie one last time. He blew her a final kiss.

"Why do I feel like I may never see him again?" asked Brie to Chantal.

"Stop talking nonsense. You will see him," said Chantal. "My intuition is never wrong. Now, let's go find my sister."

As Brie and Chantal passed the long lines bound for Paris, they saw detective Marceau with his diminutive wife. He waved at the women and walked over to greet them. He was wearing his dark sunglasses. Brie thought people who wore sunglasses all the time, including indoors, must have something to hide.

"Are you returning to Paris, detective?" asked Brie.

"Yes, I just spoke to Madame Annick. My time here has ended, and my team is confident of your security. Yesterday, I left a message for Pierre. As you know, I have colleagues in this area, so you will not be without protection, if you need it," he said.

Brie felt a sense of foreboding.

The women walked outside to find Annick, who was in the process of sending a final text to Pierre.

"It's just the three of us again," said Annick, in her cheery tone. "How about if we go to the beach? Our celebration is not over because the men have left."

"Certainly not," Chantal agreed. "Do you prefer Nice or Cannes? Or perhaps in between, at Antibes?"

"Surprise us," said Brie, feeling the rock in her throat dissipating.

* * *

Chantal decided on one of the private, pebbly beaches in Nice, not far from Boulevard Gambetta, in the heart of the city. The pebbles on the beaches in Nice contrasted with the sandy beaches in Cannes. The three women and pup Loulou settled in on *chaises* close to the water's edge.

Brie was content to sit by the sea and watch the tide roll in and out.

She could spend hours under an umbrella, breathing in the salty air. She imagined Laurent flying over the Mediterranean to Tunisia, in his beige summer suit and crisp white shirt. By now, he must be above the island of Corsica, birthplace of Napoléon. She wondered if Laurent was thinking of his Josephine, while on the way to North Africa. Even after the emperor's divorce from her, he claimed Josephine was the only woman he ever loved.

The sisters began an animated conversation about what to prepare for dinner. They agreed on Chicken Marengo, a favorite dish of the emperor himself, prepared for him on the battlefield when he won the Battle of Marengo. Chantal said there were plenty of tomatoes and mushrooms to sauté in olive oil for the sauce, with fresh herbs from her garden.

The women passed several hours at the shoreline in Nice, as the sun moved to high noon and then faded into the late afternoon light.

"No time is ever wasted by the sea," said Chantal. "The negative ions are at work to raise the mood."

Brie's thoughts were miles away, on Laurent's plane to Tunis. The universe had placed a fascinating man in her path. He was in stark contrast to the one she left behind in New York. She would let go of outcomes and allow this new story to unfold. She had to trust that she had no power over the future. The Mediterranean shone in a deep blue green. She felt at peace.

Chapter 47

The next morning, Brie went to *la boulangerie* for fresh breakfast crois-sants, with Loulou along for the walk. The streets of Cannes were less crowded than before, with the exodus of summer people the previous day. Cannes returned to a charming, quaint town once again.

Brie inhaled the fresh bread aromas and Loulou joined in with a sniff. Brie noted that the local customers were not discussing their usual gossip. Instead, they had worry on their faces. She heard them talking in anxious tones about a terrorist bombing. She became alarmed, crying out for details, as one man showed her the breaking news on his phone. All Brie could see was "Tunisia" and "the French Embassy." She felt a sharp pain in her chest, as she rushed out of the bakery without purchasing any-thing. She ran home to watch the news, with Loulou in tow.

At *Villa du Ciel*, she found Chantal and Annick glued to the televi-sion screen, as disturbing photos of the French Embassy building in Tunis, in shambles, emerged. The women looked up in horror when Brie entered. Annick's hand covered her mouth. Chantal's eyes were glazed over.

They watched in silence as the cars parked near the Embassy went up in flames, their windows smashed. The reporter stated that details were sketchy coming out of Tunis. Brie fought hard to not imagine the worst about Laurent and his safety. This had been a major attack. It was apparent that the perpetrators had waited for the full French delegation to return to the Embassy after a summer hiatus. During the summer, the Embassy always operated with a skeleton crew. The French Government was in the process of sending a rescue team from Paris to Tunis, to investigate and join the Tunisian officials in the search for survivors.

The women looked at each other with shock. They tried to comfort Brie, who was overwhelmed by the news. She screamed "No, no" at the television. She sobbed as she inched closer to the screen, as if this movement forward would somehow give her the information she craved. "Is Laurent alive?"

Brie was frantic and attempted to call Laurent's phone. The call could not be completed. It failed over and over. Tunis was one hour earlier than Nice. She thought about Madame Fifi's Tarot reading in which the Tower and the Death cards appeared. Brie's hands were shaking, but she could not stop calling Laurent's number.

"Come and sit down," said Annick to Brie, attempting to comfort her friend. "I will try to call Pierre." Pierre's phone went to voice mail. "He must be out making his rounds at the hospital."

Chantal chimed in, "Laurent is tough and resourceful. He will find a way to safety." She was brave enough to utter his name. Chantal was astute at sizing up people, noting their strengths and weaknesses.

The newscaster reported that it was a suspected terrorist cell that may have infiltrated Tunisia from a neighboring country. The region had been unstable for years.

Brie went to her room to take her blood pressure and find her medication. Her heart was pounding. She longed for a positive outcome to this tragedy. She knew it was out of her control. She felt her hopes sinking, as she flashed on the Louis Malle film, *Ascenseur pour l'échafaud*. She imagined an elevator car going down a bottomless elevator shaft. She had to hold onto good thoughts, yet she was encased in a dark silence.

Annick came into the guest room to find her friend crying. Brie sat at the edge of the bed, her head in her hands. Annick sat down next to her.

"Please come out and be with us. You are not alone," said Annick.

"I know. *Merci beaucoup*," said Brie, giving Annick a big hug.

Chapter 48

No encouraging updates came out of Tunis for the rest of the day, except for the news that the Parisian team had arrived in Tunisia and were coordinating the search for survivors with the Tunisians.

By evening, Brie was more anxious than ever. She twirled the bracelet Laurent had given her around her wrist obsessively.

"I need to take a walk by myself and clear my head," she said to the sisters.

"I'll go with you," offered Chantal.

"Please, I need to be alone right now," insisted Brie. "I think you understand."

Brie left the *Villa du Ciel* and walked, aimlessly, toward Cannes village. She was adrift on the Rue d'Antibes, staring into the shop windows, as the shopkeepers were closing for the day. It was early September, so the crowds had dispersed, and Cannes was free of the last of the vast numbers of visitors. The streets were virtually deserted.

There was a slight chill in the air now. A touch of early Autumn. Mistral winds had arrived on the southern coast of France. Brie, who wore a sleeveless dress, shivered and drew her arms across her chest.

She was startled by a bold figure who flew out at her from a hidden alleyway. He was a tall man, with dark hair. She thought she was hallucinating. The man grabbed her and tried to push her toward a large, Black SUV with dark tinted windows, parked at the curb. Brie resisted with all her strength, somehow remembering her recent defense training.

"Stop it, you bitch!" she heard the man say in English. The voice was unmistakable to her. It was the voice of Jack Taylor, her ex-husband. She could smell his hot breath on her face. Her visceral fear was all-consuming.

"Don't fight me, Brie! Get in the damn car," he said, with escalating anger. She was all too familiar with his rage, as his harsh words burned in her heart.

Brie knew she could *not* get into that car. She tried to hit him in the face, reaching for his eyes and pushing up his nose, but she cut her hand on his sharp metal sunglasses. Blood was flowing over his shirt and covering her pale linen dress. She pulled away from his muscular frame, but he was quick to pull her back into his grip.

She started to scream louder, "No, no, no, no!"

He attempted to cover her mouth with his hand. She tried to bite his hand, as she moved with lightening speed.

"We're going to have a little talk," he yelled, wiping away the streaming blood, as he grabbed for her neck.

She pulled him closer to her, and with all the strength she had, fueled by the emotions from the day's terrifying events in Tunis, she smashed her knee into his crotch with a power she never knew she held inside. He tried to grab her leg. Instead, he fell to the ground, moaning. She watched him writhing in pain in surreal slow motion.

In seconds, Brie heard Police sirens. Police cars surrounded Brie and Jack. They quickly placed Jack in handcuffs. He glared at her with his dark, piercing eyes, his sunglasses broken in slivers on the ground. Brie's look was one of doom. An officer walked Brie to safety, helping her into a nearby police van. Then, she spotted Chantal standing outside the van. Brie realized it was Chantal who had called the police. She waved at her friend, who must have followed her. Chantal nodded in her direction with a solemn expression.

"Do you know the identity of the man who attacked you, madame?" asked the police officer.

"His name is Jack Taylor, from New York," said Brie, in a clear voice. "He's wanted by the police."

"The infamous Jack Taylor?" asked the police officer, his eyebrows arched in disbelief.

"The criminal who escaped custody in New York, during his extradition," added Chantal.

"Very interesting," said the police officer. "I remember his arrest in Monte Carlo."

"He's my estranged husband," mumbled Brie.

The policeman looked at her with his eyes widened.

She turned to Chantal. "It's a good thing you decided to follow me," said Brie. "Who knows where I would be now?"

"I knew I couldn't leave you alone in your distracted state of mind," said Chantal. "But you handled yourself like a pro." She smiled.

Brie didn't feel like a pro. Some inner strength took over and allowed her to triumph. It shocked her that Jack showed up again in France, risking his freedom to track her down.

* * *

Annick joined the women at the *Commissaire de Police* headquarters. Chantal had called her. Brie was in a state of shock, yet the chief insisted on asking her more questions.

"She's been through a tough day, *Monsieur le Chef*," said Annick.

"I've taken note of that, madame," said the Chief.

"No, Chief," Chantal said. "Something else has happened in addition to this attack. We believe our diplomat friend was in the Embassy in Tunis during today's bombing. He's missing."

"Oh, I see. That *is* unfortunate," said the chief.

"She's in a state of deep anguish," added Annick, examining her friend's face.

"Still, we must get the information, while it's fresh in the victim's mind," he insisted. "My officers have filled me in on the identity of the attacker. Fingerprints and facial recognition confirm your statement. We concur that if Monsieur Taylor hadn't made his way to France to reconnect with Madame Taylor, we might never have apprehended him."

He turned to Brie. "You should be commended, madame."

"How do you think he got here? He was on a no-fly list," said Brie, still woozy, in a strained voice.

"Perhaps he arrived by boat, with a forged passport. It's difficult to say at this time," said the chief. "No matter; we're relieved to have the perpetrator back in custody. He will not escape us again. I can assure you of that."

The chief, who identified himself as Chief Inspector Du Pont, continued the interrogation behind closed doors. He went into detailed questions about what Brie knew about Jack's activities. Brie explained that she had no knowledge of Jack Taylor's alleged crimes. He'd kept her in the dark. The chief was ultimately convinced, after hours of questioning, that Brie was telling the truth. By that point, she was exhausted, her body limp.

Brie told the Chief Inspector about the young man with the ponytail, who had been following her, both in Paris and here on the *Côte d'Azur*. The chief confirmed he was aware of those details. He had met with Detective Inspector Marceau earlier in the summer. Brie was surprised these two men knew each other, although their formal manner and detached analysis were the same.

"We don't yet know the identity of that suspect. We will, however, have that knowledge before too long. Go home and rest, madame. We will contact you when we gather further information," said the Chief Inspector.

Brie thanked the inspector, her body sore from what felt was like a street fight. She had never fought physically with anyone. Jack Taylor had the strength of an athlete. She had reacted to him without giving it a second thought, fighting for her own survival.

Chapter 49

Brie fell asleep in the back seat of the Peugeot, while Chantal drove them back to *Villa du Ciel*. Once inside the house, Brie attempted to phone Laurent, without success. She was exhausted and crawled into bed without dinner. Annick attempted to feed her friend some Chicken Marengo, but Brie couldn't lift her head from the pillow. Her strength during the attack must have come from an adrenaline rush. The only other time she had an experience even close to such hysterical strength was when Chloe was a baby. The 80-pound Kensington Pram collapsed and baby Chloe almost fell under her carriage in Central Park. Brie had caught the baby in time and lifted the heavy carriage by herself, to rescue her child.

* * *

While Brie slept, Pierre called Annick from Paris with some news.

The badly injured members of the French Embassy delegation, from the Tunis attack, had been airlifted to the Paris hospital where Pierre was on staff. Doctor Girard came upon a severely wounded Laurent, who had sustained a major chest injury. The patient had lost a lot of blood. During surgery, the doctors discovered the physical damage Laurent sustained was only inches from his heart. He was lucky and he would survive. He was now in intensive care and not allowed visitors.

"Please convey to Brie that we have her man under our care," said Pierre. "I've just been with him, to check his heart. He is sedated, but alive. Etienne is with him, as we speak."

"Thank God!" said Annick. "How incredible that Laurent is safely with my husband and my son. You can't imagine what our days have been like here."

She proceeded to tell Pierre all about Jack Taylor's surprise attack on Brie. She explained how Chantal was on scene to assist during the police intervention.

"At long last, the elusive criminal is back in custody," said Annick.

"The only thing that brought Jack out of hiding was Brie. She inadvertently lured him into the open," said Pierre.

"It was a dangerous business, and she could have been killed," said Annick.

"We never should have left her out of our sight," said Pierre. "How could Jack have gotten back into France? He was on every no-fly list and his passport had been confiscated."

"That is my question," said Annick, sighing. "The authorities think he could have entered Europe by boat with a forged passport."

"By boat? Extraordinary! I'll contact Detective Marceau to be sure he is informed of Jack's arrest. He's worked with the Chief Inspector in Cannes. Their goal was to put Jack Taylor away for life," said Pierre. "After all, he was involved with a murder."

"A murder? You never told me about that," Annick could barely hold her phone.

"I won't go into all that, right now," said Pierre.

"Okay. I won't wake Brie. I'll tell her the comforting news about Laurent's survival after she has had her sleep. You can tell me about the murder another time," said Annick. *"Bonne nuit."*

"Bonne nuit, mon amour," replied Pierre.

* * *

Brie awoke in the middle of the night, her heart racing. She saw a short message on her phone from an unknown number. It said:

"I survived."

It was signed, *"Your Napoléon."*

Brie cried out at the sight of his message. She had no words. It was the message she had prayed for and the one she hoped to receive. She slept until daybreak.

Chapter 50

Brie entered the kitchen of the *Villa du Ciel* to find Annick and Chantal reading the morning papers. The story about the Tunis bombing was all over the front page. It explained that survivors were being transported to a hospital in Paris from the destroyed Embassy in Tunis.

"I got a mysterious text that Laurent survived," said Brie, in a fog, wondering if she had dreamt it.

Annick ran up to her. "Did you overhear me speaking to Pierre last night?" she asked.

"No, I think I got a message from him," said Brie. When she looked on her phone, the message was gone. "I thought…maybe I did hear something in my sleep? Is it true?" asked Brie.

Annick explained what Pierre had said. Laurent was being treated at the hospital in Paris. He would recover. Brie's heart was filled with emotion and all she could do was cry with relief. Laurent was alive and Jack was back in custody. She felt a lightness throughout her body.

"There's a short article on page two about Jack Taylor being arrested in Cannes. The details are sparse," said Chantal, looking at Brie, whose eyes widened. "No matter," Chantal continued. "We know the outcome. Our own Superwoman brought him to justice." She nodded at Brie.

Brie managed a smile, gazing back at Chantal.

"With your help, my friend," said Brie. "I ought to contact my sister Lisa. I wonder if she's heard the news?"

Brie wobbled on her legs as she walked back to her bedroom to make the call.

"Two incredible stories," said Lisa. "I read about Jack. Shocking that he turned up in France. I thought the authorities confiscated his passport. I had no idea your Laurent was connected to the terrorism in Tunis."

"Nothing had prepared me for either of those terrifying events," said Brie, shaking. She explained more of the shocking details to Lisa about Jack's attack.

"Crazy! How are you feeling now?" asked Lisa.

"Remarkably calm, under the circumstances," she replied, taking a deep breath.

"Do you want me to talk to Chloe for you? With the time difference, I would be more likely to reach her on West Coast time," said Lisa.

"That would be great. I don't want to disturb her in the middle of the night or during a film shoot. I hesitate to worry her in any way," said Brie.

"Cool. I know my niece. I'll explain both occurrences in a simple manner," said Lisa. "Chloe was never a big fan of Jack, anyhow. It'll be good news for her."

"I appreciate your help on this," said Brie.

"I have you, Sis. Leave it to Aunt Lisa."

"I will. I didn't want to send a long email," said Brie.

"No worries. I'll talk to Chloe tomorrow," Lisa said.

* * *

When she hung up with Lisa, Brie received a call from Attorney Jeff Klein in New York. She became concerned when she saw his name on her phone screen.

"My dear," said Jeff, clearing his throat. "I read that Jack has been taken back into custody."

"He came after me, Jeff." She paused, swallowing with effort. "I was lucky the police were alerted in time," said Brie. "It was frightening."

"I can only imagine," said Jeff. "The reports here are slim. I noticed a headline in the *New York Times* about his arrest in Cannes. The article explained some of the history of the international gambling ring with Jack as kingpin. So, are you okay? Planning to remain in France?"

"I have no plans to return to New York anytime soon," said Brie. She coughed.

She reflected on the years from her childhood, teen years, and throughout her career in the city. She had twinges of missing New York, the island of Manhattan. It had been her home for a long time. Now, her home front was shifting. She could be moving towards a new home in Europe.

"I'd like to change my last name from Taylor back to my birth name Beaumont," she said.

"I'll take care of the paperwork for you and continue to look after any legal fallout, my dear. With the name change, you will need to get a new passport," said Jeff.

"I understand," said Brie. "Thank you for your concern."

"You take care. Whoever could imagine my charming old friend Jack would end up in prison?" asked Jeff. "He became erratic. It occurred to me that he changed after his parents and sister died in that car crash."

"Yes! He admitted to driving recklessly on that perilous, snowy mountain road in Switzerland," she said. "He may have felt responsible."

"He's a daredevil. Always has been. He craves risk," said Jeff.

"I guess neither of us knew the real man or his motivations. I married a mystery man and I thought I knew him," said Brie.

"He's that iceberg we talked about. Danger lurking below the surface," Jeff said.

As she hung up, Brie sensed an arctic shiver in her bones. Perhaps Jack couldn't handle his wife needing him after her heart surgery. His emotions ran cold and hers were recovering from frostbite.

Chapter 51

Three weeks later, Annick accompanied Brie to the hospital in Paris to be with Laurent, who remained in Intensive Care for those initial weeks. He had been in and out of consciousness, upgraded from critical to serious condition. The patient was finally transferred to a regular hospital room and his team of doctors cleared him for visitors.

Pierre had spoken to Annick, recommending the women delay their visit until most of the horrific tubes and medical machinery were removed and Laurent's condition had stabilized.

When Brie entered Laurent's hospital room, she saw the patient looking vulnerable and thin. Nothing could have prepared her for this day. Laurent's light brown hair was matted. He opened his eyes when he heard footsteps and spoke her name. "Brie, *mon amour*," his voice was weak. She sat down next to him. "You have no idea how happy I am to see you alive," she said.

"I'm happy to be alive," he said, with a subtle twinkle in his eye. She was careful not to touch his bandaged chest. "Kiss me," he said. She hesitated, drawing back. She feared hurting him. "I don't have the plague, you know," said Laurent.

Brie sat by Laurent's side, kissing his lips with a gentle touch. He pulled her closer, entangling Brie in his IV line. Alarms rang.

Outside in the corridor, Annick was conversing with her son Etienne, who came in immediately to check on Laurent. He turned to Brie. "Don't excite him too much."

He checked Laurent's IVs. Brie recoiled, taking a breath. She didn't dare take any chances with Laurent in such a delicate condition.

Etienne walked out of the room and continued to speak with his mother. "Laurent was fortunate," he said to Annick. "We didn't expect him to live." His eyes were focused on Annick, who was teary.

"I'm relieved to know that Laurent has the doctors Girard, the best medical team possible, looking after him," said Annick. She hugged her son.

An hour later, Laurent's son Tristan entered the room. He was easy to recognize as he looked very much like his father—tall, light brown hair with those blue-green eyes.

"*Bonjour.* You must be Brie," he said as he put out his hand. "I've been waiting to meet you. My father has been asking for you every day since he gained consciousness."

Brie shook Tristan's hand. She wanted to hug him. "I've been waiting weeks to see him." Brie began to weep, with relief. "Please excuse me for being so emotional."

"I understand," said Tristan, embracing her. We've all had a bad shock with this terrible event.

He stepped back to peer out the doorway of the hospital room. "I see my Aunt Solange is on her way down the corridor."

A tall, svelte, elegant woman approached. She was solemn and formal, extending her hand to Brie. "Solange. I'm Laurent's sister," she said. Solange was impeccable in her tailored dress: a dark suit with a classic

Chanel scarf, dark-haired and very Parisian. She kissed Tristan, then looked over at Laurent, who was dozing. "My brother must be heavily medicated for his pain." An uncomfortable silence followed her comment.

She turned to Brie. "I hear you are American," she said. Brie was more casual in her light blue silk blouse, navy slacks and blazer. Solange whispered something to Tristan in French about New Yorkers being a rare breed, flashing Brie a wicked look. Brie cringed when she overheard Laurent's sister's comment. *Je parle français*, she thought to herself. She knew French women were very protective of their men, no matter what their relationship.

Brie wondered which other members of Laurent's family and colleagues might visit the hospital and when they could arrive. She wanted to mentally prepare herself to meet them. Laurent, a proud father, had only ever talked to her about his son.

* * *

Days later, Brie was seated on Laurent's bed, holding his hand. She made a habit of spending every afternoon with him, although he slept most of the time. Tristan, along with Laurent's other family members and some French government officials, visited in the evenings or on weekends. Many of Laurent's relatives lived and worked in Normandy, near the city of Rouen. Tristan studied at the prestigious Sciences Po in Paris.

Annick, who was back to her professorship at the Sorbonne, accompanied Brie to the hospital on the weekends. The Doctor's Girard, Pierre and Etienne, made their rounds in the early mornings. Brie preferred to be alone with Laurent. At his request, she read to him. He liked passages from the poems of Verlaine, especially *Chanson d'automne* and *Il pleure dans mon Coeur*. He recited the musical French poems with her, as he knew many of them by heart.

One afternoon, Detective Marceau appeared in the doorway, and popped his head into Laurent's room.

"How is Monsieur de Laval?" he asked, with concern on his face.

"It will be a slow recovery, but the doctors are optimistic," said Brie, forcing a smile. "Thank you for coming."

"May I speak to you for a moment, madame?" whispered the detective. "Out here in the corridor, so as not to disturb monsieur."

Brie stepped outside the door, concerned with what was on the detective's agenda. It had been weeks since Jack Taylor's arrest in Cannes and she only had Laurent's wellbeing on her mind.

"I spoke with Dr. Girard this morning," Began the detective. "He requested that I talk directly with you about some additional information we've discovered."

"Oh?" said Brie, wrinkling her brow, mildly annoyed by this distraction.

"Yes, the young man with the ponytail, who has been following you for the past several months, is the son of Monsieur Taylor."

"The son? I don't understand," said Brie, surprised. To her knowledge, Jack didn't have children. Here was another one of Jack's many secrets revealed.

"Yes, the young man confessed. We did a DNA test on him. It turned out that he was the product of a past relationship your ex-husband had with a woman from Eastern Europe. The young man had only recently met Monsieur Taylor, his biological father. It was Monsieur Taylor who put the young man on the case to keep tabs on you, when his previously hired private investigator demanded payment to continue his services. Monsieur Taylor's funds ran out, as you know, and he had to come up with an alternate plan to keep track of you in Europe." The detective's eyes were laser beamed on Brie. She felt fidgety, buttoning and unbuttoning her blazer.

Brie shook her head. "I don't know what to say," she said. "I knew nothing about being followed until I got to Paris. Nor did I know Jack had a son. He told me he had no children." *More of Jack's iceberg was being revealed*, she thought.

"The young man has no major criminal record," said the detective.

Brie began to pace down the hospital corridor, with the detective following her. She wanted to get out of earshot of Laurent's room.

"We're keeping in close contact with this young man, hoping he will help us to put together the puzzle that has continued to unravel," said the detective. "His name is Danté, and he lives on the outskirts, *le banlieu* we call it, of Paris."

"Well, thank you for the information, but I'm focused on another matter, as you can see," said Brie. Her concern was with Laurent, and she was in a rush to return to his bedside.

"Understandable. I will leave you to the patient. My best wishes to Monsieur de Laval for his complete recovery," said the detective, with a slight bow.

Brie wondered how much more would be uncovered about Jack's past that had been kept secret, but the thought quickly passed from her mind.

Chapter 52

A few days later, Chloe called from Los Angeles to speak to her mother. "Aunt Lisa contacted me with some scary news about Jack," she said. "We had a long talk and I want to join you in Paris, after we wrap on this picture."

"I'd love to have you here with me, sweetie. Did Aunt Lisa explain about Laurent?"

"Yes, what a double whammy for you, Mom. I'm so glad Laurent survived the attack."

"Thanks, honey. I'm extremely relieved," said Brie. "So, whenever you are free, fly over. Laurent would enjoy meeting you and his son Tristan, who studies at Sciences Po, will be here," said Brie.

"Sounds great. I'll let you know when I have a specific time frame," said Chloe. "Hey, mom, where did you learn those defense moves Aunt Lisa spoke about?"

"Oh, I took a class," said Brie, nonchalantly.

"Must have been some intense class, mom. Did you lift weights?"

Mother and daughter both laughed at that thought. "You could say I've gotten stronger. Chantal now calls me Superwoman," said Brie.

She thought back to fighting off her ex-husband on that deserted street in Cannes. The whole episode felt to Brie like it had happened in a terrible dream.

"How about if I contact our costume department and have them design a Superwoman outfit for you?" asked Chloe, giggling.

"I'm sure the updated Superwoman look will become the new craze in Paris for the upcoming season," said Brie. "I envision a one-piece swimsuit."

Brie was happy that Lisa managed to explain the whole sordid affair to Chloe, who was able to handle it with humor, although she, herself, was not at that point in her processing of the Jack factor.

"I like that idea. You're amazing, Mom. I love you."

"Love you, too, sweetie! See you here in Paris," Brie said, glancing at a photo on her phone of her with Chloe that they had taken at the Cannes Film Festival. She looked forward to hugging her daughter in person.

Chapter 53

The time was fast approaching for Laurent's release from the hospital.

His plan was to return to his Paris residence, just off the *Rue Cler* in the 7th *arrondissement*, not far from *La Tour Eiffel*. His sister Solange arranged for a private nurse to attend to him, as needed, during the day. In addition, Brie offered to stay with Laurent.

"I would appreciate having you with me," said Laurent, in response to her offer. "As they say in America, you won't have to ask me twice." He had a passionate shine in his eyes.

Brie was radiant as she walked beside Laurent's wheelchair toward the hospital exit. His son Tristan, along with Pierre, Etienne, and a group of other physicians and nurses joined them, as Tristan and a nurse helped Laurent into his waiting car, his driver placing the patient's suitcase into the trunk. A few members of the French Press were there to cover the story. Laurent's face was awash with serenity, as he conveyed his gratitude to the doctors and nurses who saved his life. They all applauded.

* * *

Laurent's luxury apartment had an enchanting view of the Eiffel Tower. The décor, modern and inviting, was similar to the blues and grays of his cottage in the south. He would be on medical leave from the Embassy, with no specific assignment return date to another post. The future would be determined by the time it would take for his full recovery.

Laurent sat on his cushy sofa, propped up by artful pillows. "I've been in a hospital bed for way too long and it feels good to be home." He cautiously leaned back, gazing at *La Tour Eiffel* through the French doors. He motioned to Brie to sit down next to him, and she complied.

He unbuttoned his shirt and looked at her. "You see, now we have matching scars." She was transfixed by his wound, noticing how similar it was, in placement and size, to her own heart scar.

"*Oui, mon amour,* we do," she replied. She kissed him on the cheek and felt quiet fireworks in her heart. She was grateful to be sitting with Laurent, at his home in Paris, with the Eiffel Tower in front of them. She could have never imagined a more perfect outcome. They watched the impressionist sunset. The pinks and mauves promised a clear day to follow.

Laurent spoke about his desire to spend Noël and the winter holidays at his cottage in Mougins.

"Would you like that?" he asked her. She nodded in agreement, giving him a sultry look. "I'd love Christmas in the south of France and perhaps New Years' in Paris. If you are feeling up to travel in a month or two," said Brie. "Let's wait and see what the doctors recommend."

"I have the best medicine right here with me," he said, holding her close. "In a month, I'll be able to climb *Mont Blanc.*"

Brie's heart was full. She understood what they shared, and she trusted enough to allow her new life to unfold. It was a shared *histoire d'amour.* Their story. Brie and Laurent breathed in unison. Moments of adventure in Paris awaited outside their doorstep.

ACKNOWLEDGEMENTS

A sincere thank you to my dear friend Olga Vezeris, editor extraordinaire, for her expert guidance and encouragement during the many revisions of my manuscript. I could not have successfully moved forward without her assistance.

Thank you to the women of Creative Souls, so much more than a writing group, for their wisdom and support. And, to Dr. Marsha Lupi for her advice and friendship.

Much appreciation to Coco Tanner Smith, for her brilliant technical knowledge and devotion to this project.

Love to my talented daughter, Nico. Music and art are the universal languages.

Thank you to my scholarly students, who continue to nurture my creativity.

Much gratitude to the French people. Their language and culture have been my inspiration for decades.

Finally, deep admiration and love to my dear sister Wendy, for her never-ending love and care. She is my shining light in all endeavors.

AUTHOR BIO

Lynn Heyman, a New York City native, has had an illustrious career teaching French language and literature. She studied and spent years in Paris and throughout France, where she returns often.

A seasoned world traveler, she now resides near San Diego, California.